P9-ELX-796

THE SAFEST LIES

THE
SAFEST
LIES

MEGAN MIRANDA

EMBER

This is a work of fiction. Names, characters, places, and incidents either are the product of the author's imagination or are used fictitiously. Any resemblance to actual persons, living or dead, events, or locales is entirely coincidental.

Text copyright © 2016 by Megan Miranda
Cover art copyright © 2016 by Getty/Valentin Casarsa

All rights reserved. Published in the United States by Ember, an imprint of Random House Children's Books, a division of Penguin Random House LLC, New York. Originally published in hardcover in the United States by Crown Books for Young Readers, an imprint of Random House Children's Books, New York, in 2016.

Ember and the E colophon are registered trademarks of Penguin Random House LLC.

Visit us on the Web! randomhouseteens.com

Educators and librarians, for a variety of teaching tools,
visit us at RHTeachersLibrarians.com

The Library of Congress has cataloged the hardcover edition of this work as follows:
Names: Miranda, Megan.
Title: The safest lies / Megan Miranda.
Description: First Edition. | New York : Crown Books for Young Readers, [2016]
Summary: "When Kelsey's agoraphobic mother disappears after years of claiming the kidnappers she escaped from were coming back for her, Kelsey quickly discovers that her mother isn't who she thought she was—and she's not the abductor's only target" —Provided by publisher.
Identifiers: LCCN 2015024031 | ISBN 978-0-553-53751-2 (hardback) |
ISBN 978-0-553-53753-6 (ebook)
Subjects: | CYAC: Mothers and daughters—Fiction. | Identity—Fiction. |
Fear—Fiction. | Kidnapping—Fiction. | BISAC: JUVENILE FICTION /
Love & Romance. | JUVENILE FICTION / Action & Adventure / Survival Stories. |
JUVENILE FICTION / Action & Adventure / General.
Classification: LCC PZ7.M67352 Saf 2016 | DDC [Fic]—dc23

ISBN 978-0-553-53754-3 (pbk.)

Printed in the United States of America
10 9 8 7 6 5 4 3 2 1
First Ember Edition 2017

Random House Children's Books supports the First Amendment
and celebrates the right to read.

CHAPTER 1

The black iron gates used to be my favorite thing about the house.

Back when I was younger, they reminded me of secret gardens and hidden treasures, all the great mysteries I had read about in children's books.

This was the setting of fairy tales. The vegetation creeping upward in places, ivy and weeds tangling with the bars, and the way they'd light up in a storm, encircling the house—a stark surprise against the darkness.

And we were on the inside.

It was better to see it from this direction, on the way out. It looked different as I grew older. From the other side, through a different filter. A glance over my shoulder as I walked away, and all I could see were the cameras over the entrances. The sterile, boxed walls of the house beyond. The shadow behind the tinted window.

I didn't realize, for a long time, that *this* was the secret.

Still, there was a familiarity to the iron gates, and I couldn't help tapping them as I passed each morning, a routine goodbye as I left for the day. In the summer, the bars would be hot from the sun. And in the winter, when I was bundled up in wool, sometimes I'd feel a spark underneath the cold, like I could sense the current of electricity that was running through the top.

Mostly, though, they felt like home.

Today, my palm came away damp, coated with morning dew. Everything glistened in the mountain sunrise.

Now that I was beyond the gates, and because I saw my mother's shadow, there was a routine I was supposed to stick to:

Check the backseat through the windows before unlocking the car door.

Start the car and count to twenty so the engine had time to settle.

Wave to my mother, watching from the front window.

Two hands on the wheel as I navigated the unpaved driveway made of gravel, and then the winding mountain roads on the way to school.

The rest of the day was a tally of hours, a routine I knew by heart. Swap this Wednesday for any other Wednesday and nobody would notice. My mother said there's a safety to routine, but I didn't exactly agree. Routines could be learned. Routines could be *predicted*. But it would be a mistake to say that. Honestly, it was a mistake to even *think* that.

Here was the rest of my Wednesday routine:

Arrive at school early enough to get a parking spot near a streetlight, since I'd be leaving late. Avoid the crowded hallway, hope Mr. Graham opened his classroom early. Claim my seat in the back of math class, and coast through the day, mostly unnoticed.

Mostly.

My books were already out and I'd just about finished the morning problems when Ryan Baker swept into class.

"Hey, Kelsey," he said as he slid into his seat, just as the bell rang.

"Hi, Ryan," I said. This was also part of the routine. Ryan looked the way Ryan always looked, which was: brown hair that never fell the same way twice; legs too long for the desk beneath him, so they stretched under the seat in front or to the aisle between us (today: aisle); jeans, brown lace-up boots, T-shirt. Autumn in Vermont meant a sweatshirt for me, but apparently Ryan hadn't gotten there yet.

Today he was wearing a dark blue shirt that said VOLUNTEER, and he caught me staring. I didn't know if it was supposed to be ironic or not.

His fingers drummed on the desk. His knee bounced in the aisle.

I almost asked him, on impulse, but then Mr. Graham called me up to the board for a problem, and Ryan started drawing on his wrist with blue ink, and by the time I returned to my seat, the moment had passed.

First period was mostly quiet and mostly still. People yawned, people stretched, occasionally someone rested their head on their desk and hoped Mr. Graham didn't notice. Everyone slowly came to life over the span of ninety minutes.

But Ryan always seemed the opposite—all coiled energy, even at eight a.m. Rushing into class, his leg bouncing under his desk, his hands continually drawing patterns. His energy was contagious. So by the time the bell rang, I was the one coiled to jump. I'd spring from my seat, wave goodbye, head down the hall toward English, and pretend we hadn't once shared the most embarrassing conversation of my life.

The rest of the daily routine: English, lunch, science, history. Faces I'd grown accustomed to seeing over the last two years. Names I knew well, people I knew casually. The day passing by in a comfortable string of sameness. Blink too long and you might miss it.

Wednesday also meant tutoring after school to meet the volunteer component for graduation. Since I was a year ahead of most everyone in my grade, taking mostly senior classes, this was the easiest way to fulfill it.

Today I was scheduled to start with Leo Johnson, a senior taking sophomore science who I kind of knew from the Lodge. *Kind of knew* because (a) Leo was the type of person that everyone kind of knew, and (b) Ryan and I shared a shift at the Lodge twice a week over the summer, and they were friends. Which meant when Leo came in, he would occasionally nod at me, and even less occasionally mention me by name.

He dropped his notebook on the table across from me. "Hi, my name is Leo, and I'm failing." He flashed me a smile.

"Yeah, hi, we know each other already."

He slouched, narrowing his eyes. "Yes, but did you also know I was failing?"

"Seeing as you're assigned to be here after school on a Wednesday, I kind of assumed. Even more telling that you didn't bring any books."

He tipped his head to the side and scrunched up his mouth like he was thinking something through.

I looked at the clock. Only two minutes had passed. He didn't even have a pencil. "Look, I get credit whether I help you or we just sit here staring at each other. Just let me know which you prefer."

He stifled a laugh. "Okay, Kelsey Thomas," he said. "I get it now." He gestured to my stack of textbooks. "Let's do this. I'm told I do need to pass this class for graduation."

Leo turned out not to be the worst student in the world, though he was possibly the most easily distracted. He paused to talk to any person walking by the library entrance, and he checked the clock every five minutes or so.

His head shot up again an hour into our session when he heard footsteps in the hall, and he called, "Hey, Baker!" even though it was the library and he echoed. Leo was the type who didn't mind the attention—good or bad.

Ryan slowed at the library entrance but didn't quite stop. "Gotta run. Later, man." Then his eye caught mine, and he lifted his hand in a half wave. "Bye, Kelsey."

I half raised my hand in response.

Leo laughed under his breath. When I looked back at him, he was still grinning.

"What?"

"Nothing."

I felt my face heating up. I gripped the pencil harder and jabbed it at the paper, waiting for Leo to refocus on the problem.

Thanks to my mother, I was way ahead in terms of school material. But I was too far behind in everything else. I assumed this was how Leo must've felt, staring at these problems like they were written in a code he'd never seen before.

This was the code of high school. I had yet to crack it.

* * *

Leo and I both got our credit forms signed by the librarian, who took off just as fast as we did, locking up behind us.

"Been a pleasure, Kelsey," Leo said as he flew by, a gust of wind as I rifled through my purse for my phone.

The evening routine: call my mom, grab a soda, drive straight home.

"On my way," I said when she picked up.

"See you soon," she said. Her voice was like music. A homing device. I heard dishes in the background and knew she had already started dinner. This was her routine, too.

I hung up, and Leo was gone. The librarian was gone. The halls were silent and empty, except for the hum of the vending machines tucked into the corner. I slid a crisp dollar from my wallet, fed it to the machine. The gears churned, and in the emptiness, I started imagining all the things I could not see.

I felt myself taking note of the exits, an old habit: the front double doors through the lobby, the fire exits at the end of each hall, the windows off any classroom that had been left unlocked. . . .

I shook the thought, grabbed the soda, and jogged out the double front doors, my steps echoing, my keys jangling in my purse. I kept jogging until I made it to the ring of light around my car in the nearly empty lot.

It was twilight, and there was a breeze kicking in

through the mountains, and the shadows of the surrounding trees within the overhead lights looked a lot like the shadows of the black metal gates at home, when they were lit up in a thunderstorm.

I ran through the morning routine again, in reverse: check the backseat, start the engine, let it warm up. My phone in my bag, my bag beside me, nothing but gnats and mist caught in the headlights.

This was a good day. This was a normal day. A blur in a string of others, passing in typical fashion.

The reflectors on the double yellow line caught my headlights on the drive with a predictable regularity, almost hypnotic.

October came with a chill at night, and I wished I'd brought my coat. I leaned forward, turned the dial to hot, pressed the on button, and listened to the rush of air surging toward the vents as I leaned back in my seat.

A burst of heat.
A flash of light.
The world in motion.

I didn't know the air could scream.

CHAPTER 2

Don't be afraid.

The voice sounded far away, like it had to travel through water, or glass, before it reached me. And then there was that static—a radio? White noise, crackling like electricity, singeing my nerves.

You're okay.

Warm fingers at my neck, and the voice, getting sharper. My limbs were too heavy, like I'd fallen asleep with an arm and a leg hanging off the edge of my bed, and now everything tingled with pins and needles— sluggish and removed—as I tried to shift positions. My eyelids fluttered as I searched for the muted walls of my room.

"Can you hear me?" A voice that was not mine, not my mother's, not Jan's—but familiar nonetheless. A guy's voice. *Not my bedroom.*

I opened my eyes, and nothing made sense—not the feeling of blood rushing in the wrong direction, or the lack of gravity where it should've been, or my dark hair, falling in a cascade across my face. Not the sound of my own breathing echoing inside my head, or the scent of burning rubber, or the dull thudding behind my eyelids, which I'd opted to close again.

But.

Don't be afraid. You're okay.

Okay.

"Hey, I'm going to get you out of here. Everything's fine."

Everything's fine. I repeated it to myself, like my mother would do. But even as I let the words roll through my mind, like soft blankets tucked up to my chin, I felt the fear starting up, creeping slowly inside.

"Where am I?" I asked. There was a pressure in my head, a stiffness through my neck and shoulders, a subtle throbbing in my joints as my limbs were coming back to life.

"Thank God." The voice was coming from behind me somewhere. Vaguely familiar. But before I could latch on to it, something mechanical and high-pitched started whirring in the distance. The static—sharper now, and clearer.

"What's that?" I asked.

"You're okay. Don't panic."

Which meant that (a) I probably was not okay, and (b) I probably had reason to panic.

I attempted to twist around, but a strap cut across my lap and my chest, and metal pressed painfully up against my side, and when I attempted to push my hair out of my face, I could only see white billowing in front of my face, like a sheet. I was trapped.

Not okay.

Reason to panic.

Out. Get out.

I pushed against the metal for leverage as my breath started coming too fast.

The other person sucked in a breath, wrapped an arm around the seat to still me. "Also," he said, "don't move."

His arm was shaking. *I* was shaking.

There were other voices now, farther away, and the humming of the equipment grew louder. "Coming down," someone called.

"Okay," the voice called back. And then to me, "Listen, you're okay, you've been in an accident, but we're going to get you out now. It'll be a little loud is all."

I was in an accident? *The bend of the road and the reflectors in the double yellow line. Headlights, and I cut the wheel, and the sound of metal—*

Oh God, how long had I been here? Had my mom tried to call? Was she panicking already, unable to reach me? I pushed my hair aside again, tucking it into my collar. I moved my arms around, feeling for my bag. Best I could tell, I was hanging—kind of diagonally and forward, and my purse had been on the seat beside me. So that would mean . . .

I reached my arms over my head, but the metal was

too close, warped and bent, and I couldn't feel any bag. "Really," he said. "Don't. Move."

"I need my purse. I need my phone. I need to call my mom." My breath hitched. He didn't understand. I had to tell her I was okay. *You're okay.*

"We'll call her in a few minutes. But you need to keep still for now. What's your name?"

"Kelsey," I said.

A pause, and then, "Kelsey Thomas?"

"Yes." Someone who knew me, then. Must be someone from school. Or the Lodge, or the neighborhood, maybe. I strained to look in the rearview mirror, which was closer to me than it should've been. The world appeared disjointed.

The mirror was cracked and askew—I could see branches, the rock making up the wall in the side of the mountain, but not my rescuer's face. "Ryan," he said, as if he understood I was grasping for something. "Baker," he added.

"Ryan from my math class?" I asked, which was only one of the many things I could've said, but it was the first in my head, and the first out of my mouth.

A slow, steady breath. "Yeah. Ryan from your math class."

I was surrounded by metal and white pillows, and I was presumably upside down, but I could wiggle my toes, and I could breathe, and I could think, and I was having a conversation with Ryan Baker from my math class, so I tallied off the things I was not: paralyzed;

suffocating; unconscious; dead. My mother said it made her feel better to list the things she *was*—always starting with *safe*—but I preferred to carve out my safety with a process of elimination.

"The other car?" I asked.

He sucked in a breath. "Kelsey, I'm going to cut you out of your seat belt, but not until they remove the back panel. It'll just take a minute."

A minute. The air bags were in my face, and I felt the first pinprick of panic—that I would suffocate here, or that the car would explode between this moment and the next. I grasped for the reassurance of Ryan's words—*you're okay*—but it was too late. The thought had already planted itself in my head. An explosion. A fire. All the ways I could die, flipping through my mind in rapid succession.

"Cut me out *now*."

"No, that's not a good idea."

Illogical fears, that's what my mother's therapist, Jan, would say. Not something that would actually happen. Remember the difference. I could move the air bags aside and I'd be fine. Ryan from my math class would cut my seat belt and I'd be out, and then I'd find my phone and call my mother and she'd list off the things that were okay before she got to the fact that I'd ruined the car.

I pressed down on the inflated air bags, pushing them lower, away from my face, to prove it to myself.

"Wait, Kelsey. Don't."

But his words were too late—I'd already gotten a glimpse of precisely what he didn't want me seeing, and all the air drained from my body.

There was absolutely nothing *fine* about it.

The windshield was gone. And there was nothing below me. No pavement, no rocks, no grass or tilted view down the road. There was *nothing*. I was hanging toward air. Air and distant rock and fog—

"Oh my God," I said. And suddenly, I was perfectly, completely oriented.

Behind me were rocks. To my side, I could just make out the rough thick bark of a branch. There was a leaf resting on the air bag, the tips browned and starting to curl with the changing weather. I heard something creak.

"Are we over the cliff? We are, aren't we? We're in a tree over the goddamn cliff!" My shaking hands fumbled for the buckle as the pinpoint of panic crossed over into full-out hyperventilation.

"I told you not to panic!"

"Get me out!"

His hands gripped my arms from behind. He was pressed up against the seat, and I heard his voice through the fabric in a low plea. "Please stop moving. *Please*. Do not do *anything* to move the car."

And if I wasn't panicking before—I certainly was *now*.

I let the hair fall over my face again, and I closed my eyes, and I gritted my teeth, and I tried to think of anything, *anything*, other than the fact that I was hanging, suspended from a branch, over the edge of a cliff.

Jan would call this a legitimate fear. Not like a meteor crashing into our house, or getting trapped inside the freezer in the basement, or being forced to talk to Cole—all of which were so unlikely as to never happen, and were therefore irrational. But *this*, this was a legitimate fear: a thing that might happen. I was hanging upside down from a car stuck in the branches of a tree hanging over the edge of a cliff. The only thing holding me in was the thin strip of cloth from a seat belt.

"How do I get out?" I shouted over the whirring behind us. "How the hell am I getting out of here?"

"They're cutting out the back windshield. Then I'll cut the seat belt and take you with me. I have a harness."

A harness. Oh God, we needed a harness.

"It's just you?" I asked.

"It's the safest plan," he mumbled.

Ryan from my math class was possibly the last person in the world I'd want in charge of this plan. Ryan Baker, who could not remember the difference between sine and cosine. Who tattooed meaningless, intricate patterns on the inside of his forearm with pen instead of taking notes each class. My future was in the hands of someone who didn't understand basic trigonometry. What if he got the angle wrong? Misjudged the timing? How could I trust someone who didn't understand the geometry of a right triangle?

This seat belt was strapped across my chest at a right angle. The branches and the car and the cliff— all angles. This was a goddamn real-world application.

Fear: I might die today. I might die a minute from now.

Worse: if I moved, I'd also potentially kill Ryan Baker.

"What the hell are you doing here?" I asked.

"I'm a volunteer firefighter."

"I want a real one," I said, my voice high and tight.

"I *am* a real one."

"A different one!"

"Trust me, I would not object. But I'm the lightest one. Least chance of making the car fall out of the tree."

And there it was: the car could fall. They knew it, too. They had to make a *plan* for it. Falling, dying, was a real thing that could really happen, right now.

"You're not even that *light*," I said. He was decidedly taller than me, broad-shouldered, more lean-muscled than bulky—but definitely not *light*. I felt tears forming at the corners of my eyes, and I tried to pray. *Please please please.* But the branch still creaked below us.

"We're going to be fine," he said. But he sounded like he was trying to convince himself, too.

I settled on the deep breathing that Jan taught my mom, and my mom taught me.

The car lurched, and I braced my hands on the steering wheel, my stomach settling as the car stilled, and then lurching again as it tilted, dangling precipitously.

I heard Ryan's breath catch through the fabric of the seat.

"I think maybe this would be a good time to quit," I said.

If he responded, I couldn't tell, because the saw or whatever they were using was cutting through the panel, and the contact of machine on metal shook my insides, vibrated my back molars. Ryan grabbed my arms—either to comfort me or to keep me still, I wasn't sure.

I'm not paralyzed; I'm not unconscious; I'm not bleeding out; I'm not drowning.

And then the noise stopped, and Ryan's arm draped over my shoulder, holding out a belt with a clip. "Put this around your waist. Carefully." Our hands were both shaking, and I laughed as I grabbed the strap, bordering on delirium. Everything about this moment was ridiculous: from Ryan to the strap that would supposedly save me to the goddamn leaf curling on the air bag, parts of it still soft and green—like it didn't realize it was already dead.

I did as he said with as little movement as possible. The strap connected in front, and there was a small metal clip where it latched. "Okay," he said. "Here we go." He handed me a rope with another clip attached. "Connect this."

I did.

I saw the blade of the knife just beside my shoulder. "Okay, I'm going to cut you out, but you're attached to me now, and I'm attached to the guardrail above, so even if you're hanging, you'll be okay. But we need to *move*."

The car lurched, and I screamed. I had a feeling if the car fell now, I would *not* be okay. And neither would Ryan. Something about the force of the car being greater than the force of the rope holding us up. There was surely some math involved that he didn't understand.

"Let's go!" A voice of authority from outside. Older. Capable. "Out, now!"

Ryan wrapped a hand around my arm and used his other arm to slice through the fabric of the seat belt. I swung toward the middle of the seats, twisting around to face Ryan as the belt released. We were connected by a short distance of rope, clipped to the front of both of our harnesses. His hands gripped the slack between us.

"See?" he said. I swayed gently back and forth, reaching for his shoulder as he started to say something else.

Then there was a slow crunch from somewhere underneath us, and a long creak as the car tilted forward, and I saw it in Ryan's eyes just as my hand connected with his shoulder.

A quick snap that I heard at the same time I felt the tension of the rope above us release. I fell back, losing my grip on Ryan. He reached for me, but it was pointless. We were cut loose from the guardrail.

We were *falling*.

CHAPTER 3

I frantically reached for nothing, for *anything*. My fingers clawed at the fabric of the air bag as I hurtled through the open windshield—but I was still falling, my arms and legs skimming metal, a bruising pain as my elbows hooked into a groove. My body came abruptly to a stop, my legs dangling below, the chilled night air empty and endless all around me.

One second of relief, half a breath, and then I saw a body sailing by in a blur, fingers grasping for anything, nails and skin scraping on metal and *me*, and the impossible pressure on my hips as his weight tugged the rope connecting us, the added pressure making my elbows dislodge from their hold.

My eyes widened, and I slammed my hands down as I slid. My fingers desperately searching for a hold—and finally locking into the groove of the windshield once more.

Part of my weight was still on the hood of the car—but my legs dangled over, along with Ryan.

Don't look. Heights had, surprisingly, never been a fear of mine. Dying, on the other hand . . . I stared up at my hands instead. My fingers, the grip of my knuckles, were the only thing keeping us from going over.

Ryan kept jerking the rope, swinging back and forth, and I felt the metal cutting into my fingers, my grip slipping. "Stop moving! Ryan! Don't move!" I yelled.

He stilled, and I tried to slow my breathing. I closed my eyes, concentrating on the muscles in my hands, my arms, my shoulders.

List the things I am not. Go: *I'm not falling yet; I'm not dead yet.*

I risked a look to the side, noticed a wheel well to my left, and strained my leg toward it, until I could place some of my weight on the tire. I hooked my foot around it for leverage, dragging myself closer until my other leg could reach. With our weight supported, I started to move, sliding my fingers along the edge of the empty windshield, until both feet were firmly on the tire, though the harness on my waist, and Ryan's weight below, made every movement painful and strained. I wedged my elbows back into the groove of the windshield. "Okay," I called. "Can you make it?"

He didn't speak, but I felt the tug of the rope, over and over, as he must've been pulling himself up, hand over hand, until he could use the car for leverage. Finally he stood on the wheel, an arm around my back, one side of his face resting on the hood of the car and the other turned toward me. His breathing was labored and his eyes were wide, and we stared at each other in silence until the voice of another fireman cut through the night. "Baker! You guys okay, man?"

"Okay!" he called back.

They lowered another line down the outside of the car, which Ryan then hooked into his harness again. He wrapped both arms around me, and I did the same to him, and he called, "All set!"

I felt his muscles trembling from his shoulders down to his fingers. His eyes never left mine as they pulled us up to safety.

Ryan was shaking even worse than I was. Another firefighter clapped him on the shoulder. "Nice work, kid. Take a breather."

"Kelsey," Ryan said, "you can let go now."

I had my arms hooked around his shoulders, my body pressed tight to his own, even as I felt the ground solid and stable beneath us.

"Right, okay," I said. His eyes were gray and staring directly into mine as I backed away. He was dressed like the rest of his team—oversized pants and a blue T-shirt under suspenders. But surrounded by the rest of them now, he looked younger, as if he were playing dress-up in someone else's clothes, and I felt the urge to smooth the messy brown hair back from his forehead.

"Hey, we're not dead," I said, which was by far the stupidest thing I could've said out loud.

The side of his mouth tipped up, and then his whole face broke into a smile. "No, we're not," he said.

"Come on." A woman in uniform gestured to the ambulance. "Let's get you checked out."

I scanned the surroundings—the cars stopped on both sides, people with their phones out, police keeping everyone back. "Where's the other car?" I asked. "Is everyone okay?"

She tilted her head, a hand on my back, pushing me along. "There's no other car," she said.

The heat kicked in, a flash of headlights, and I cut the wheel—

"No, there was," I said.

She stopped for a moment, peering closely into each of my eyes, leaning so close I could see myself reflected in her pupils. "There isn't," she said.

"Are you *sure*?" I thought of the high mountain walls, the steep drop-off of the cliffs.

"We're sure," she said.

As I walked away, I heard the second firefighter ask Ryan, "You know that girl?"

"Yeah," he said. "She's in my math class."

Okay, so.

Before Ryan Baker was Ryan from my math class, he was the guy I worked with at the Lodge during the summer, where we'd trade off manning the register or checking people in or running equipment back and forth. We had developed a code—a tap on the shoulder to switch jobs, a wave goodbye, turning around simultaneously to stifle the laughter over the guy in ski pants in July. And a routine when our boss left— Ryan would sit on the counter and talk and ask me questions and laugh, and it was my favorite thing of the summer, the thing I looked forward to every day on the way to work.

And then at the end of the summer, on our last day, he'd said, "Hey, do you want to do something sometime?"

Yes, I thought. "Yes," I said.

"Okay." His face broke into a smile, and I heard someone whistle. Leo and AJ and Mark were nearby, clustered near the front door.

And I wasn't sure what I'd just agreed to, so I said, "Wait. What does that mean?"

And then Ryan looked over his shoulder, where we could both see his friends waiting for him, and said, "What do you want it to mean?"

"Is this a trick question?"

It felt like a trick question.

"No. Uh." Leo said something indecipherable behind him. "Look," Ryan said, his face unreadable. "It doesn't have to mean anything."

"Oh. Okay."

And just like that, he left. No exchange of numbers,

no plans for later. And when school started up the next week and I found myself assigned to the seat beside him in math, both of us just pretended it hadn't happened.

There were probably some social cues I wasn't aware of, some high school mating-ritual dance I'd never learned—or maybe *do something sometime* meant *meet me in the back closet after work.*

I bet he had not expected *do something sometime* would mean rappelling into my dangling car and cutting me out of my seat belt, then hanging from a harness attached to my waist instead of falling to his death.

Hey, remember that time we did something? Good times.

"I just want to go home. I need to see my mom," I told the woman looking me over. She didn't look much older than me, to be honest. God, where were the adults in charge?

"You were unconscious, Kelsey. We need to check that out at the hospital. Your mom can meet us there."

"No, she can't." She *couldn't.* "I need to call her. I need my phone."

The lights were too bright from all the cars on the road, headlights shining directly at us, and I squinted, feeling a headache brewing.

Ryan weaved through the cluster of cars and emergency vehicles haphazardly parked around the site, holding his arm limply in front of him, apparently also needing to get checked out in the ambulance. He paused, handed me his phone with his good arm. "Sorry," he said, "I don't think yours made it." I took it from his outstretched hand and dialed home while he shifted foot to foot, pretending not to pay attention. I had to try twice before I got the right numbers with the tremble in my hands, which I'm sure he noticed.

It rang four times, like I knew it would, before the automated voice of the answering machine instructed me in a robotic tone to *please leave a message.*

I lowered my voice. "Mom, it's just me. Pick up."

"Kelsey?" I could hear her brain working overtime: *Daughter calls from phone that's not hers. Where's the danger?*

"Hey, I'm okay, but I had a car accident, I'm so sorry, but they're making me go to the hospital to be sure. But I'm totally fine, I promise."

She sucked in a breath. "I'll call Jan."

"No," I said. "I'm really fine. I just need a ride home. I'll call the car service when I'm ready. Oh, and I think I lost my phone."

I heard her exhale slowly, could picture her closing her eyes, doing that breathing thing, picturing me alive, and safe, and home. "You're fine," she said. "And you're with the doctors. And you'll be home soon." The good before the bad.

"Sorry about the car."

"It's okay. You're safe. We're not talking about the car again." A pause. "But I think I have to call Jan."

I handed Ryan back his phone, and the too-young-to-be-in-charge medic ushered me into the back of the ambulance.

"Hey, hold on," Ryan said.

I held on. My grip on the door handle, my feet on the metal loading dock, so I towered over him. He looked like he had a thousand things he wanted to say to me. I had things I wanted to say to him, too. But where to start? Where to even start?

"You need a ride home from the hospital?"

"I can call someone." The car service was one of the first numbers I'd memorized when I was younger.

"I'll be there anyway. So."

So. Communication: not our strength.

"Okay. If I see you there . . ."

He nodded. "I'll find you when I'm done."

As the ambulance drove off, I saw him through the back windows, talking to the other firefighters. But the image that stuck in my head was his face, the moment I'd reached for him. The moment he knew we were going to fall.

Don't be afraid, he'd said in a whisper, before he knew I was alive, or conscious.

You're okay, he'd said, before he knew whether that was true.

I'd clung to those words, made them into something I could believe in. But in hindsight, I wondered if maybe he'd only been talking to himself.

CHAPTER 4

The emergency room of Covington City Hospital had pictures of Vermont's Green Mountains on the walls—which I guess were supposed to be comforting. If only I hadn't just plummeted off the edge of those same mountains. And the landscapes were interspersed with health notices to *Please Wear a Mask* if you were feeling ill.

The medic insisted on bringing me inside with a wheelchair—protocol, she claimed—but I stood up as soon as we were safely inside the lobby, despite the look she gave me. I glanced around the room at the sea of strangers—all watching me back.

I heard periodic beeping, a loudspeaker crackle, a baby crying. Everything was unfamiliar—the angular walls, the sounds, the sharp scent of cleanser—and I stayed close to the medic as she led me through the lobby. I checked over my shoulder, saw the double doors we'd entered. But there were no windows, no other exits except more doors leading to more halls. I could see the fluorescent glow through the glass panels. A labyrinth of rooms I'd never find my way out of alone.

I also didn't see Ryan anywhere—maybe he was already getting looked at. Maybe he was on a different floor. Maybe he'd never find me in the sea of strangers. The medic led me past a bunch of people who looked like they should definitely be wearing masks, past the police hovering near the hallway entrances, to a narrow bed surrounded by blue curtains. I hadn't stopped shaking since being pulled from the car.

"Probably just the leftover adrenaline," she said, watching me stare at my own hands. I curled my fingers in.

"Yeah," I said. Not the fact that my hands had barely kept me from falling, or the fear that was oozing out of every pore, turning me anxious and paralyzed.

It's just the unknown, that's what Jan would say. It's how I got through the first month of high school last year, after it was strongly suggested that I attend our local school instead of having my mother homeschool me any longer. *Strong suggestions* were things my mother took pretty seriously. And me leaving the house on a regular basis was a big condition of her custody agreement with Jan and the Department of Family Services. Jan was the one who got me a summer job, for that very reason.

The medic patted my shoulder awkwardly before

leaving the area as a woman in scrubs pulled the curtain aside.

I'm not stuck in the car anymore; I'm not hanging from a cliff; I'm not in danger. And slowly, the shaking subsided.

The doctor kept shining a light in my eyes, asking me to follow her finger, even as the police officer questioned me. I didn't have a bump on my head, I didn't recall hitting my head, but the fact remained that I had been unresponsive until Ryan Baker crawled into my car. I wondered, briefly, how long that had been.

"Were you on the phone?" the police officer asked.

"My phone was in my bag." Both of which were now over a cliff.

The doctor's fingers traced patterns on my skull, which was not at all unpleasant—a direct contrast to the officer's line of questioning.

"Had you been drinking?" he asked.

"Other than caffeine? No."

"So, you were tired then? Did you fall asleep at the wheel?"

Of course I was tired. I'd been at school for eight hours, and then spent two more hours tutoring Leo Johnson in chemistry. But these were the types of questions people asked my mom, who had learned to err on the side of caution, on the side of lying. Always too much to lose.

"Not really," I said. "A soda was just the cheapest thing in the school vending machine. There was a car heading my way, on my side of the street. *That's* why I drove off the road."

"What did this car look like?"

It had been dark. I closed my eyes, tried to remember. *One glance away. The heat kicking on. The glare of headlights, and I cut the wheel . . .* "All I saw were the lights."

The doctor was moving my head gently back and forth.

"There's no sign of another car," the police officer said.

I closed my eyes, tried to see it again—maybe the glare had been from my own high beams reflecting off the median. What had I really seen? It had only lasted a fraction of a second. Now that I revisited it, I started to doubt my own memory.

"Did you check the bottom of the cliff?" I asked.

He looked at me like I'd made a distasteful joke, but I was serious. He nodded to the doctor. "That'll be all, Kelsey. Do me a favor and fill in your birthdate, phone number, and address, in case we have any more questions."

"Sure." I took the clipboard from his hand.

The officer pulled the curtain back as he left, and Ryan stood just outside, leaning against the desk at reception. I smiled involuntarily, and he half waved back. He was something familiar, and suddenly safe, and it reminded me of all those times at the Lodge, before things turned awkward, when he'd sit on top of the counter, smiling at me while I talked.

There was now a bandage wrapped around his upper arm, disappearing inside the sleeve of his shirt, and I wondered whether he'd gotten that from climbing in my car or if it was from the fall. The doctors chatted him up, patted his shoulder—he was still in uniform, and looked completely at home.

"Looks like someone's here to check up on you," the doctor said.

"He's my ride home," I said. And when she raised an eyebrow, I added, "He's in my math class."

She ran her hands over my arms, my sides, my back. I winced when she pressed my left arm, felt my body tense when her fingers skimmed my elbows. "You can expect some bruising," she said.

She scanned my body quickly, turning over my hands, gently uncurling my fingers. "Ouch," she said. Her eyes flicked up to my face and back down again. "Any idea how this happened?"

The deep line ran across all four fingers of both hands, the skin scraped raw. I resisted the urge to ball them back up. A secret—how close we truly came.

"No," I said. "I don't know." A small lie. A learned habit.

She pressed her lips together as she treated and bandaged each one. "Are your parents coming?" she asked. "There's still a bunch of paperwork to take care of before we can release you. And we need your insurance information."

"No, but . . ." The thought trailed off as two teenagers approached the desk Ryan was leaning against. I heard the guy say my name as the girl's gaze flitted around the room, eventually settling on me. She tapped her brother's arm, and I shrank into myself.

Cole and Emma. Jan's children. Both exes of mine, in one way or another.

Jan's son, Cole, was also first-boyfriend Cole, even though it was back when he was fifteen and I was fourteen, and he probably only did it because he wasn't supposed to. Or maybe just because I was always *there*.

Jan used to take me to "socialize" with her children—it was healthy, she told my mom. It was a step. A safe step. She brought me around to birthday parties, or out on excursions, for *years*. Until I turned fourteen and I wasn't just a girl his mom made them hang out with anymore. There were probably rules against this, with Jan.

He'd told me he liked my freckles and I told him I'd had them forever, hadn't he noticed? He'd shrugged. He'd kissed me. A month later, Jan found out and told Cole to put an end to it, and when I confronted him about it, he shrugged again, and that was the end of that. At first, I'd thought he was a coward, not standing up to his mom. Then I realized he probably didn't *care*. He shrugged. The end.

I have since come to loathe all boys who shrug.

Rumor had it that he broke up with his last girl-friend through a text, and that he forgot to break up with the one before that *at all* before moving on. So, honestly, I guess it could've been worse.

An unfortunate by-product of the Cole breakup was that Emma eventually became ex-best-friend Emma, as well. Sadly, never to be replaced. My neighbor Annika was probably the closest thing I had to one now—when she wasn't away at boarding school.

Cole, at least, had let me know in no uncertain terms that whatever we had was over. The shrug. With Emma, it was more of a drifting. There was no big falling-out; she just stopped answering her phone. Our friendship just kind of fizzled, like a sparkler burning down to your fingers. By the time you realize you were being burned, it was too late—the damage done, the spark already extinguished.

She'd gone on to become someone else—new friends, different crowd—while I remained left behind, painfully the same. *A work in progress*, Jan called me. Always in progress.

I assumed Jan had had a Talk with her children about privacy and such, because as far as I knew, neither had told anyone about my mother. And last year, when I found myself wandering the school halls for the first time, their faces were the only ones I recognized—their eyes momentarily meeting my own, then sliding quickly away. Three years later, and it was as if we'd never known each other at all.

Still, both of them were metaphorical bombs, as far as I was concerned. I couldn't make eye contact without seeing myself reflected in their eyes—in their mother's dinnertime conversation, in her papers. I did not like what I saw.

Cole was the one to speak first. "Mom's taking a night course. And our dad's away at work. So here we are."

"Thanks," I said. First word spoken in over three years. Not too hard. Like ripping off a Band-Aid.

But then he shrugged. *No big deal. Whatever. We're done.* Take your pick.

Cole had my medical consent forms, the ones that Jan had used before to get me treated. The ones she needed to get me released. Because I was seventeen, and therefore not capable of making decisions for myself.

Emma was sixteen, had grown into her wide-set eyes, had also developed curves and a mean streak, if rumors were to be believed. Cole had only gotten taller, had filled out from football and lacrosse, and had his pick of girls, which he rotated through at an alarming pace.

"What's Ryan Baker doing here?" Emma asked, like we were still friends—as if she hadn't systematically ignored me until I stopped trying. And then, when Ryan turned at his name, she leaned into her hip and cocked her head—a study in flirtation—and said, "Are you okay?"

"Yeah. Just a few stitches," he said.

"How much longer?" Cole asked the doctor, not making eye contact with me.

"Thank you for bringing the papers. But I have a ride," I said.

"My mom said—"

"Ryan's driving me." I liked this version of me a lot better. The girl who got rides home from people she vaguely knew, who did not need to rely on the generosity of ex-friends. Resourceful. Resilient.

"Okay, fine." Cole let the papers drop into my lap, his hands held up like he was relieving himself of some great responsibility. "I do have better things to do, you know."

I wondered what Cole had been doing before his mom sent him here, because his aggravation at me seemed a little stronger than a one-month relationship more than three years earlier should warrant— especially one that ended with a shrug.

"Blame your mother," I said, because that hurt.

"Or yours," he said, which hurt even more, because he was right.

The ticking bomb. They knew the truth. *I know, I know, I know who you are.*

Who am I? Usually, I'm nothing. A student in your math class. Kelsey Thomas? A shrug. A girl in a sea of faces, passing unremarkably in the hall. Most of the time, I'm fine. Steady hands, steady course, X-ing out the boxes of the calendar—a string of days that blur together in typical fashion.

Other times, out of nowhere, I become afraid, like her. So afraid that I cannot move. Sometimes, for no reason that I can understand, I do nothing but lie in bed, like my mother does, needing the four walls and the silence. I sometimes become so paralyzed that I pretend to be physically ill, just so I can remain, unmoving, in the safety of my room. To know, at any moment, at *every* moment, that I am okay. I am safe.

But that's nothing compared to my mother.

I'm the daughter of a woman completely ruled by fear. We live on a very fine line.

And they know.

After the papers were processed and the doctor released me to go home, leaving me with a pamphlet on how to watch out for signs of an internal head injury, I unwound the bandages from my hands and quickly looked myself over in the mirror. Nothing visible for my mother to worry over unnecessarily. I slid off the bed and joined Ryan at the front desk, where he was working his way through a bowl of lollipops. People kept smiling at him as they passed, like they couldn't help themselves.

"Those your friends?" he asked, his tongue unnaturally red from the candy.

"No," I said. "Their mom had paperwork the hospital needed. Long story."

"Is she your guardian or something?"

"Not exactly," I said, following him out into the parking lot. Jan wasn't something I wanted to elaborate on, or explain.

"But your mom's sick, right?" My shoulders stiffened on impulse, and he visibly cringed. "Sorry, I didn't mean to just say that."

I guess there was some sort of talk, if Ryan had heard that. "Yes, she is." It was the truth, but not in the way he meant it. Not cancer or something terminal. But it *was* an illness. Simpler to let them assume it was something physical in nature. Something they could understand.

Seeing Jan was part of my mother's deal to keep me. Jan was assigned by the state. I've come to rely on her, but I also don't totally trust her, because she reports to someone else, who decides my fate. My mother relies on her even more, and trusts her even less.

Especially since that article she wrote, that was decidedly about me.

My fear.

There was this study, before, that she referred to in the paper, on *epigenetics and fear*. How scientists repeatedly scared mice with specific odors—fear conditioning, it's called—and then watched as their future offspring seemed to be scared of those same scents. They did it with cherry blossoms—I could not imagine being scared of cherry blossoms, but to each their own, I guess. Anyway, this was the basis of her article. Evolution in progress. A sign that gene expression can be altered. That fear can be passed down, conditioned, woven into the very core of us, down to the expression of our DNA.

Her article became the subject of a peer review discussion. Were my fears the product of my childhood? Was I fed them as an infant, held to my mother's chest? Did the tension leech from her body into mine? Did I absorb some physical cues from her? Did she weave them into bedtime stories, whispered to me in the dark? Or—and this is Jan—was there something tying mine to hers, that goes deeper, all the way to my DNA?

On the one hand, I wasn't a mouse.

But I remembered, just as Jan must have, when she took me and Emma to that nail salon while the back rooms were being worked on, and all the hairs on my arms stood on end from the scent of the cleaning fluid, and I threw up my burrito all over the cheap linoleum floor.

The scent of caustic cleaners, Jan wrote in that paper. Though this was a violation of our privacy, we had too much to lose.

Careful, always careful. The word like an echo, always there, always a warning. There were too many ways she could lose me.

CHAPTER 5

Ryan drove a Jeep with a soft top, and doors he could remove in the nice weather, which I'd seen him do when he pulled up to the Lodge in the summer. I could tally the ways my mother would deem this car unsafe. Then again, mine was over a cliff, and his was not.

"Where do you live?" he asked as he opened my door.

"Do you know Sterling Cross? It's this neighborhood at the end of—"

"Yeah," he said as he shut the door. "I know it."

His phone chimed in the space between us as we exited the parking lot, but he ignored it.

"So," I said, "firefighter, huh? Aren't you a little young?"

"I turned eighteen last month, but I've wanted to do it my whole life. My dad just retired. My grandfather was a firefighter before him, too. The department is practically my family. We were all just waiting to make it official." He smiled to himself. "It's in my blood."

His phone chimed again.

"Are you going to check it?" I asked. If it was my mother, and I ignored it more than once, she'd start to panic.

His hands tightened on the wheel, and his eyes slid over to me for a fraction of a second. "Not while I'm driving. I've seen enough accidents, thanks," he said.

And then I was back there, hanging, my fingers scrambling for purchase. . . . "I wasn't texting, in case you were wondering," I said. I picked up his phone, felt him cut his eyes to me again. "A Holly wants to know if you're going to the party at Julian's tonight."

He shifted in his seat. "Uh."

"She says she really hopes you'll be there. The *really* is in all caps, by the way. So I think she means it."

"Kelsey?"

"Yeah?"

"Are you okay?"

"Just a few scratches. More than I can say for you." I caught myself staring at his bandage.

"No, I mean are you *okay*?" he asked.

"Oh." I put his phone back. "I don't know." We drove through the mountain pass, and I concentrated on the floorboard instead of the double yellow line, and the narrow shoulder of the road, and the dark night stretching out below us. "Ask me tomorrow."

"Put your number in my phone, and I'll ask you to-morrow."

"My phone is gone," I said.

His thumbs were drumming on the steering wheel, all nervous energy, and it was starting to catch.

He's asking for your number, Kelsey. Don't be a moron.

"For when you get a new one, then," he said.

Meaning: I lived in Sterling Cross, I could afford a new phone. And I *would* get a new one soon, because it was doubtful I'd be let out of the house without one.

"Okay." I added my number to his phone, like he asked.

"Where to?" He pulled into the entrance of Sterling Cross, which was one windy road you had to travel a few miles down until it forked off in several directions, each road leading to a single lot with a stand-alone house. There were only ten houses in the neighbor-hood, and most were some type of mansion trying to disguise itself as a humble log cabin—*mountain chic*, Annika called it, when I'd pointed this out to her.

Mine was the only one that didn't follow the trend. Cole and Emma used to call my place the House of Horrors when Jan would pick me up, and after, I couldn't see it without looking at it the same way. The house was white and clean and boxy—an exte-rior that looked slightly industrial with its perfect, hard angles, like cement blocks. The windows were sleek and tinted, and it was set down a slope, so you couldn't really see it from the road. There was nothing really scary about it, once you were inside. But the metal fence was high and spiked and covered in ivy—and that's not even counting the wire running along the top—and you could see the bars over some of the windows, which was I guess how they got the *Horrors* part.

"Here's fine," I said at the turn for my road.

Ryan laughed. "Pretty sure you don't have to be embarrassed about where you live."

We weren't rich, like he thought. My mother came into a lot of money, once upon a time, and she'd used up most of it to buy this place, set it up, set *us* up. She worked from home as a bookkeeper, and we got by just fine. But we lived there not because of the prestige of the houses or the property. We lived here because the houses themselves were all set far apart, and there was only one road in or out, funneled down a finger of land with steep, treacherous terrain on both sides. And people left us alone. Everyone here kept to themselves. It was safe.

"Okay," I said. It was dark on the drive in, and the lights would've been off if Mom hadn't been waiting up for me. "Turn right here," I said. But now the front of the house was lit by big spotlights, exposing everything.

It was exactly as I feared. Spikes illuminated, the top of the house—the steep slopes and sharp angles of the roof—just visible from the street, making it look larger than it was. And the camera over the gate, the keypad awaiting my thumbprint.

Ryan looked from me to the house and back again. He unbuckled his seat belt and twisted in his seat, the engine still running.

"Well, thanks for the ride." I raised my hand to wave, and his eyes narrowed.

He reached out and grabbed my wrist, his gaze searching my palm. No, he was staring at my fingers. I balled them up, but then he grabbed the other hand. "Jesus," he said. I followed his line of sight to the deep red crease across my fingers. The indentation from the metal. The only thing that had kept us from falling. He ran his fingers just below the raw skin, and I shivered.

My hands started to shake again, and I replayed that moment, my elbows losing their grip, my fingers grasping for anything, and I pulled them back, balled them into fists. "See you in math," I said, my voice shaking, along with my hands.

"Kelsey, wait—"

But I couldn't wait. I needed to be inside, with my mother. Behind the gates, behind the walls.

"Thank you, Ryan," I said as I stepped out of the car.

His eyes locked on mine as I stood before the gate, awaiting my fingerprint. I didn't want him to see this part. I didn't want him to *know* this part.

"I'll see you tomorrow," I called.

I waved goodbye, and eventually he caved. "Okay,

tomorrow, then," he said. I waited until he was around the first curve before letting myself inside the gate.

My mother was standing in the foyer, in front of the common area and between the hallways that snaked out into the two wings of the one-level house. She kept touching her shoulder through her loose shirt—an old habit—and she'd been crying. I'd barely had time to lock the door behind me, and she was pulling me to her, gripping me tight, and then holding me back by my shoulders. "Oh, thank God!" She took a quick breath, almost like she was gasping for air. Then pulled me to her again. "Imagine my surprise to turn on the news and see my daughter's car *over a cliff.* Kelsey, *God.*" I felt her fingers pressing into my spine.

"It looks worse than it was, Mom."

I waited until she slowly released me. Her long blond hair moved over her shoulders as she shook her head, her eyes closed. "I knew it was too soon. I shouldn't have listened to Jan. You're too young to drive."

You're too young to be living like this, I wanted to say. She was. So young. She looked young enough to be Jan's daughter, even.

"Mom. Look at me. Mom, I'm fine. Nothing's broken. Nothing hurts. See?" I needed to get out of this room before she had me walking her through it all. "I just want a shower," I said. "And a nap."

I handed her my hospital forms, knew she'd spend

an hour looking over everything, researching the hospital coding on her own, reading up on potential head injuries—an outlet for the fear. But she didn't, at first. She stared at me, picking me apart, her hand brushing over the chemical burn scars on the back of her shoulder again. I grabbed her hand to get her to stop.

She has no memory of her abduction, just the fear that came with her when she left. Taken from her home just outside Atlanta, Georgia, in the spring of her junior year of high school, she escaped from wherever she was held more than a year later, with no memory of her time there.

An entire year. Gone.

Sometimes I'd catch her staring at me, like she was trying to see something more. Pick me apart, like she could read the fabric of my existence.

Nobody knew anything about the man who had held her. Well, that's not entirely true. We knew some things. We knew he was most likely white, with brown eyes, and taller than average.

This was what I could deduce from the fact that my mother had blue eyes and I did not. And from the fact that I was paler than her, even though I spent a lot of time out in the sun in the backyard. And I already towered over her. Maybe he had freckles, too.

So. There were some things we knew.

Subtract the half of me that was her, and what was left?

"Don't tell me it's *not that bad*," she said. She put her

hand to her mouth, shook her head, pulled me toward her. "I don't know what I'd do," she said, hugging me for eternity. "The car is *gone*. It could've been—"

"I'm safe," I said, my chest constricting.

Back in my room, down the opposite hall, I tried to take comfort in the four walls, and the bed, neatly made. The mountains out the window, which used to keep us safe.

The car was *gone*, my mother said—it fell. It fell, and it was gone, like I would have fallen, like I would've been gone, had Ryan not pulled me out.

I peeled off my clothes, and I stood in the shower, bracing myself against the wall, and I began to cry.

I remembered how peaceful it had been, the emptiness. The quiet of the unthinking mind, at rest. Listening to someone else's words, and believing them, before I became myself again. Before my mind started working overtime, beginning the vicious cycle. I latched on to fears, the beautiful familiarity of them. And they crawled like spiders across my skin, until the only solution was to give myself over to them, in stillness.

And now here I was, revisiting the fall, as I would be all night, relentless and unstoppable.

Maybe it was ingrained in my DNA, and I had no hope of overcoming these moments, and everything Jan said was pointless. Maybe I learned it from my

mother, the way we locked our doors, remained behind walls, constantly demanding confirmation of our
safety. Maybe it was her fault I'd be up all night, staring at this wall.

Not like Ryan, who I imagined going out with
friends, celebrating his daring survival with underage
drinking, and Holly and other girls draping themselves
over him, calling him a hero, and him being all *It was
nothing. Just some trigonometry. A little muscle, that's
all.*

And me, staring at the empty wall, like it was the
darkness over the edge of the cliff. Just me and my
breathing, replaying it over and over, seeing how close
we'd come—one missed grip, one second of slipped
concentration. The crease across the skin of my fingers, throbbing and raw.

The thought would circle and dig and circle some
more, until I felt empty without it.

How close we'd come.

How close to gone.

CHAPTER 6

I stayed home from school the next day, which wasn't my mom's idea, exactly, but I didn't get out of bed Thursday morning, and she didn't ask me to. We had to wait for the insurance money before replacing the car, and Jan was looking into the bus situation— but in the meantime, nobody mentioned anything about me and school. It seemed to be an agreed-upon decision, especially since I didn't have a new phone yet, which meant Mom couldn't track me if she wanted to.

I wondered if anyone had recovered my phone, my bag, my key ring with the purple clip that I'd hook through my belt loop for safekeeping. If it was all still at the bottom of the cliff, inside the car, wedged between crushed metal and deflated air bags.

I dreamed the same thing whether I was sleeping or awake—an endless fall, with no bottom. The car too slick, or my fingers too slow, and the air rushing up as I plummeted into darkness.

I'd just read a short story for English about a man sentenced to death by hanging over a bridge, and as he fell, the rope broke, and he escaped—falling into the river, swimming to evade capture, making his way home—only to feel the noose tighten when he finally arrived. The whole escape a fabrication of his mind. A slow and inevitable demise. That whole time, he'd just been falling in slow motion.

I sat in the dim light of my room and stared at my fingers, at the red line and the swollen skin, like proof.

I wasn't falling. I'd held on. I'd made it home.

I was in my bed, surrounded by my four walls, with the sound of my mom banging pots and pans around in the kitchen, which was yet another stress-relief strategy via Jan. And one of my least favorites. She'd serve up casseroles big enough for eight people, and we'd have to eat them for an entire week, and she'd apologize, knowing it was terrible, but eating it anyway.

To be fair, cooking did tend to relax her—keeping her hands busy, her mind occupied with a list of ingredients, a simple task to focus on. If it worked, if she broke free of whatever was haunting her, she'd eventually cave and let me order pizza or Chinese for delivery.

This was not one of those times.

For two days, she called me out for meals—the casserole crisp where it should be soft, soggy where it should be crisp—and I slunk back to my room after. She didn't argue. I wondered, if I went to her office, if

I'd find the pictures from the accident up on the computer screen. Or if this time it would be something worse.

She had a bad habit of seeking them out, robberies and kidnappings, missing children and acts of violence. Even before her kidnapping, her life had been a struggle. It must've been so easy for her to only see the dangers. This was something I didn't tell Jan about. I didn't know if it was making her worse—more fearful of the world beyond our walls—or whether it might help. If it reminded her: she had escaped, when so many did not.

I stared at my fingers again. I had lived. And so had she.

Mom knocked on the bedroom door as I was waking on what I thought was Saturday morning, but when I checked the clock, it was already after noon. "Jan's here," she said. Code: *Get out of bed. Look alive.*

It was a big deal if Jan was here for a session on a weekend. Her husband worked as some sort of consultant and traveled during the week, so they tried to keep weekends free, for family time. If Jan was here on a weekend, there must've been a reason, and that made me nervous.

The last few days had blurred together—I'd been in the same pajamas for at least a day and a half. I opened the windows to air out the room, but left the outside metal window grate closed. I had a key so I could swing the bars open, also for safety reasons (in the event of a fire), but for now the locked bars were what I needed. I changed out of my pajamas and splashed water on my face.

Jan had brownish-gray hair cut in a mom-bob, and she was dressed in her work slacks and blouse, even though it was the weekend. "Kelsey, my dear," she said when I emerged from the room—hair in a bun to hide the fact it hadn't been washed, foundation to hide the dark circles, smile to hide the fact that I still hadn't shaken the moment, the one that circled and dug and made itself at home: one second, one muscle cramp, between here and gone.

"Hi, Jan," I said, taking the package from her out-stretched hand. The new phone my mom had re-quested, in a box that must've been sitting outside the gate since yesterday—I hoped Jan hadn't noticed. "Oh, I didn't know it had arrived yet," I said.

"Same number," my mom said. "Just need to pro-gram it again."

"Kelsey," Jan said, taking her normal seat in the living room, in the loveseat across from the couch. "Sit, please. Let's talk." Beside her on the floor was a brown box with no lid, filled with my missing things. My backpack, dirty and singed, my purse, the strap dangling from a single side, the red umbrella that used to be in the backseat, the spokes bent at unnatural angles, the handle either crushed or melted.

It all smelled faintly chemical, like gasoline. I pressed my lips together, tasting it in the air, and wondered if Mom could sense it, too. But she was looking beyond Jan, through the large windows at the back of the living room, her head tilted slightly to the side. I followed her gaze and saw a girl sitting on the stone wall past the gate, kicking her legs.

An exit, thank God. "It's Annika," I said. "I was just on my way out," I added.

My mom raised an eyebrow, but said nothing.

Jan twisted around on the couch, squinting. "How can you even see that far?"

Annika was an easily identifiable blur, even from the distance: her hair exceeded normal volume by at least three hundred percent, she was always wearing colors that would somehow catch the eye, and she had the inability to sit still. Besides, this was where she'd always wait for me. It was as close as she ever got.

The stone wall at the edge of the property was our first line of defense, though it was more of a deterrent than an official barrier. There was an open gap in the front of the wall, a makeshift driveway where I used to park my car. Then came the high metal fence, with a discreet electrical cable lining the top and a locked gate toward the back, and another in the front, encircling the yard. There was a small stand-alone booth with a door and a window just inside the gated entrance, to the left, I guess in case someone actually hired a security guard to man the gate.

But between the fence and the outer wall the weeds ran wild, vegetation climbing up the stone, thick and unruly. "It looks like the perfect place for snakes," Annika had complained, and I had to agree. She never came any closer. Her side of the wall was all mowed and landscaped with shrubbery and a pond with a constantly running fountain.

"It's her," I said, with one more glance to the box at Jan's feet. "I have to go. Can we talk later?" Because I couldn't completely brush Jan off. There were lines to walk, after all.

"All right," Jan said. "Listen, I've spoken to the school. It's too late to add on to the bus route, so Cole and Emma will be picking you up Monday morning. At least until you get the car situation taken care of."

I considered it one of my greater accomplishments that I kept my face passive and my thoughts unvoiced. "That would be great," I said, because of all the things I'd either inherited or learned from my mother, the art of the lie was the most useful.

Annika swung her legs like a little kid, the heels of her shoes bouncing against the wall. She wore gray tights and black Mary Janes and a purple skirt so short it was a good thing the tights were opaque.

"I've been calling you all day," she said once I got close enough to hear.

"I'm sorry, I lost my phone." I leaned against the wall beside her.

"Oh, I was starting to wonder," she said, leaning closer, her eyes roaming over me from head to toe. She scrunched up her nose at my bun. "I *heard.*"

The scream of metal, the rush of air, the scent of burning rubber, and my nails skimming metal—

I placed my hands flat against the stone wall, trying to ground myself. *You made it. You're here.*

She patted the spot beside her on the ledge, and I used the grooves between the uneven stones for footing.

To me, Annika always seemed like she came from a different world. She layered her clothes, unmatching: bright tights under plaid skirts, or the other way around, boho tops and jewelry that chimed like music when she walked, and long, wavy hair she'd coil around ribbons or push back from her face with a scarf or bandanna.

She also had this vaguely unplaceable accent, not quite European, but something deliberate and alluring.

"It's from all the travel," she'd told me once. A year of school in France as a child, another in England, before her mom divorced her State Department husband and settled here with Annika and her older brother, who was off at college now.

"I cannot believe," she was saying as I hauled myself up beside her, "that I had to hear about this from my mother, of all people. Normal people tend to call their friends when they nearly die, you know." Annika looked at me the way I imagined I must look at her: like she was caught between being captivated and confused. I thought it was probably why we remained good friends, despite the long stretches of silence, the distance, and the differences. She was foreign, and interesting, and unplaceable, like her accent. And I was the same to her. Our worlds were so far from each other that they circled back around and almost touched again.

"I didn't nearly die," I said. I felt her gaze on the side of my face, wondered if she could read the lie in my expression. Wondered what normal people tended to say, or not say, to their friends. "I had a car crash. And I wasn't really in the mood to relive it."

"That's not what the papers say," she said, the corners of her lips tipping down. They were shiny, covered in a pink gloss that might've even had sparkles, and it was hard to take anything she said too seriously.

"The papers?"

"Mm," she said, turning sideways, her hands on the stone between us, her nails painted electric blue. "According to Thursday's paper," she began, using some faux-official voice, "thanks to classmate and volunteer firefighter Ryan Something-or-other, Kelsey Thomas, the young woman miraculously pulled from the car over Benjamin's Cliff, walks away without a scratch." Her fingers circled my wrist, warm in the autumn chill. "Someone took a picture of your car after it fell. Quite the sight, Kels." She paused, and in that gap, I pictured it—the car, falling. Me, still clinging to the edge. "So don't tell me you didn't nearly die. A reporter showed up last night, hoping us neighbors might have a status update for them. Nosy bastards."

I felt my shoulders deflate, my back slumping. "Ugh," I said. My name. In the newspaper. My mom was going to flip. She was big on privacy—so big, in fact, that I was probably the only student not on one of the vast assortment of social networking sites. I only had an email account because it was required from school so teachers could send us assignments. I was sure she wouldn't have gotten me a phone if it didn't also double as a GPS. "Isn't that illegal to print my name? I'm a minor."

"Apparently not," she said. "Or else someone missed that memo." I decided this was something best kept from my mother, for her own peace of mind.

"You home for a while?" I asked, itching to change the subject.

"Fall break. Just the week." Annika's newest boarding school worked on some nontraditional schedule, not really adhering to typical holidays, and I could never remember when she was supposed to be home. "I emailed you when I got home last night, when I couldn't reach you."

"Oh, sorry," I said. I'd never made it to Mom's office and the computer. I was used to using my phone for email, and I wasn't working on any school projects. I had barely made it out of my room at all—mostly on autopilot, to the kitchen and back again—until the fear of Jan seeing me this way knocked me out of my stupor.

"I even tried your home line," Annika said. "Busy signal. All day."

"Really?"

"Yeah. I just tried it again before I came out here."

"Huh. I'll check it." Maybe it had been knocked off the cradle. I hadn't heard it ring since the accident, now that she mentioned it.

"So, listen, you want to come over tomorrow? I'm sentenced to *family time* today with Brett home from college for the weekend, but he's going out tomorrow, so I should be free at least part of the day."

"I can't come over," I said, shaking my head. "Maybe later next week but . . . not now." Not when it took three days to leave the house. Not when I already felt the vastness, as my mom called it, of the open air. The feeling of all the things that could go wrong the farther I walked from my door.

"Sure. Later, then," she said. This was another reason I thought we got along so well. We didn't ask too many questions. I never asked why she kept changing schools, and she never asked why I lived behind bars and gates and wires.

I slid off the wall, back to my side of the property, an invisible tether—the promise of safe, and predictable.

She stared at the weeds, squeezed her eyes shut, and dropped down after me. "Hey," she said, hand on my arm. "You're okay, right?"

I wasn't sure if Annika knew about my mom, or what she suspected, but she must've known something. The leash I was kept on, the things I couldn't do, the fact that we always went to her house instead of my own.

"Yes," I said. "I'm okay." *The darkness over the edge, the grip of my fingers . . .*

I felt an ache in the bruise on my shoulder, my elbows, and the line across my hands.

Annika shuddered and picked her feet up, one exaggerated step at a time, like there might really be snakes in the grass. I uncurled my hand, overwhelmed with the sudden impulse to show her the line across my fingers—that maybe she would understand—

"Annika?" A woman's voice, from the other side of the wall.

Annika rolled her eyes. "Gotta run." But before she climbed back over the wall, she pulled me toward her, squeezed me tight, the ribbons in her hair tickling my neck. "I'm glad you're okay, Kelsey darling." Then she air-kissed my cheek, which was something only Annika could get away with, before finding a foothold in the stone wall.

CHAPTER 7

Back inside, Mom's office door was closed, and Jan's car was still parked just outside the front gate. They were probably having an official session. The box of my recovered items was still on the living room floor. I stepped around it and picked up the phone line—it had been left off the hook. I hung it up, picked it up again, heard a catch, a click, and then the dial tone. If it hadn't been working before, at least it was now.

Just as I hung up, a shrill ring cut through the silent living room. I let it ring twice, until the number flashed on the caller ID. Something local that I didn't recognize. And then I remembered that my cell had been out of commission, and I'd called home from Ryan's phone, and, in an uncharacteristic surge of irrational hope, I thought maybe he was checking in, like he said he would. I held the phone to my ear. "Hello?"

But it was a woman. "Am I speaking with Kelsey Thomas?"

"Yes," I said slowly, shifting the phone from shoulder to shoulder, my eyes on the closed door of the office.

"I'm Moira Little, and I was hoping to get a quote from you for a piece I'm writing for the *Covington City Gazette*."

"Uh," I said, "no comment." That was a thing, right? Would that be printed in the paper? *Ryan Baker, hero, rescues Kelsey Thomas, who has no comment.* "Listen," I added, keeping my voice low, "it's just, I'm not supposed to do this."

"Give quotes to reporters?"

Among other things. "Yes." *Ryan Baker, hero, rescues Kelsey Thomas, who is not supposed to give quotes to reporters.* "No," I said, "I mean, I'm just happy to be alive."

Silence, and then, "There's a slight discrepancy between the police report and your school paperwork. Are you the Kelsey Thomas born on September seventh or November seventh?"

It was a simple question—I'd turned seventeen last month, in September, and she probably only wanted my age for whatever she was writing. But my mother had taught me to guard my privacy. I heard her voice, an echo in my head: *Careful.* So I settled on a neutral answer, an answer this woman could presumably get anywhere. "I'm seventeen," I mumbled.

"And will we be seeing you Monday?"

"Uh," I said. Was she asking if I was going back to school? Or whether I was planning to show up at her office? I felt like I was missing half the conversation. "Maybe," I said. That seemed like the safest answer. "Bye now."

And I thought that possibly my mother had left the phone off the hook for a reason.

I went to my room and started the process of reconfiguring the new cell phone. As soon as I had it all set up, it started beeping, downloading a bunch of texts from the last few days. First, a string from Annika— Where are you? Omg, I heard. I'm home. Call me, doll— and an indication of a voice mail as well. Then a bunch of texts from an unknown number, and I felt my smile growing involuntarily as I read through the messages.

> Hey, it's Ryan. Checking in . . .
>
> I didn't see you at school. What's going on?
>
> Are you okay?
>
> Hmm, okay, not much for texting, huh? Call me when you get this.
>
> Okay, from the non-response, it has just occurred to me that you probably don't have a new phone yet.

**And now I feel like a stalker. Man, I wish I
could delete those.**

Oh God, please say something.

I heard Jan and my mother in the living room—
session over, I assumed. I hoped Jan didn't notice I was
back from visiting Annika just yet.

Hey, I wrote. Phone acquired.

He wrote back almost immediately:

**So, just pretend I didn't send like half of
those, okay? It was a weird few days . . .**

Consider it done.

The phone rang in my hand, and my heart ended
up in my stomach when I saw his number displayed. I
answered quickly so nobody else would hear.

"Hi," I said, trying to keep my voice low. But it
came out all breathy, like I was trying to seduce him
or something. I cleared my throat. Flopped back on
my bed. Died.

"Hey," he said. "So . . . you okay?"

"Sure. I guess so." I lay on my back, staring at the
ceiling, which my mother had painted pale blue when
I was a baby, complete with white clouds.

"Are you coming back to school?" he asked.

"Yes. On Monday. Did I miss anything interesting?"

"Is that a joke? Are you making a joke, Kelsey Thomas? I didn't know you were that funny."

"Oh yeah. Math must be super-boring without me." I put my hand over my eyes, my smile stretching to beyond-stupid levels. But that was the great thing about the phone—you could smile stupidly to yourself and not feel embarrassed by it.

Ryan was choosing not to speak at the moment, and I pushed myself up on my elbows, worried I'd said something wrong. This would not be a surprise.

"So," he said, "what have you been up to the last few days while playing hooky?"

"Nothing," I said. Embarrassingly nothing. And now there was nothing on the other end of the line. *Say something, Kelsey.* "I keep dreaming about it," I said, then squeezed my eyes shut. Pitfall of the phone: you could say something stupid, with no possibility of deleting the statement.

I waited for Ryan to do the *Hey, my mom's calling, gotta run* bit, but instead he said, "Me too."

I sat up, balled my pillow in my lap. "I keep thinking about this story we read in English about a man about to be hung, who dreamed an entire escape in the moment he fell, never realizing he was still falling in slow motion, on the way to being dead."

Please, somebody save me from myself.

A pause from Ryan Baker, who must've been

reevaluating his decision to call and check in on me. "So . . . you think we might still be falling? Right now?"

"No. *No.*" God, this was why I didn't try to flirt. "I just keep thinking about it."

But I wondered if he felt it too, wherever he was, the gust of air coming in through the window, off the mountains—like we were rushing through it still.

"I haven't slept," he said. "At first I thought it was just too much adrenaline, but now I don't know. Every time I close my eyes, I think maybe they won't open again." He paused. "So, there's that."

I shifted on my mattress, tipping my head back on the pillow again. "We're hilarious," I said.

He laughed. "You really are funny," he said.

"So . . . ," I said.

"So . . . you're kind of okay, but kind of not, and we've established that I'm the same. And I have to work the rest of the weekend. I'll see you Monday, then?"

"Yes," I said. "See you in math class."

His laughter filled my head as I hung up the phone.

Something woke me Sunday morning, and it took me a moment to realize it was the sound of my phone vibrating on the bedside table. I rubbed my eyes, trying to focus, as I opened the message from Ryan. It was a picture of the firehouse—all brick and red paint, like a cartoon—with the caption **Home for the next 14 hours.**

I texted back: Looks like fun.

By the time I got out of the shower, I had another message from him. This time, a picture of the bathroom floor, with a mop and a bucket, caption: **Not exactly. This is what I get to do here most of the time. Sorry to shatter the illusion.**

I went to the window, positioned the phone between the bars of the grate, and snapped a picture of the mountains in the distance. I sent it to Ryan with the caption Illusion: peaceful and serene. To the people who've never driven off the side of one.

A few minutes later, he sent a picture of the protective gear the firefighters wear, hanging from a peg. **Illusion: nothing can touch you.**

When Mom called me out for lunch, leftover casserole lumped on a plate, I quickly snapped a picture before she sat down: Illusion: edible.

She had dark circles under her eyes—a telltale sign that she wasn't sleeping. But she was out of her room, and she was cooking, and she smirked as I slid the phone under the table. "You sure are glued to that thing today," she said. And she had this faint smile, like she knew.

Faced with deciding between two equally difficult options—talking to my mom about who I was texting or eating her food—I took the martyr stance, shoved a heap of food in my mouth, and gave her an exaggerated thumbs-up.

"Is there something you want to tell me?" she asked, moving the food around on her plate.

"Delish," I said, still chewing.

She sighed. "I hoped we wouldn't be like other mothers and daughters."

"Don't worry. We're not," I said, chasing the bite with an entire glass of water.

She cringed but said nothing. And I remembered that she'd grown up in a home without a mother at all, and with a father she probably wished had not existed, either. I remembered all that had happened after, and that she was doing the best she could.

"It was a joke, Mom."

"Mm," she answered, pushing the food around her plate.

After lunch, I had another picture from him, the backs of several men hovering around a kitchen. It looked like they were cooking. Caption: **I'll fight you for title of worst lunch.**

"Kelsey?" Mom called from her office. "I'm about to place the grocery order. Anything you need?"

I stood behind her at the computer, scanned her list on the grocery-delivery site, and said, "Shampoo, please."

"I just bought you shampoo," she said.

"It's terrible. It doesn't do anything except sit on top of my hair." Mom had the perfectly straight, no-need-to-style type of hair. I, on the other hand, did not. "Go back to the old kind."

She sighed, but placed the order. I saw she'd set the delivery time for after school Tuesday, so I'd be here to take it in. This office was where she spent most of her time, for work and for research. This computer was her lifeline. Security screens stood guard in the upper corners of the room, and pictures of the two of us lined the walls, a timeline from infancy to now. And beside the door, a shadow box framed my first artwork—a swirling mess of finger paint—where it had hung for as long as I could remember.

I shifted from foot to foot. "Any word on the car insurance?" I asked.

My mom raised her eyes from the screen for just a moment, then went back to staring at the bright light, her eyes unmoving. "No," she said.

I searched for the box of returned things from my car, thinking about sending a picture to Ryan, sure he would understand, that it would need no caption to say what I was feeling—but I couldn't find it. Mom must've moved it, or trashed it. I hurried back to my room, planning out my next photo message, but found a message waiting for me again:

Is this Ryan's girlfriend???

It had been sitting unanswered for over twenty minutes.

The phone chimed when it was still in my hand:

Sorry. I work with assholes. Gotta go.

I debated how to respond for an embarrassing amount of time, finally settling on See you tomorrow. A literary masterpiece.

I didn't hear from Ryan again that night, and I slept fitfully, thinking I heard the vibration of my phone every time I drifted off. It was just after midnight, and I checked my phone one more time, but there was nothing there. *Pathetic, Kelsey.* I rolled over, pulling the sheets up to my chin, and heard a shout. I bolted upright in bed, tiptoed out into the dark hallway, feeling for the light switch.

I checked the alarm display next to the front door—the red light, the house armed and ready. "Mom?" I whispered.

I heard a sharp intake of air from her room, like a wheezing gasp. The word "No." And I was running.

My feet skidded along the cold, tiled floor. Her door was closed, as she always kept it. I turned the handle, held my breath. The door creaked as I pushed it open, and Mom sat upright in bed, breathing heavily, the whites of her eyes catching the glow from the hall light. "I thought I heard you . . . ," I said.

Her eyes skimmed the walls around her, and I imagined what she was checking for. Spiders, crawling over the walls, the furniture, *her*. It was the only thing I ever knew about her nightmares. "The spiders, get them off," she'd once said, half-asleep, as I tried to shake her awake.

I'd told Jan once, back when she first came into our lives. That Mom was afraid of spiders. And Jan must've told Mom, because after Jan left, she grabbed my arm, tighter than ever, and shook me—asking where I'd heard that.

"In your nightmare," I'd told her, and she released my arm. I knew better than to ask again.

I dreamed of them too after that. Spiders spilling out of the corners of a room. Spiders crawling over her skinny, pale body as she lay curled up on a cold basement floor somewhere, with burns on her back. I'd feel them myself, the spiders creeping between the covers of my bed as the fears settled in.

"Mom? Are you okay?" I asked, taking a step inside her room.

She ran a hand over her shoulder, looked at the red glowing numbers of the clock, stared at me again, like she was orienting herself. "Go to bed, Kelsey," she said.

I shivered as I closed her door—the goose bumps rising across my arms and legs—and smelled the faint whiff of gasoline-soaked gear, like a lingering memory.

CHAPTER 8

Mom **wasn't out of** her room by breakfast. *No big deal*, I thought, opening the curtains, letting in the sunlight cutting through the mountains. It didn't necessarily mean anything. She could've been catching up on sleep after the nightmare. She could be on the phone with Jan in there.

I slowly packed my backpack from last year, which I'd pulled out of the coat closet.

I checked the clock. I peeled a banana. I slammed cabinet doors.

My shoulders finally relaxed as I heard the creak of her bedroom door, and I kept my back to her as her footsteps approached, so she wouldn't see the relief on my face. "Hey," I said, holding up a banana. "Last one, want to split?"

"No, no, all yours," she said, starting the coffee. I glanced over my shoulder, saw her robe and unwashed hair, the tremor in her hand as she reached for a mug.

She must've seen me looking, because she said, "I think I'm just coming down with something."

I nodded, letting the lie slide. At least she was up, and the coffee was running, and she'd moved on to scrubbing the casserole dish, which was still soaking in the sink from last night. She was okay. Not a step back. No reason to call Jan.

"So," I said. "I'll call you after school, once I know when Cole and Emma plan on driving me home." I didn't know whether they had after-school activities, or whether Jan had discussed this already with them. I'd figure it out later.

"What?" she said, pulling her focus from the dishwasher. "Oh, yes. Okay."

"Okay. Well." I hugged her goodbye, felt the ridges of her spine pressing through her robe. She stared out the back window as I pulled away, her focus a thousand miles away.

I slid my phone into my bag. "It was a guy named Ryan," I said, and Mom turned to look at me. "Yesterday. On the phone."

"Ryan, huh?" she asked, smiling.

"Bye, Mom," I said, smiling in return.

I heard their car pull up the driveway, then stop, the engine still on. I could see them through the front window, through the gate. It looked like they were arguing. Possibly about who would ring the bell on the gate. And it looked like Emma was losing, as she was suddenly throwing open the passenger door.

"Gotta go!" I yelled, entering the code to momentarily disarm the alarm system. It beeped once, and I hit the button for the gate on the way out the door, locking it behind me (as was the protocol). The gate would close automatically after I left, thirty seconds later, if someone didn't either enter the code or a thumbprint at the fence to keep it open, or press the button inside the house, forcing it closed even sooner.

I jogged through the metal opening, tipping my head to Emma in greeting.

"I see nothing's changed," Emma said, frowning at the iron bars mechanically shutting behind me.

But all I could think, from the unfamiliar black car with the music pounding to her unflinching gaze, was *Everything's changed*. Emma kept changing, kept getting older and different and further from the girl I used to know—the one who used to play tag in the backyard and make jewelry out of gum wrappers.

"We're going to be late," Cole said, still staring straight ahead.

"We're not going to be late," I said. This was the time I left every day, and we lived *maybe* fifteen minutes away.

But Sterling Cross had a way of seeming farther away than it actually was. Despite the name, the neighborhood was not in the shape of a cross, nor did it cross through the mountains. It jutted into them, as far as the terrain would allow—man pushing against nature, carving out a space, and mostly losing. These were not houses with views of trees and mountains. This was mountains and trees with specks of houses lost inside. It must've felt like another world to them.

Emma turned down the music. "So, Kelsey," she began, like she was trying on my name. Remembering what it sounded like. "What did your mom think of the story?" she asked as we pulled out of the neighborhood.

"What story?" I asked.

I caught Emma's eyes in the rearview mirror the second before she tossed the paper through the gap in the seats. It was the Sunday paper.

Local Student to Be Honored for Bravery

The article had both of our pictures, side by side, both of us with fake school-picture smiles. And the article detailed the circumstances of the accident. Ryan Baker, eighteen-year-old volunteer firefighter, pulled classmate Kelsey Thomas from a car suspended in a tree branch, at the drop-off known as Benjamin's Cliff. The mayor's ceremony was Monday night (public, please come out to show your support!), and Ryan was going to be awarded the Mayor's Medal of Bravery. Ryan was quoted in the paper: *"Just doing what we were trained to do."* And then there was my incredibly embarrassing non-quote beside his. *"I'm just happy to be alive," says Kelsey Thomas.*

Oh. God.

The article concluded with the few public facts of our existence: *Son of a retired firefighter, Ryan lives with his parents, Jeremy and Cathy Baker, in the Pine View subdivision, along with his younger brother. Kelsey lives with her mother, Amanda Silviano, in Sterling Cross.*

I groaned, covering my face with the open paper, wishing I could teleport myself away inside of it. The reporter must've pulled Mom's former name from my original birth certificate—it was the last place it ever existed. She'd changed it, years earlier, to *escape* reporters.

"I didn't realize the accident was that bad," Emma said. "Honestly. That picture. Wow." Her voice was softer, like I'd remembered from years ago, and when I pulled the paper from my face, I imagined, for a moment, the little-girl version of her—all bouncy excitement and infectious giggle.

I scanned the article again, wondering what she was talking about. And there, at the bottom of the article, was an aerial view of my car, crushed and mangled at the bottom of the cliff.

The car is gone.

I carefully folded the paper and placed it face-down on the seat beside me, and I folded my hands in my lap, gripping them together, listening to the whistle of air hissing through a broken window seal.

* * *

First period. Math class. I slammed my locker door and took a deep breath, trying to shake some subtle, unplaceable fear. Almost that the walls were closing in, but not that. I flattened my palms against the metal locker door, trying to focus through the haze of voices and laughter. Back when I first started high school, this hallway was a mental hurdle to clear every morning—all the noise, all the people, bodies pressing as they passed, the sounds all blurring together. I couldn't hear myself think. Mom told me to just keep moving—one foot in front of the other—and before I knew it, I'd be back home again. And eventually, I'd gotten used to it.

But this. *This* was something different. Something impending and unavoidable—butterflies in the stomach, bordering on nausea. I ducked into the girls' bathroom and ran a wet paper towel over the back of my neck. And then I stared at the red line running across my fingers—still visible.

I jumped at the sound of the two-minute-warning bell, my stomach flipping once more, and then I realized: math class. I was scared of going to math class. Of seeing Ryan Baker in person after our phone conversation.

Was that normal? That couldn't be normal.

It had been so much easier talking to him on the phone. In person, we were awkward and stumbled over each other and never seemed to communicate what we were thinking. On the phone, he couldn't see me blush or smile so wide it was embarrassing. I could tell him things, and he could tell me things, buried under the caption of a picture.

Now I was going to *see* him—no screen to hide behind. And on top of that, there was that article. My ridiculous quote. *Ugh.* That was the only thing I could say to thank him?

I stood in front of the open door, saw him already at his desk, his hair falling in front of his face as his hand gripped the pen tightly, drawing an intricate pattern on his wrist, like links of a chain interlocking.

Ryan usually arrived at class just as the bell rang, sliding into his seat in the back row just as the sound cut off, like he'd been practicing his entire high school career. I was usually in my seat before the two-minute warning.

Today, the situation was reversed. Because he was brave. And I was the coward. Right.

The bell for the start of class rang, and Ryan glanced up at the doorway as I stepped inside. I waved, slight smile, and Ryan did the same.

"Hey, Kelsey," he said.

I sat at my desk. "Hi, Ryan."

It was obvious from the other students who were all gazing up from their notebooks and twisting in their chairs that the story had circulated a few times, possibly even absorbed some exaggerations based on the fact that Alyssa kept staring at my legs, like she was surprised they were still functioning and attached to my body.

The teacher called for attention, and Ryan leaned back in his chair, pen twirling between his fingers. "Nice to see you alive and well, Ms. Thomas," Mr. Graham said. "Certainly gave us all a scare."

I sunk further into my seat, searching for an adequate response. *Just happy to be alive, sir.* I settled on a mumbled "Thanks."

A school administrator gestured to Mr. Graham from the hall, and he excused himself. The room broke into hushed conversation, and I peered at Ryan from the corner of my eye. He was doing the same to me.

He resumed doodling on his wrist, his knee bouncing under his desk—and I wondered if he was as nervous as I was. I pictured his friends coming into the Lodge, the way he'd laugh along with them, agreeing to meet up later, saying goodbye with pats on the back, getting messages on his phone from girls like Holly—all of which should have made him confident. And he was, he must've been, to become a firefighter, to climb into my car. But I also remembered his voice, his words . . . *Don't be afraid.*

I tried them out. *Don't be afraid, Kelsey.*

I leaned across the aisle toward him. He raised an eyebrow, and then the corner of his mouth. "Congratulations," I whispered.

His leg stopped bouncing. The pen paused over his arm. "For what?"

"The ceremony," I said. "For the medal." He went back to the pattern on his wrist, peered at me from the corner of his eye, like he wasn't sure whether I was serious or not. "Tonight?" I added.

He shook his head, not making eye contact. "It's stupid. I told them not to do it. I told them I didn't want to," he said.

"It's not stupid," I said. He had crawled into a car dangling over a cliff. It was brave. He deserved the medal.

Mr. Graham strode back to the front of the room. "Books away! Pop quiz time." He rubbed his hands together.

A collective groan rose from the class, and someone mumbled, "You don't have to look so *excited* about it."

Mr. Graham paused at my desk as he passed out the papers. "Do you need an extension, Kelsey?"

"No," I said. I should've probably been in a higher-level class than this—Mom had gotten me ahead with all the years of homeschooling—but then I'd have nothing to take next year, as a senior.

Ryan didn't look at me for the rest of class, and he didn't ask me to wait up for him as I quickly gathered my books at the end of the period. He didn't say he'd see me later, and he didn't send me any random texts throughout the rest of the day. It was like the Ryan on the phone was one that only existed when nobody else was watching.

I'd been so sure he'd gotten to class early just for the chance to talk to me. I thought the phone conversation meant something. I thought we'd become friends, somehow. I thought I just had to be brave.

"I'm not a chauffeur service." Cole was arguing with his mother on the phone as we stood beside his car in the parking lot. He was supposed to drop me off and then go back for Emma after soccer practice. I stood outside the passenger door, unsure whether I should get in or wait for some sign from him.

I saw Ryan striding across the lot with AJ and Leo, and he slowed when he saw me.

"Let's go," Cole said, pulling my attention.

We drove in silence, which I thought was probably better than the alternative.

"Thanks for the ride," I said when we pulled into my driveway.

He leaned forward, taking in the gates, the house, and he let out a sigh. "Same time tomorrow?" he asked.

"I'll be here," I said as I exited the car.

"Hey, Kelsey?" he called after me through a lowered window.

I paused in front of the iron bars.

"For the record, I *am* glad you're okay." And then he drove away.

I saw Mom's shadow at the window, curtains pulled aside, then falling back into place, as I pressed my thumb to the security screen at the gate. She'd already unlocked the door as I was walking up the front steps. She stood back from the entrance, watching Cole drive away, then shut and locked the door behind me. Except *shut* was kind of an understatement. The door slammed, and the pictures on the entrance table shook.

I took a step backward. The house smelled like green beans and syrup, and I needed both space and air.

"So," I said, "I guess you saw."

There was something almost unrecognizable about her, this person I knew better than anyone. Something about the way she was standing, the way she was looking at me. Her hands were tightened into fists. "What? Your *picture*, and *my name* in the paper with a *quote* from you? Yes, I *saw*."

"I barely said anything, obviously," I said. "I didn't tell her your name. I mean, I told her *no comment*, but she just kept talking, and—"

She held up her hand. "What I'm upset about, Kelsey, is that you didn't *tell* me. You talked to a reporter, even though you knew I wouldn't want you to, and you thought I wouldn't find out? The story was picked up by the *state news*, for Christ's sake! It's a human-interest story now, and it has our address!"

"No," I said, "you don't understand. She called and—"

Mom fixed her eyes, cold and hard, on my own. "She

called? Where was I during this phone call? Were you trying to hide this from me?"

"God, Mom, you're completely overreacting! You were in the office with Jan!"

She took a deep breath, closed her eyes, but I could tell it wasn't working. "You don't just *pick up the phone*," she said, like I'd done something akin to handing over the nuclear launch codes to an enemy state. "That's what the answering machine is for."

"I thought it was someone I knew," I said. "Sorry!"

"Who? Did you think it was that *boy*?" I was starting to see my mother like someone from the outside—like she was being completely irrational, like this whole conversation was embarrassing and frustrating and *not* normal. Which was completely and totally true. "I raised you better than this. I raised you to *think*—"

"I thought it was Annika," I said. "Because I wasn't answering my cell." I wanted to tell her to get a grip, to *listen to herself*, but her hand kept reaching for the scars on her back, and I remembered that she had limitations, that it had taken her seventeen years, and this was as far as she'd come.

Something impossible to shake, a memory she could not reach—proof that bad things did happen. People were taken, hidden, hurt. Danger was everywhere.

And here I was, standing before her, living proof.

The oven dinged, and she strode back to the kitchen and pulled out a pungent casserole. I couldn't be in a room with this stench anymore. I couldn't be in a room with *her* anymore.

"I have homework," I said. But she reached for me with an oven-mitted hand, and I lingered near the sink.

"I feel like I'm . . ." She let the thought go, but I could tell, with the way she was still reaching for me, and the way I'd been moving back. *Like I'm losing you.*

Like I was slipping, falling . . .

It was the car, and the pictures, and me in the paper—everything out of her control.

"I'm here," I said. "And I'm fine." I took a deep breath, swallowed the lump in my throat, hated that I had to say the next part. But I did. "We're safe."

She nodded, but her hair fell in front of her face, and I couldn't read her expression. She took a knife and started hacking at the dish, and I left.

We ate in silence, both of us pushing green beans around the plate. "Mom," I said, seeing as she'd had some time to cool off. "I'm sure you saw, there's the mayor's ceremony tonight, and Ryan—"

"So, this Ryan in the paper. Is this the same Ryan that had you glued to the phone yesterday?"

"I guess," I said. "We're . . . friends." At least, I'd hoped we were. Now I wasn't so sure. Which was part of the reason I wanted to be there tonight. It felt like

I needed to—the moment had become something bigger than the both of us. It had left its mark on him, too, and I was pretty sure I was the only one who could see it.

She raised her eyes, sharpened them, like she knew what I was about to ask.

"I should be there tonight," I said. "I was going to see if Annika could take me."

"Absolutely not," she said. "I don't want you on television," she said. "You know how I feel about privacy." Oh, didn't I.

And then the walls felt too close, and the gates too high, and everything too narrow and constricting. And I wondered, for the first time, whether Jan was right—whether Mom made me this way. Whether she *kept* me this way, so I wouldn't want to leave her.

"You have to let me out of the house," I said. "You *have to*—"

"I don't *have* to do anything, Kelsey. You were just at school. That sufficiently counts as *out of the house*. The rest? That's up to the parent. That's up to *me*."

This was the first fight that I could remember truly having with her. Usually I agreed with her decisions, her ideas seeping into me, becoming my own, like fear itself.

"Just let me explain—"

"You're not going. From now on, you go straight to school, you come straight home. The discussion is over."

I took my dish to the sink well before she was finished, and slammed my bedroom door.

I turned on the music, turned it up loud enough to rattle the windows.

I called Annika and asked her what she was doing tonight.

And I prepared to do the one thing that every normal teenager must do at one point or another: I was going to sneak out.

CHAPTER 9

I set the music on a loop and kept it loud, hoping Mom would let me wallow in my anger. Sometimes the house felt too big for just the two of us—each of us on a separate hallway—but other times, like now, it felt too small. Walls closing in, stale recirculated air, doors opening, doors closing, in unnecessary ceremony.

I watched the clock from my seat at the edge of the bed, tapping my heels twice as fast as the beat.

I checked my email on my phone to pass the time. Only one, from Annika a few days earlier:

> Are you okay, doll? I've tried calling. And
> calling. I heard you almost died, and I would
> like confirmation that you aren't, in fact, dead.
> Call me soon as you get this. xoxo—An

I loved that about Annika—how she could make everything big and small at the same time. It was so different from my own life—everything over-examined and weighty.

At seven-thirty, I took the key from my desk drawer and unlocked the metal grate outside my bedroom window, swinging it open. I held my breath, listening for signs of my mother. My room faced the front, which worked in my favor, because Mom's room was down the other hall and faced the back. The dining room was the only other room with windows toward the front. Everything else—the kitchen, her office, the living room—had a clear view back to the mountains.

I sat on the windowsill, willing myself to jump the four feet to the ground, and my heart beat wildly. Everything about this moment felt magnified. The night, crisp and unexpectedly alluring. My stomach churning. The feeling of spiders crawling out from the corners of the room, coming for me.

At the last moment, I took my new cell phone from my purse and tossed it onto my bed. I wasn't sure whether my mom had some sort of alert set up, but better to play it safe. Either she had ESP for when I diverted from my route (like the time she called when I took the wrong exit and went an extra ten miles before I noticed, or the time I craved a burger and drove until I found one, with the newfound freedom of my driver's license), or she actively tracked me whenever she knew I was out, or—and this was what I was worried about—she had a perimeter set up that sent an alert to her computer when I wandered out of it.

I counted down, and tried not to think—not to let myself hear all the *maybes* circle and dig and circle some more. It was my *mother's* voice, my *mother's* warnings, my *mother's* fears, I reminded myself.

Not my own.

And then I jumped.

I braced for impact, crouching low, expecting some unknown alarm to sound—but there was nothing. I eased the metal window grate shut, but couldn't lock it from the outside. The front lights were off, which meant she was probably back in her room, or in the living room, watching TV. Maybe the office. Hopefully, she wouldn't hear the gate. Hopefully, she wouldn't see the green light next to the front door for the thirty-second span that it remained unlocked.

I hit the code in the keypad beside the fence, and the gates eased open, the mechanical gears humming in the still night. I slipped through the opening as soon as I could, then crouched in the bushes, counting to thirty. Counting, and watching the front door.

But nothing happened.

No alarm, no yelling, no Mom.

I was free.

Annika was waiting for me in her driveway, leaning against the blue sedan that she and her brother shared when they were home from school, texting on her phone. I'd had to take the long way—down my street, right on the main neighborhood road, right again on her street, which backed to mine—instead of hopping the wall connecting the backs of our properties. She jumped at the sound of rocks kicking up in her driveway as I jogged toward her.

"Well," she said, slouching against the hood, one hand on her hip, "look who's the little rebel. Honestly, after you hung up I wasn't sure if you'd actually show." She wore leggings and boots and a dress with lace trim, and I felt completely unpresentable in dark jeans and a nice shirt.

She handed me the keys.

"You're not coming?" I asked.

"Change of plans," she said, smiling. "I have a date. His name is Eli, and he does landscaping work in the neighborhood, and I think I'm in love."

"I've never heard of any Eli."

"Well, I kind of just met him. But we only have the week, so we're on an accelerated schedule." She smiled.

She slid her phone out of a disguised pocket in her dress, scrolled through, and pulled up his contact—*Eli*. His photo showed a slightly hooked nose and deep-set eyes, a bunch of mismatched parts that somehow worked together. He was looking off to the side, and his mouth was open, like he was caught midsentence, and he was vaguely squinting into the sun. Annika did this—took stealth pictures of people for her phone. Mine, I once saw, was me from a distance, sitting on the stone wall, head tipped back and eyes closed. "Stalker much?" I'd said to her the first time I saw it. But the truth was, it was my favorite picture of me that existed. For one thing, I was outside. For another, I looked completely carefree and at peace. In truth, I think I'd been about to sneeze. But, like a magician, she had somehow captured the essence of the person I wanted to be instead.

"He's picking me up at eight," Annika said. "Just do me a favor and bring this baby back in one piece."

"You're giving me your car?" I asked.

"No, I'm not *giving you my car*. I'm letting you drive it. Figure you've already driven off a cliff once, what're the chances of that happening again?"

"Not funny," I mumbled.

"Too soon?" She nudged my shoulder. "Oh, come on, it is a little bit."

I grinned. "Thank you, Annika. You're a good friend."

"Well, I heard there was a boy involved. Do me a favor, when you get back, leave the keys in the visor, yeah?"

"Okay, I won't be late," I said.

"Don't go making any promises," she said.

Annika swayed back up the front walk, and then she lingered near her door, like she was waiting for me to get in and drive off. I was frozen. I knew, in theory, I'd have to drive again. Otherwise, I'd become trapped like my mother, each of my fears chipping away little by little at the world, until all I had left was the bubble. The world shrinking, twisting, slipping—I'd always be stuck in that moment. I'd always be falling.

Annika, maybe sensing as much, called over to me, "Lightning doesn't strike the same place twice, Kels."

Which wasn't really true—turns out, despite popular opinion, lightning did not discriminate. But I got the point—what were the chances?

Take comfort in the logic, Jan would tell me. *Chance is on your side.*

I had to drive down the windy mountain roads into town, to the community center, where the ceremony was being held. I took the turns about ten miles under the speed limit, not caring that there was a car on my tail that eventually blew by me on a rare stretch of straightaway. I gripped the wheel, eyes on the yellow line, hovering so close to the center that a car on the other side honked. Any time I saw headlights, I flashed back to that foggy moment—a flash of light, a car on my side, jerking the wheel, the panic closing my throat.

I wondered if it was possible that the panic itself had knocked me unconscious. I wouldn't doubt it.

Eventually I had to pass the site of my accident. I crawled by it, overcompensating each turn of the wheel—worse than my first driver's ed lesson. The metal barrier on the side of the road had already been replaced. There were no signs anything had ever happened, except the stretch of metal was fresher, with no imperfections yet. If I'd died, there would've been flowers or teddy bears or a cross on the roadside. *We did not fall. We did not die. Everything was fine.*

It wasn't until I hit the lights in town that I relaxed my grip on the wheel. Wasn't until I exited the car and stared at my hands, slightly trembling, that I began to laugh. I'd have to tell Jan about this one day, when it was far enough away. When I wouldn't get in trouble. A fear I overcame, the picture of progress. Standing there, in the middle of the packed parking lot, I'd never felt so powerful.

I recognized a bunch of student parking stickers on the cars around mine, and some fire department bumper stickers on others as I walked up the steps to the community center. The reception area—the gymnasium, actually—was pretty crowded, with rows of folding chairs set up and reporters with cameras and notepads standing along the wall.

Out of force of habit, I found myself taking stock of the exits: the double doors behind me, an emergency exit to the side of the makeshift stage, another presumably behind the platform. I looked up: a few windows, but no way to open them. I stayed near the door, another habit I couldn't quite break. "Always take note of the exits," Mom had said, worrying her thumb over each of her fingers, until her knuckles popped, one by one. "Besides the obvious. There's always another way out. The windows. The ceiling. The floor. You have to think beyond, and you have to think *fast*."

I couldn't help picturing that now: all these people trying to funnel through the double doors in the event of an explosion or a fire. And me, caught in a stampede. I shook my head, clearing her out of there. The words of a paranoid mind. The words of fear. It wasn't too late for me.

Up front, it looked like they were about to get started. The men and women were in suits, and so was Ryan. He was fidgeting with his tie, and an older man stepped forward to straighten it for him, before placing a hand on his shoulder.

It's in my blood, Ryan had said. A family legacy. He was surrounded by a group of people who had watched him grow up, who were waiting for him to join them. He had a place he always knew he would belong.

Meanwhile, I was alone and completely out of place. I looked at my jeans, my purple shirt, my black sneakers. It hadn't occurred to me that this would be a formal affair. I mean, it was the *community center*. The basketball nets had been retracted upward, toward the ceiling, but this was a place where people worked out. At least I was wearing my nice jeans. And at least I'd put some product in my hair. My curls were shiny and tamed, and I guess that counted for something.

A hush fell over the crowd as the people up front started assembling themselves into order, in a straight row. A man who must've been the mayor made his way to the podium.

I saw Ryan scan the crowd, the seats, but he never got to me. His gaze drifted back to the floor, and he took a deep breath. If I didn't know any better, I'd guess he was nervous. He'd already done the hard part—me, the car, the fall. All he had to do now was stand there while other people in suits said nice things about him.

I noticed several people from our class in the chairs near the aisle—the guys I'd see Ryan with at school, in the halls, or the ones who stopped by the Lodge during the summer, looking for him. Mark and AJ and Leo, in khakis and button-downs. AJ had his girlfriend with him. There were also a few vaguely familiar faces, who I thought must've been from his fire department. One of them, standing behind Ryan, was watching me back, and I didn't know whether it was because I was severely underdressed or because he remembered me. Had he been there that night? The only person I remembered was Ryan—the promise in his words, making me believe. Even the medic's face had faded away. I understood how my mother could've forgotten everything after her imprisonment. Everything else was buried under a layer of fear, and I didn't want to poke at it too hard.

The other firefighter leaned forward, whispered something into Ryan's ear, and Ryan's eyes scanned the crowd, settling on me. His face didn't change, but he started raising his hand. But then the microphone snapped on, and the mayor's quick intake of breath echoed through the room before he let out a booming "Good evening!"

The crowd settled, and even Ryan turned his focus to the mayor.

And then there was an all-too-familiar voice in my ear, a minty whisper, and a jangle of bracelets. "Hey there, you."

Emma stood beside me with two of her girlfriends. At least Cole didn't seem to be here.

"Hi, Emma," I whispered. "What are you doing here?" *And are we friends again? I didn't get the memo.*

She nodded her head toward the girl beside her, leaning against the wall. "Holly wanted to come. For Ryan." She smiled again, all teeth. I made myself smile back.

Holly-in-the-flesh was slightly less scary than the Holly-of-my-mind, who I'd turned into a vacant texting machine who chewed gum and had long, manicured nails. The Holly who had actually texted Ryan (all caps, super-excited) was rather sweet-looking, with dimples and wavy strawberry-blond hair, phone nowhere in sight.

"Shh," someone said. The room echoed, like a gymnasium. It *was* a gymnasium after all.

The mayor was now talking about acts of bravery, and the average person, and looking out for our neighbors, and how community was built on the shoulders of people like this.

There were two people receiving the medal. One woman, for performing the Heimlich on a stranger at the Italian restaurant in town (heroic, yes, but brave?), and Ryan. "According to Chief Nicholas," the mayor said, "Mr. Baker insisted he be the one to climb into Ms. Thomas's car. There was no moment of hesitation." Ryan hadn't told me that part. *I'm the lightest* is what he'd said. *Least chance of making the car fall.*

Even from here, I could see the heat rising on Ryan's face. God, heroic much? Emma and Holly were whispering beside me, and I swear one of them audibly sighed.

The mayor pinned something to his jacket, shook his hand, and everyone applauded.

Everyone stood, and Ryan disappeared. I shifted to the side, stood on my toes—the room was all noise and activity again.

Emma turned to her friends. "You should invite Ryan," I heard her saying, probably to Holly.

"To my house?" Holly responded.

"Yes. Tell him we'll be there, no adults, heroes welcome."

I turned away, needing air and space and *home* again.

"Excuse me." I bumped into a woman with a badge clipped to her blazer and a notepad in her hand. She was smiling, big and bright, like I was exactly what she was looking for. "Kelsey, right? I thought I saw you come in."

I strained to see the front of the room again, and I caught a glimpse of Ryan trying to push through the crowd, heading this way—maybe to see Holly, who was still talking to Emma.

Holly shook my resolve, and my confidence. I didn't know, after all, what had happened at the party after the hospital. I didn't know if Holly was his girlfriend, and I was just someone he could talk to about that night. If everything about that moment in the car shone brighter than it should, took on more meaning. Near-death experiences bonding people together— that was a thing, right? But it didn't *mean* anything, unless I stayed there, stuck in that terrifying moment.

The woman beside me kept pressing—her hand on my arm now, like walls closing in. "It's so great that you came," she added. "Wonderful for you to show your support. Can I get a quick picture?" She jutted her head toward Ryan, who had just broken through the group in the middle, and was shaking free of the latest person who stopped him to shake his hand. "Of the two of you together? The readers would love that."

"You've got the wrong person," I said, backpedaling out the double doors. This was all a mistake. I should've sent him a message first. Let him know I was coming. Let him tell me about Holly first. I should've worn something different, arrived a little earlier. Convinced Annika to come with me so I wouldn't feel this blind rush of terror—because I'd learned in high school, after years of being homeschooled, that loneliness was something felt more powerfully in a crowd.

I fumbled for Annika's keys in my purse—heard footsteps behind me and started running. My hands shook as I turned the key in the ignition, and I peeled out of the parking lot. But I couldn't slow my heart. I couldn't shake the nerves. And I couldn't shake the headlights, always just a curve behind.

CHAPTER 10

The headlights were gone by the time I pulled into Annika's driveway. Nobody came out at the sound of the car on the gravel. Amazing, that people could come and go so freely, without someone keeping tabs on them. I left the keys in the visor like she'd asked and started walking back up the road, arms folded across my stomach in the dark. I didn't want to go through the back, hopping the wall, where my mom was much more likely to notice.

The mountains were darker against the moonlit sky—the world, shadows on shadows.

I stayed on the roads, striding quickly in the gap between the streetlights, but I stopped when I turned onto my drive. A car with its engine running. A car was *here*.

There were no other houses on this part of the street. It was too late for a delivery. If it was Jan, my mom would probably knock on my door, and I'd be found out. I moved faster, keeping to the bushes, trying to work out how to slip through the gate and climb through the window with neither of them noticing.

The engine turned off, and I froze. I eased my body slowly around the corner, until I could see the car. A green Jeep, just like Ryan's—

Before I could stop myself, I had jogged alongside the car, which was practically in view of the front gate. If someone leaned to the side in the front window, they might be able to see him.

He was going to get me busted. As I approached the car, I saw him still sitting in the driver's seat, texting on his phone. His tie was undone, and so was the top collar button, and his jacket was tossed in a heap on the passenger seat.

I tapped the car window, and he jumped, dropping the phone into his lap.

He let out a relieved sigh as he opened the car door. "You scared the crap out of me."

"What are you doing here?" I whispered, while making hand motions for him to *keep it down*.

"I tried to catch you when you left. I saw you pull into the development, but . . . then I couldn't find you." He grabbed his phone. "I've been writing to you." He showed me a string of open text messages, then turned the phone back to himself. "Um, you can delete them now." He looked down at his shoes, which had probably been shiny a few hours earlier, but were now coated in a layer of fine dust.

"I was borrowing a friend's car," I said. "I left it at her house. And my phone's in my room."

"Oh," he said.

"I wasn't supposed to go out," I said. "So I left the phone, which also has GPS tracking, you know?"

He raised an eyebrow. Maybe he didn't know.

"The thing is," he said, just as I said, "What did I do?"

"What?" he asked.

"I did something wrong."

"You didn't," he said.

"It sure seems like it," I said. "Because we were talking, and it was nice, and then in class you just . . . stopped. And went back to ignoring me."

"I wasn't ignoring . . . ," he said, and winced. "Sorry. It's not you, Kelsey."

I was pretty sure that was a line. *It's not you, it's me.* Famous. And final. Like a shrug from Cole. I raised an eyebrow at him in return. I remembered Holly's adorable dimples.

He shook his head. "You don't understand." He wasn't whispering anymore, and I didn't try to stop him. He was working his way up to something, stepping a little closer. "I feel like such a poseur," he said. "I don't deserve this. Here. Take it." He already had the medal for bravery in his hand, and now he was thrusting it at me.

I laughed, pushed it back toward him. "No way, what am I supposed to do with this? *I* was terrified."

He took a step closer. "I'd be dead if it wasn't for you."

I shook my head. "No, you wouldn't. You wouldn't have been in the car in the first place. *I'd* be dead. . . ."

"I was hanging in midair, Kelsey. You held us up with . . ." His eyes drifted to my hands, and I balled them up. I couldn't look at the gash across my fingers—raw and starting to scab over—without reliving it all, and now it seemed he couldn't, either.

"Look," I said. "You chose to climb into my car. I held us up because . . . well, because what was the other choice? It was an instinct."

His eyes went wide, and he laughed. "Well, I'm glad your instinct was to *not let go*." He was looking at my hands again, but he was smiling.

"Self-preservation," I added, half laughing. "Pretty sure it's what anyone would do."

This time, his gaze shifted from my hands to my arms, my neck, my mouth. He lowered his voice, took a step closer. "No, I don't think so."

He shifted his weight from foot to foot, kicking up rocks in the driveway, and it made him seem younger than a man receiving a bravery medal on a podium.

"So, I want to try something again," he said, his lips curving up into a smile. God, I loved that look. "Do you want to do something sometime?"

I smiled back, big and stupid, and didn't even bother trying to stop it. "Yes. But maybe we should specify this time."

"Hang out. Somewhere. Sometime."

I heard my heartbeat echo inside my head—not nerves, not quite, but something close. "You mean besides upside down in my car?"

"Yeah. Definitely besides that. Like . . . my house. Or the movies. Or the park. Or here, right now." He gestured to the iron gate in front of us, the house hidden behind it.

I chewed the inside of my cheek, picturing Ryan filling up my room with that smile. "I'm not allowed to have people over. I'm also not exactly supposed to be out right now. It's going to be hard enough for me to sneak back in alone."

Ryan was eyeing the keypad, the camera, the gate. "Why all the precautions?" he asked.

"Makes her feel safe," I said before I could stop myself. This was a trick I had taught myself: act before the fear. And now there was a dare in my words. What kind of person would he be? What would he do with the information?

He nodded slowly. "My dad has a closet of guns, same reason. I don't really get why we need more than one. Sometimes I think he's preparing for the zombie apocalypse."

"No guns here. We're only good with keeping zombies out. If they breach, we're screwed."

I turned to go, my hand connecting with his, leaving the medal with him. He grabbed my elbow as I approached the gate, spinning me back around, his hand trailing from my elbow to my hand. "So there's no confusion this time," he said, and his cheeks flushed, "I'm asking you out."

Then he backed away, his hands in the pockets of his suit pants. He was smiling, but he was also waiting.

"And I'm saying yes," I said.

He leaned against his car, and before I could talk my way out of it, before I could let all the fears work their way into my head, all the uncertainty, before I could question what I should do or should say, or shouldn't do or shouldn't say, I took three quick steps toward him, and I stood on my toes, and he said, "Oh—" in the second before my lips connected with his, and then his hands were around my back, and he was pulling me closer, and I melted—my body sinking into his. I felt his lips curl into a smile as I pulled away.

"Bye, Ryan," I said.

He laughed. "Bye, Kelsey."

I turned back to the gate, still smiling. I could see the house lights on in the background. I'd probably be caught. I didn't even care. Ryan was still watching me from beside his car. And I didn't wait for him to leave first this time.

I pressed my thumb to the keypad, but nothing happened. Maybe they were shaking with adrenaline. I tried again, first wiping my hands on the side of my pants. Again, nothing happened. No click.

Something soured in my stomach, in my mouth—and my hands started shaking again, for a very different reason.

"What's the matter?" Ryan called. He started walking toward me. I leaned to the side and looked up at the cameras, where I'd usually see a faint red light—but there was none. I felt the wrongness through every pore of my body. I pushed at the gate, and it opened on its own, and my heart plummeted into my stomach.

The system was off, and the gate was unlocked.

"Something's wrong," I said.

CHAPTER 11

Ryan **followed me through** the gate, which no longer automatically closed behind us. The gate would normally be unlocked only if someone entered the override code to hold it open, or if the electricity was out. But I could see lights *on* inside.

"Stay here," I said, once we got to the porch. "I don't want her freaking out."

Understatement. If she realized I was missing, that would be the least of my concerns.

I checked the front door handle, but it was unlocked. And when I pushed open the door, there was no beep of the alarm. The air felt different, too. Like the expanse of the world—*the vastness*, my mom would say—was inside the house. Too much, too unknown.

"Mom?" I called, and the word echoed off the tiled floors, the white walls. "Are you okay?"

The first thing I noticed was the silence. The music I'd left running in my room was off. There were no footsteps. No shuffling in the halls. Just the slow drip of a faucet from somewhere beyond.

I left the front door cracked open for Ryan as I checked each room. She wasn't in her bedroom, or the office, or the living room. I passed the foyer again on the way down the hall to my room, barely registering Ryan standing in the open doorway.

My stomach dropped as I approached my room. My door was open, and she'd definitely been in here. I stood in the entrance, assessing the damage. My phone was thrown onto the floor. My desk drawers were pulled open. The floor was a mess of clothes and paper and electronics. I nudged a pile with the side of my foot and picked up my phone, placing it on my desk.

There was a chill to the room, like her anger lingered. Something had happened to change the taste in the room. Something empty and hollow and unusual. It was no longer safe and known and *mine*.

The hairs on my arms stood on end—this was not her typical behavior. This was a version of her I didn't know.

"Mom?" I called again, more tentatively.

The alarm was off, and nobody was here. I picked up the landline phone in the living room, and it clicked, repeatedly—no dial tone.

I opened the door behind the kitchen—it was also uncharacteristically unlocked—and called her name into the dark of the backyard. Went back to the hall, slid the lock at the top of the basement door, stood in the entrance as the door creaked open. The lights were off and it had been locked, but still, I called her name. Only a chilled gust of air came back.

I heard footsteps behind me, and turned to find Ryan standing in the foyer, his eyes roaming over the bright rooms, the white walls, the immaculately clean surfaces. "What's the matter?" he asked.

I stared at him, trying to find the words, terrified of giving voice to them. The thing I had never imagined. Never even so much as feared. It snuck up on me, this one, and I felt myself getting sucked down with it.

"I can't find my mom," I whispered.

Ryan paced the foyer, picked up a picture of the two of us from the entryway table. He held it close to his face, his eyes shifting from her face to my own. "This is your mom?" he asked.

My mother was young and beautiful—she was thirty-five, but looked even younger in her casual clothes, long hair, makeup-free face. She looked perfect, in that picture. *We* looked perfect together. Big smiles, windows behind us, sunlight streaming through. "Yes," I said.

"So give her a call," he said. "See where she is if you're that worried."

If I was that worried . . .

I took a deep breath. Took the picture from his

hand, felt a tug in my chest as my eyes searched her frozen face. Tried to tamp down the panic, steady my hands, steady my voice.

"She hasn't left the house in seventeen years," I said.

Ryan held my gaze as the words settled in, and I noticed him processing, refitting everything he thought he understood about me and my family. He opened his mouth, closed it again. Seemed to reconsider everything he was thinking. "Okay," he said, "so let's double-check."

And even in this moment of terror—even as this emptiness was clawing at the inside of my skull, and the uncertainty turned into panic, my breath coming too fast—I found myself falling further for Ryan. That he could just take it in stride, and do what needed to be done. He walked down the hall, and I could imagine him doing this in his uniform, assessing the threats, trying to calm those inside. He projected calm and confidence, and I wished I could do the same. At the moment, I wished I could be anyone other than me.

"Mrs. Thomas?" Ryan called, walking back into the kitchen with me, opening the closest door, which was her office.

"Mandy," I said. Nobody called her Mrs. Thomas, and anyway, she wasn't a Mrs. She went by Mandy, or she went by Mom.

"Mandy?" he repeated, stepping inside the office. He checked under the desk, and I opened the closet, and it suddenly occurred to me what we were looking for. My mom, shut down from the fear. Or worse, unresponsive.

I led him down to her bedroom, where her door was open and her bed still unmade. The bathroom, bright from the LED lightbulbs. The shower door, clear. No place to hide. Everything about the house was out in the open. Even as a child playing hide-and-seek, there weren't many good hiding spots, besides sliding under the bed, stealing myself away in the dark corner of a closet, or curling up in a ball inside the cabinets.

There was the basement, but the basement was off-limits.

I opened the bathroom cabinets now, even though it made no sense, just to get a whiff of everything that was her—the lotion and mouthwash and the soaps stored in mega-packs near the back.

Ryan kept calling her name.

The kitchen still had the scent of dinner; the pan was soaking in the deep sink. The faucet was faintly dripping, and I reached out to hit the handle, turning it all the way off.

"Mom?" I called again. The room itself seemed to echo. I pulled back the curtains, caught our reflection in the windows that faced the mountains.

I led Ryan down the other hall to my room, which

was the only place in disarray. I gestured toward the mess on the floor, the drawers left ajar. "I didn't do this," I said. "She must've known I snuck out."

"So maybe she went looking for you," he said.

"Even if that were possible, she would've left a note, don't you think? Left the alarm on?" My throat was tightening. "Ryan, she couldn't come to the hospital after the crash. What could've been so worrisome that she'd actually leave?"

He touched my elbow gently. "Maybe she called someone first."

I nodded. Yes. Too bad the landline was down and I couldn't just hit Redial on it to find out. I'd have to call on my cell. But first, there was one more place to check. I didn't want to have to call Jan unless I was sure. I opened the door in the hall, just before the kitchen, and stood at the top of the basement steps again. Neither of us ever went down here much—it had a secondary lock near the top, from back when I was a kid who might go wandering. To keep me out of the darkness.

The basement had always terrified me. The dark corners, the absence of windows. I pictured my mother tied up in one for over a year, with nobody around who could hear her scream. I pictured burns on her shoulders, and spiders crawling over her on the damp floor. Neither of us went in the basement alone.

Mom kept everything from my childhood down there. All my artwork, all my old baby clothes, stored in plastic bins and labeled with permanent marker. Boxes of chemistry kits and electronics we used to do homemade projects with, back when she homeschooled me—a volcano bubbling over on the kitchen counter, colorful smoke I'd dance around in the backyard while she watched from the window, smiling.

"Mom?" I called.

Maybe she came down here, and maybe she slipped and fell. Maybe she was looking for something. Maybe the fears overwhelmed her—me gone, the alarm off—and she locked herself down here. But the lights were off. . . .

I used to imagine monsters sneaking up from the basement at night, that that was the reason for the lock at the top of the door. I used to think my mother knew about the monsters, but didn't want me to worry.

A silly thought. The lock worked from the inside too—a precautionary measure, so we could never be trapped. And she didn't think of my own worrying much. She raised me on it, taught me to look for it, to find it. To live with it.

I ran my fingers against the wall until I found the switch, then started down the steps. The basement was still unfinished, with bulbs hanging directly from the ceiling. We searched around the stacks of bins, but there was no sign of my mother.

One more thing. One more possibility . . .

I stood in front of the far wall, staring at the subtle

lines that marked the door. As far as I knew, it hadn't been opened in years.

The door wasn't hidden, but it did blend in to the natural delineations in the stone wall. I flipped open the compartment that looked like a circuit breaker, exposing the dial, like a safe.

"What's that?" Ryan asked.

The panic room. "One more place to check," I said.

Jan was the only one who called it the panic room. Mom told me it was the safe room. The room that, regardless of what was happening in the world around us, we would always be safe in. Jan twisted it around, made it into the place we would only go in a panic. I used to see it like my mother did—a last resort. Reinforced walls, safe against acts of God, that could withstand even a tornado. Fireproof walls that would last until help could arrive. A radio so we could hear about what was happening outside, and food and supplies to last us the duration. This was a room I should always feel safe in.

But the way Jan asked me about it, years later, twisted it around in my head, turned it into something dark and ugly and full of shame. "Tell me about the panic room, Kelsey," she'd said, sitting across the couch from me. "How often does your mother close herself up in there?"

"I don't know," I said, even though I did. Rarely. Very rarely. But suddenly I didn't know if that was a safe answer.

"Does she ever bring you in there with her?"

With this, I knew the answer wasn't safe. "No," I said. I was ten years old, and I had just learned the power of a lie. Jan smiled.

Mom used to bring cards to play in there. Once, we had dinner out of dehydrated food and stored bottles of water, blankets rolled up like sleeping bags on the blue carpet. It was an adventure, she'd said, and I'd believed her.

But it was also a drill. If the alarm sounded, the protocol was to come down here immediately. No matter what. This was the safest plan.

There were only two people in the world who knew the code. It didn't matter how many times Jan had said it was safer to have a backup, or to be sure to write it down—*What if we got locked inside, knocked unconscious? How would someone get us out?*

That fear, apparently, didn't measure up to the other. Only my mother and I knew the code. *Meaningless, and therefore unbreakable*, she had said. As far as I knew, my mother hadn't been in there in years—not since Jan came into our lives. She was getting better. She *was*.

But. If the alarm shorted, somehow taking the gate offline with it, and she didn't feel safe, she could've locked herself down in the basement, and then inside the room. She could've gone to my room first, trying to bring me there with her. But there were limitations to her bravery. It all made sense. And when she couldn't find me, maybe she left the front door open for my return.

My mother in the panic room would be a setback. My mother in the panic room might be a reason to have our living arrangement reassessed. My mother in the panic room would be reason to lie.

Hope and dread, swirling in the pit of my stomach.

Ryan narrowed his eyes at the dial.

"Turn around," I said to Ryan. Not because I didn't trust him, but because my mother would want it this way. If she was in here . . . If she was in here, it was a problem.

CHAPTER 12

I spun the wheel three times, in a way that was second nature even though I hadn't tried it in years. As the locks clicked open and the door unlatched, I pushed gently on the door and said, "Mom? It's me. I'm coming in."

The door was thick and the room dark and stale, and even before I had it open, I knew it was empty. The lights flickered on automatically, a crass fluorescent compared to the rest of the basement. The blue rug that my mom had put down so we could sit comfortably, playing cards. The shelves full of any possible emergency precaution, ordered from every end-of-the-world vendor site. It was, I could see now, nothing more than a sterile closet, with too-close walls, fluorescent lights, bottles of water and food that would keep. A fire extinguisher, fire blankets, and a black-and-white video feed from the security cameras, beside a phone.

I stayed in the entrance—I could see everything

from here. I could see it was empty. It looked small, and cold, and I understood why Jan would be worried if my mother had kept us in here. I pulled the door shut, my hand on the wall until I felt it latch.

"What was that?" Ryan asked.

I shook my head. "The safe room. For emergencies." Not looking at Ryan, not wanting to see what he thought of that. Whether he saw it as a safe room or a panic room. Like the black iron gates, it looked different now, from the other side.

A chill ran over me, but it could've been from the basement itself.

"I need to check my phone," I said. "Maybe she called." But even I could hear the desperation in my voice.

Ryan led the way back upstairs, followed me back to my room, for my phone.

The first thing I saw was a string of messages from him:

I'm outside. Can we talk?

I'm sorry about earlier.

There are things I have to say to you.

I turned to look at Ryan, and he was cringing to himself. "Yeah, um, you can ignore those. . . ."

But Mom hadn't tried to call me. Neither had Jan.

Ryan was rolling up the sleeves of his dress shirt,

keeping his hands busy, trying to find something to do. The impossibility of this moment only worked to increase my dread: *Ryan Baker is standing in your bedroom, and nobody cares.*

I closed my eyes, trying to think like my mother. If she knew I was missing, who might she call? She knew I'd talked to Annika. Maybe she'd called her, maybe Annika had tried to cover for me and ended up making it worse.

Ryan leaned against my dresser as I dialed Annika.

I heard music in the background when she picked up. "Back so soon?" she answered.

"Did my mom call you?" I asked.

"Did your mom . . . what? No. Did she find out? Are you in trouble?"

"No, I can't . . ." I ran my hand down my face. Too many people knowing about my mother was still a fear of mine. I didn't want the whole world knowing the extent of her condition. "Did you happen to see her? I'm not asking if you were spying, but you know, you can see my house from the wall, and maybe you were sitting on the wall or something. . . ."

The music was off now. "Kelsey, is everything okay?"

"I don't know," I said. "She's not here, and it's not . . . like her . . . not to tell me."

"Just like it's not like you to tell her when you're leaving, right?" I could hear the smile in her voice.

"Annika, it's important."

"I know, I'm sorry. Eli picked me up at eight, and

we've been out since then. I didn't see her. She didn't call me."

I heard someone say something in the background, and I assumed it was Eli. "It's my neighbor," Annika responded, her voice muffled though the receiver.

"Maybe she called your mom?" I asked.

"My mom's driving Brett back to college. Nobody's there." She paused. "Do you want me to come over? We're in the car already, I can be there in thirty," she said.

"No, it's okay. Enjoy your date, Annika."

Ryan moved to sit beside me on the bed—and again I thought of how ridiculous this was: *Ryan Baker is on your bed.* And I started to laugh.

"Everything okay?" he asked.

I shook my head. "You're sitting on my bed, and my mother is missing. And I kissed you ten minutes ago."

His lips quirked up in a half smile. "I know you did." And now he was staring at my mouth again, like he was replaying it. "I liked ten minutes ago."

But he didn't understand—everything about ten minutes ago was gone. Everything from then to now was impossible.

"This can't be real," I said. I stared at the phone in my hand, because I knew what I had to do. I had to call Jan. I had to find out if she knew something, without giving anything away.

White lies. Little lies. Like my mother taught me. *Careful.*

I called Jan's cell, but it went to voice mail after a single ring. Which meant she saw it was me and hit End. Which meant she was probably in a late meeting with a patient. Or at the class Cole had mentioned. If she knew something about my mom, she would've picked up. I was sure. I was pretty sure.

I typed: Did my mom call you?

And then: Did something happen? But I changed my mind, deleting the second line before hitting Send.

But it was too late—all those *somethings* started working their way into my head, circling and circling.

My phone beeped in response, and my heart jumped along with it.

Text from Jan: No. Is everything okay? In a seminar.

Was everything okay? Not even close. My mother didn't call Annika, or Jan, or me. The possibilities were shrinking. Wherever Mom was, she was not okay.

"Kelsey?" Ryan asked, reaching for my hand.

Ryan was watching me closely. Between the ceremony and this moment, his hair had gradually become disheveled, like it usually was at school, and his dress shirt had turned casual, with the collar unbuttoned and the sleeves rolled up, and he was beginning to look, once again, like someone who had been playing a part—stuck in someone else's clothes—who was slowly unmaking himself.

He looked, all at once, both uncomfortable and unsure, alone with me in this house where something was very *not right*. Like my thoughts were catching. I remembered his face the moment we fell. His words as he crawled inside my car. But I also remembered the way he'd held on to me, promising we'd be okay. The way he thought that *I* was the brave one.

Think, Kelsey. If my mother noticed I was missing, would she try to come after me? Was it possible? Would she *try*? "The front booth," I whispered. "And the backyard. We need to check them both."

The booth near the front gate was not made like the rest of the house. It was wooden and painted white, but the grain was starting to show, with weather and time. The door didn't have a lock. Though small and enclosed, nothing about this booth was safe. Even the floorboards echoed. As a kid, I'd been afraid to play inside it.

The windows to the front and side were thin and rattled when I pulled the door open. The room was empty.

Inside, it smelled of must and gasoline and exposed wood. Everything was coated with a thick layer of dust and pollen. There was only room for one person to sit, in a chair that was no longer here. Red plastic containers of gasoline for the generator were stored under the control panel—and had been for as long as I could remember. Everything about this room was undisturbed.

There were no safe answers left. My mother had not

tried to come after me and then lost her nerve at the gate.

I quickly shut the door again, staring at Ryan.

He must've read something in my face, because he said, "There's still the whole yard." As if we might find her curled up in the weeds, hidden from our sight, just waiting to be found. As if words alone could turn into hope. He reached a hand out for me, and I took it.

I followed him in the darkness, and I felt the vastness, as my mother called it. All the danger, all the possibility, existing in the places I could only imagine.

"Mom?" I called repeatedly, as we made our way along the edge of the gate, until we could be sure there was nowhere left to hide.

I shivered in the night air, and I felt too exposed all of a sudden. Like my mother would be, standing in this very spot. My eyes darted from shadow to shadow in the darkness. There could be people watching, from every corner of the woods. My blood was thrumming.

Inside. Inside was safety.

"Let's go," I whispered. I led the way back into the house, locking the doors behind me on instinct. I wandered down the hall, my hands trailing along the walls, trying to orient myself. Like I was waking in a strange place for the first time.

The alarm was off, and she was missing.

What the hell was going on?

* * *

I sat down at the kitchen table and stared at my cell, hoping it would miraculously provide answers. Ryan hopped up on the countertop, like he used to do at the Lodge. Like my two worlds were overlapping. As if I could be both people at once.

"Should we call someone else?" he asked.

Ryan was not nearly as worried as I was—because Ryan didn't understand how improbable this situation truly was. The fear was too great. It had no boundaries. It seeped into every aspect of our lives, binding her here. I imagined it like the ivy, creeping up the iron gates. Tangling together until you couldn't see one without the other.

"Kelsey?"

Ryan Baker, who asked you out, is hanging out in your kitchen in suit pants and a button-down shirt, two feet away from you, with his brown hair falling in his eyes, waiting for you to do something. Snap out of it, Kelsey.

I didn't want to explain how delicate my situation in this house was already. I was always just one moment from being pulled. One call from Jan, or one call to the police, and the whole thing might tip too far, my whole life might slip away from me.

"She doesn't have a car," I finally said. And then I gave voice to the thought that had begun in my room when I was texting Jan. The thought that dug in and circled and wouldn't let go. "What if someone broke in and hurt her?"

Lightning striking twice. Her biggest fear.

He pushed off the counter. Surveyed the room. "Is anything missing?"

"No," I said. "I don't think so."

Because that was why people broke into homes, in Ryan's world. Not to take people. Not to keep them, and hurt them, and ruin them.

He looked around the room, his eyes lingering on the closed doors, the locked windows. "It doesn't look like a break-in to me, Kelsey."

I nodded. Except. Except we had locks and security and a panic room for a reason. What if her fears were not so ungrounded? What if she knew the danger was real? That someone was still out there, just waiting for a chance?

The fears started skittering along my skin, threatening to shut me down. I wanted to give myself over to them. Crawl into bed, stare at the walls, surround myself with them.

Ryan grabbed my shoulder, crouching beside me so his face was just inches away, his eyes wide and worried. "You okay? You look pale. Like you might pass out."

My mouth had gone dry, and it felt almost like my throat was closing off, the air scratching along the surface, and I was a balloon, drifting farther and farther away. . . .

"Kelsey?" he called, but his voice was on another planet. Didn't he see?

My mother was gone.

My mother was gone.

CHAPTER 13

Jan didn't come into our lives until I was nine.

Before that, we'd been coasting along at a pretty decent clip, under the radar.

And *under the radar* was my mother's number one goal. Jan and I were the only ones who knew who my mother had once been. She told Jan because she had to. She told me because it was always just the two of us against the world. And what she wasn't able to tell me herself I could find out easily enough with an Internet search.

Amanda Silviano was famous.

She was famous for the horror. For the media circus. For the tragedy of what had happened to her, and also what happened because of it. She was one of those names that lingered. Elizabeth Smart. Jaycee Lee Dugard. Girls taken and kept, like so many others. But she was one of the few: girls miraculously found again.

The difference was she no longer had a place to return.

The Amanda Silviano in the news stories was raised in a middle-class neighborhood by a single father. She lived in a beige ranch with a white picket fence, in a grid of houses that looked exactly the same. I'd seen the pictures from old articles. Her father reported her missing—kidnapped—after coming home one morning from working the night shift to find the house ransacked. The front windows had been smashed in. The neighbors had heard a scream.

My mother was beautiful, and seventeen, and a Girl Who Followed the Rules. The perfect trifecta for media attention. The attention got more police involvement, and then more *people* involvement. And then the allegations began. Allegations of a long history of abuse. The cigarette burns. The black eye. The reports from her classmates. The screams, not so unusual, the neighbors said. But nobody had spoken up. Nobody had protected her, then or later. Only in hindsight did anybody care.

It was a past that, in the eyes of the public, could only lead to one single truth: that he was guilty. And that perhaps this was a cover-up. Perhaps his daughter was dead and buried, and he had staged the whole thing.

He was vilified. The police brought him in for questioning. He took, and failed, a lie detector test. He was all but declared guilty, before a trial, and he overdosed on sleeping pills as rumors of his impending arrest swirled. Impossible to tell whether it was accidental or not. *Suicide over the Guilt*, one headline claimed.

But then, later that year, my mother reappeared—alive. She escaped from the man who truly held her. She was found running on the edge of a highway, in the woods of Pennsylvania, delirious, dirty, smelling of gasoline—and four months pregnant. The hospital ID'd her, and the reporters were there almost as fast as the police. She was alive, and *what a tragedy*, they said, what had happened to her father. What a tragedy, what they themselves had done.

Is it any surprise she changed her name? She checked herself out of the hospital as soon as she could, and she left. She took the money that her father had left her, and she used it to set us up here. Given the media circus surrounding her reappearance, her request to have the records sealed on her name change was granted.

She had no memory of her abduction, and I had no memory of her ever leaving the house.

Though I believed, based on the fact that she would never talk about her life before her abduction, either, that she was more than happy to leave all of Amanda Silviano behind. To become someone new. To give us both a fresh start.

She took classes online, eventually finding herself some part-time bookkeeping work for a local business.

She slowly set up a life for herself, one where she could provide for the both of us without ever having to leave these walls. I played out in the backyard, inside the gate, while my mother watched from the kitchen. I'd turn to see her, always at the window, smiling and watching. I was healthy and loved, and I grew and thrived.

She registered me as homeschooled. I took the state tests. I scored well. I hadn't had a checkup, or a vaccine, which wasn't illegal then—but it raised some flags with social services, over time.

But sometime between year seven and eight, something happened. I'm not sure what, exactly. But Child Protection showed up, and they asked me questions without my mom around, and I said something—I said something troubling, about the kids on TV, and how dangerous it was for them, playing in the woods. Something that made them realize that neither of us had left the property since soon after I'd been born.

I was temporarily removed, just for forty-eight hours, but my mother went into a fit. It was not the best reaction, truly. I remember this well, because it was the first time I'd been away from home. Sometimes, when I walk into a new place for the first time, that same feeling overwhelms me, and I remember disappearing into myself—trying to scream, but finding no air.

But even then, even when her daughter was taken

from her, even when she did not know where I was, *even then*, she did not leave the house. She did not try to find me.

She waited for them to return me, and then she fought hard to keep me.

But that was how I knew she wouldn't leave just because I wasn't home.

She couldn't.

It was impossible.

Ryan had made himself at home in the kitchen, gotten me some juice, looked at me sideways, and pushed me into a chair anytime I'd stand and start pacing. I felt numb and removed, like I was still floating above my body somehow. This was really not how I imagined my first date with Ryan going.

Hey, remember that other *time we did something? Where we sat silently in the kitchen while I tried to figure out what happened to my mother?* Right. Good times, part two.

Ryan looked through the pantry and ate a cookie before sliding one in front of me, too.

He took out his phone, and that's what jarred me back to the present. "We should call the police," he said, "if you think . . . something happened. We need to call."

Something happened. Yes, something happened. But

what? The *what* changed everything, and I couldn't make a decision until I knew.

It was such a delicate balance, and I needed him to understand. It felt like a confession, though, and I was so used to keeping these things to myself, *for* myself. But he was waiting, tapping his fingers—listening. I took a deep breath. "If I call the police, I won't be able to live here anymore. And she needs me here." *And I need her.* "Just . . . I need to look around. I need to figure out what happened first."

He put his phone on the counter, like a concession. He didn't ask one of the thousands of questions he could've asked based on what I'd told him. Instead, he ran his fingers through his hair, pushing it back from his face. "Okay," he said. "Other than the alarm being off, was anything else different?"

"No," I said, and then I felt my eyes growing wide, drying out, the buzzing in my ears. *No, no, no.*

The doors were all locked when I left, but my window . . .

I pushed back from the table, the chair abruptly screeching against the tile, and ran to my room, my hands brushing the walls, realizing why I'd felt that chill—why it was colder in my room, like something had happened here. Not my mother's anger.

The window.

It was ajar, and the grate was pushed open, when I was sure I'd left it closed. "Oh God," I said.

She could've pushed it open looking for me, or . . . someone could've gotten in.

If something had happened, it could've started right here, in this room, because I'd left the window unlocked.

"What is it?" Ryan asked, standing in the entrance, his arms braced against the doorjamb, tension leeching from me to him.

But it was something more—something I could feel starting up again, so familiar it was almost welcome, the one thing I understood. The way the hairs stood up on my arms, the goose bumps on my legs, the nausea in my gut. The reason Jan wrote that article about me.

These were the things that had hurt my mother: the chemical burns on her back, the man who had taken her. It's why, Jan thought—and *wrote*—I couldn't bear the scent of anything chemically acrid.

Was there something here, then, that my body understood? Something passed along to me from my mother? Fears were learned, but they were also inherited. Natural selection. Run from the lion. Jump away from the tiny, poisonous insects. They exist for a reason—we *survive* because of them.

So what was it about a hollow, empty room? What was really to fear here? The night air, the scent of pine, all things I was familiar with.

The scars on her back, a man who held her—all of this changed her.

I remembered how she'd spend the days watching

the news, reading through articles, focusing on all the horrible things that people were doing to each other.

She'd read them out loud, and she'd ask me: *You are trapped in a trunk, what would you do?* Or *There's a mass shooting, how do you escape?*

She taught me to find the fears. She taught me to see them everywhere. It was our most basic instinct.

What had she taught me to fear about this moment?

It wasn't Ryan, or the night, or the chill. It was none of those things.

It ran deeper. Simpler. The empty, hollow room. The empty, sterile house. The emptiness.

That I was alone now.

The only thing possibly worse: that I had brought it upon myself.

I wandered around the room, slightly untethered, vaguely aware of Ryan following behind me. I saw the room in a new light—the mess, the drawers pulled open—and pictured, instead, someone crawling inside the unlocked window. Not my mother looking for me, but a stranger. I reached for the grate through the window, which was slightly ajar. Not quite how I'd left it.

Ryan reached for my arm. "Talk to me," he said.

"I snuck out," I said. "I left this unlocked. This is all because of me." One way or another, it came back to this decision.

She was unreasonable, I'd thought. An unlocked

window grate wasn't a big deal. Lightning wouldn't strike twice.

But I was wrong. I was so wrong.

He moved closer, put a hand on my shoulder, closed his eyes for a moment, as if he was steeling himself for what came next. "Look, Kelsey, I'm going to say it again. If you believe someone came into the house, then we need to call the police."

Spoken like someone who had never been forcibly removed from his home.

I shook my head, unable to make a decision. I'd never had to before. I did what my mom, or Jan, told me to do. I feared what she feared. I loved what she loved. And the one time I made a decision for myself— sneaking out—I paid the consequences.

I wanted to sink into my bed, feel the familiar comforter, the four walls, the spiders crawling across my skin. All of it, if it meant knowing my mother was down the hall.

"Kelsey," Ryan said. "You have to do something."

There was a fifty percent chance it would be the wrong thing. Either way, I was the one who'd have to suffer the consequences. Not him.

"Let me think," I said, holding up my hands.

My mother didn't have a cell phone to call—there was no reason. She never left. She had her computer, and the landline, and the alarm system.

"Okay. If I can get the alarm back on," I said, "then she must've turned it off herself, or it was an electrical surge, and we wait. If I can't . . . then someone cut it, and I'll call. Okay?"

"Sure," Ryan said, sounding slightly less than sure.

The idea was taking root—that there was some sort of electrical surge, taking out the alarm system and the phone line. Frying anything on the grid. I just had to reboot the system. It had happened once before, in a really bad thunderstorm, when I was little. I watched my mom come down to the basement, after the backup generator had kicked on a few moments later, and reboot the alarm system.

I felt like I was tracing her footsteps, following the path to the basement, to the circuit breaker.

"Hold on," I said. I flipped everything off—the house going dark, and momentarily cold, and in the basement, our breathing seemed too loud. I listened for any other sounds. I was sure, in that moment, I'd hear someone breathing through the walls, if they were here.

Ryan's hand brushed my arm as all the equipment wound down. His fingers circled my elbow, and I felt his body pressing closer, his fingers holding firmer—as if he wanted us both to be sure.

"Just a sec," I said, and then I turned everything back on. The house came to life. The lights, the hum of the freezer along the back wall, air moving through the vents up above.

Then I went to the main alarm box on the wall, pushed the reset button, and listened as the house let off a low beep—*ready to arm*. "Everything should be back up now," I said.

"So," he said, "everything's okay?" His face like the moment before we fell, when I reached for him—on the cusp of relief.

Then there was silence, and suddenly in the stillness it occurred to me that I'd been overreacting. That there must be some simple explanation—an electrical surge, the police showing up at the gate, my mother letting them in. Maybe she'd had a health scare. Maybe she was in the hospital at this very moment, and someone was trying to call—but with the electrical surge, they couldn't reach me.

"The alarm works fine. Which means—"

"What's that?" Ryan asked, his head tilted to the side. He walked slowly toward the steps.

I thought he was talking about the alarm beep, or the vibration of the equipment above, coming back to life—but then I heard it, too. The faint hum of an engine revving. The slow crunch of gravel under tires, getting nearer.

"Oh," I said.

I pictured the police, coming to tell me something about my mom. Something I wasn't ready to hear. Maybe she'd been hurt, or felt sick, and called 911. Maybe she'd panicked about me, called 911, and they came, couldn't calm her, took her away.

I placed a hand to my stomach as I walked up the stairs. This was it. This was the moment my life would change. I could feel how pivotal it was, the police showing up—my mom *not okay* and everyone learning the truth. The only place I'd ever known would no longer be mine.

I pulled back the front curtains, but I didn't see any car.

The night was dark—darker, because of the lights reflected in the windows. But I thought I saw a shadow moving toward the front gate. I flipped on the outside lights on instinct, and whatever I thought was moving stopped. Everything within me turned on edge. Something prickled at the back of my neck, and for once, I didn't try to ignore it.

"Turn off the lights, Ryan," I said.

Slowly they shut down, one by one, my image dimming, and then disappearing, in the reflection.

There it was, just beyond the ring of light shining at the front gate—a shadow. From a tree? Or a person, watching the house?

My fingers fumbled at the alarm pad beside the door. I pressed and held the Arm key, listened to the house beep twice, letting me know we were safe. The gate was locked. A current was running once again through the wire at the top of the fence, with its high, spiked bars.

"What is it?" Ryan asked. I could feel his breath on the side of my face in the darkness.

I backed away from the window, not wanting to be seen.

I tried to talk myself out of the impending panic: *I see the danger everywhere. I see the danger in everything. It isn't real. Irrational fears.*

I tapped the glass with my index finger. "Tell me what you see," I whispered.

Ryan frowned, then leaned close to the window, his breath fogging the glass. "The bars of the gate. Trees." He leaned toward the side. "I can kinda see the edge of my car."

"That's it? Look at the shadow at the edge of the light."

He shook his head. "I don't see anything."

I stood beside him at the window, shoulder to shoulder, to point it out—but the shadow was gone.

I backed away from the window, panic lodged in my skull, words stuck in my throat. I ran to my room, fumbled for that key in the top drawer, and pulled the window grate shut, turning the lock and pushing the glass shut.

"Kelsey? What's happening?" Ryan had followed me to my room, and he was watching me, focusing on my shaking hand, still gripping the key. And I wondered whether he was asking what was happening outside, or what was happening to *me*.

Paranoia. A trick of light. My mind making me see things that weren't there. This was the fear talking. Crawling out from the corners, turning the safe into every different horrifying possibility. Impractical fears of things that would never happen. I was falling apart in front of Ryan Baker, and I couldn't even stop myself.

But my mother was missing.

My mother was gone. . . .

I ignored the question in his voice and ran back to the front window. There was nothing there. I moved from window to window, tracing the perimeter of the house—my eyes tracking the iron bars, a familiar comfort. I pulled open the living room curtains, and turned on the back lights, just as a shadow darted quickly behind the rails of the back gate.

The entire room was buzzing.

I saw it. I was sure.

"Ryan," I said, my voice wavering. "Call the police."

CHAPTER 14

I had my back against the wall while Ryan still stood at the window with his phone in his hand, peering out into the dark between the gap of curtains. The difference between me and Ryan could be best summed up right here. I was hiding, imagining the worst, and he was curiously assessing the scene. He was not panicking unnecessarily, imagining all the terrible things people might do to each other.

I craned my neck to see the alarm console beside the front door, the red light, the word *Armed*, and let out a slow breath.

Ryan held the phone to his ear, his face pressed into the beige curtains, like he was about to give a practical, firsthand account of what he was looking at. *There are shadows moving around the house. Right, no big deal, but you don't understand, someone is missing.*

Maybe my imagination was running away with me—maybe these were just a slew of illogical fears that I'd succumbed to, with nobody here to pull me out. Maybe I was taking Ryan down with me. Fear was contagious like that.

Two minutes later, and I was already second-guessing what I saw. How could I trust myself, when I heard my mother's words echoing back? It could've been the wind moving branches, a trick of the light, clouds moving across the moon, an animal even.

I looked at Ryan, about to voice my thoughts. "Maybe . . . ," I began.

But then he pulled back from the window, lowered the phone, frowned at the display. The light of the phone display lit up his face in the dark, an eerie, un-natural glow. He tried again. Frowned again.

"What?" I asked.

"The call won't go through. I can't get any service," he said.

My phone was on the kitchen table, where I'd wasted time staring at it, debating what to do. Doing *nothing.*

Move, Kelsey. Do something.

I walked across the room, feeling for the furniture as I passed—dark shapes in a darker room. My limbs tingled like they had when I'd woken in the car, hang-ing upside down—like they understood, even before I did, the wrongness of the situation.

I squinted against the bright display in the dark and dialed 911, but as soon as I hit Enter, the call dropped. I looked at the display—*Searching for service.* I shook my head at Ryan, then said, "Same here," in case he couldn't see me. I picked up the corded phone hanging from the wall, but all I heard was the faint click, the dead air.

"Try sending someone a message," I said. Jan. I'd text Jan. I need help, I wrote, but a message popped up in response: *Failure to send.*

I looked over at Ryan, and from the way he was staring at the phone, he was getting the same result. I walked toward him, half his body in shadow. His eyes were wide, his body still and contained, and I recognized his expression from the moment we felt the cable snap. The knowledge that we were falling. The realization that it was all out of our control . . .

"What's happening?" he asked.

"I don't know," I said, going back to the gap between the curtains. I stared at the alarm beside the front door, still flashing *Armed*.

The feeling of spiders crawling across my skin. Everything about the situation whispering *Wrong*. Like a cold breath across the back of my neck.

"Could be an electrical surge," he said. "Like you said before. Rolling blackouts or something . . ." He was grasping for anything—nails and skin on metal and me—just like when he fell.

"For cell phones, too?" I asked.

He stepped back from the window, pressed his lips together, and he didn't answer. He was doing the same thing I was—trying to find a reasonable explanation, to tamp down the paranoia, or the fear, but one of us had to say it. One of us had to face it.

"Or," I said slowly, instinctively grabbing his arm, pulling him back from the window, "something's blocking our calls."

Something. Some*one*.

I hadn't made a decision, and now it was too late. My fault. My inaction. And now we both had to pay for it.

Our eyes locked, his mouth slightly open. "You saw someone out there?" he asked. "You're sure?"

"Yes," I said, and I felt acid rising in the back of my throat.

He quickly scanned the walls, the doors, the windows, jerked the curtains closed and backed toward the center of the house, pulling me with him. Even in the dark, I could tell he was closing his eyes. "This place is a fortress," he whispered. "It's okay."

This place was not a fortress. It was built to withstand a strong storm—to provide for us if we couldn't reach the outside world for a week or two. It was built to protect us from intruders—until help could arrive. It was designed to alert, to alarm, to tell us to call for help, or to run. None of which were options at the moment.

"There are cameras in my mom's office," I said. His arm brushed against mine, and our fingers linked together as we made our way through the darkened hall.

"It could be nothing," he said. "It could be anything."

He meant it to be reassuring, but his hand was cold and his grip was tight, and I wondered, once more, whether he was talking to himself.

"Ryan, we need help," I said. Just to make sure he understood—this house was not a fortress.

The blinds in Mom's office were slanted open, and I reached up to close them before turning on the screens for the security cameras around the property. I didn't want to draw attention to ourselves. I wanted to see without being seen. It felt like the upper hand, even if we were, at the moment, trapped.

I watched the screens flicker to life as Ryan stood beside me. The light reflected off the pictures and the framed artwork lining the walls, but everything seemed colorless and dull. The screens were black-and-white, grainy and pixelated, and I could only see the area illuminated by the outside lights—like a stark, oval orb. The gates remained closed.

Fortress, I told myself, trying to make it so.

"I still don't see anything. Tell me exactly what you saw," he said.

I closed my eyes, replaying it. "I saw a shadow out front, and then it was gone." I shivered. "And when I turned on the back lights, I saw a shadow dive to stay hidden."

He looked over his shoulder, at the windows closed up tight. "So it could just be neighborhood kids or something," he said. But he pressed his lips together, and he didn't look at me when he said it.

I said nothing in response.

Ryan was watching the video feeds on the wall above us, frowning. He must've been able to feel all the pieces crushing in on us, each one more wrong than the last. My mother gone, the phone line out, our cell phones blocked, a shadow out back. He could explain away each on its own, but all together? No, he couldn't. And he knew it.

He turned to face me, and he placed his hands around my shoulders, as if this alone could keep me safe. "They'll leave," he said. "They'll realize we're here, and that we see them, and they'll leave. People don't *want* to rob a house with people home, Kelsey."

As if we could wait it out and be fine. I rested my forehead against Ryan's chest for one heartbeat, two, before I pulled myself together.

"In the basement," I said, pulling back. "We have everything down there, in case of emergency. There has to be a way to make a call."

In the safe room, we had anything we might need, in any possible emergency situation—and now I needed them.

We kept the lights off.

I felt my way through the dark hallway, stumbling around the corners, until I found the basement door.

There was nothing. No source of light. No ambient glare from the streetlights far away or the moonlight through the windows. I didn't know the way by heart in the common rooms, not the way I knew the steps from my bedroom light switch to my bed, or the way I could count the paces as I ran down the hall to my mom's room when I was little and prone to nightmares that I could never remember.

She'd curl her body around mine, and I knew nothing could happen to me as long as she was there.

The dark was not a fear of mine. The dark was my home. I could hide inside it, with the four walls of my bedroom keeping me safe, and go still—and nothing could touch me.

But even that wasn't true. This house was not made of impenetrable steel. It never occurred to me we might not be safe enough here, with the bars and the alarm and the reinforced locks and the grates over the windows. But take away our phones, cut the alarm, and we were on our own. It was all just a matter of time.

Ryan trailed behind me, a hand on my shoulder, another on my waist, following my lead until I eased the basement door shut behind us and flipped on the overhead bulbs, which seemed to dance in the dark.

We bumped up against boxes and each other as we raced through the stacks, even in the light, on the way to the safe room. I didn't bother hiding the code from Ryan this time: 23-12-37, and we were in. The security feeds flickered to life as the power turned on. But all I could see were dark, stationary objects in the orbs of light. The black iron fence, lit up and circling the house in a pattern I knew by heart.

There were plastic boxes lining the shelves from floor to ceiling on the three remaining walls. Flashlights with batteries and other light sources, boxed food, blankets and bottles of water. I tried to remember what she'd said about the radio—something about communication, even without electricity, even without phones. She'd truly prepared for everything.

I pulled the boxes down, one at a time, but Ryan stayed outside the door. "You can come in," I said, pulling down the clear tubs that looked like they held electronics.

"I wasn't sure if you wanted me to."

I had asked him to turn around earlier. I had wanted to keep this from him. The darker parts of my life, the scarier parts. The part of me that was *my* blood. I had wanted to be anyone other than who I was. But there was no hiding anymore.

"Here," I said, sliding one of the containers across the floor, closer to him. I opened the top, but Ryan was looking past it—past *me*—his face scrunched up in confusion. "Do you guys have a safe room inside a safe room or something?"

"Huh?" I dropped the flashlights I'd grabbed from the top of the box. Turned around. Saw what Ryan was talking about. The corner of the blue rug was folded up, caught on the corner of the crate, and in the floor was another compartment. A small square, completely flat, like a large bathroom tile, but with a tiny hole the size of my finger, to pull it up.

"Oh." I removed the square tile and leaned it against the back wall.

It wasn't deep—just the size of a safe, everything resting on a square piece of wood below. Inside were zippered, opaque pouches. I unzipped the first, and knew immediately why it was hidden. Cash. Large stacks of crisp hundred-dollar bills bound together with rubber bands.

"Whoa," Ryan said.

"Oh," I repeated.

There were two pouches like this, stacked full of money. Right. This made sense, if I thought like my mother. Without electricity, there would be no electronic banking. She was just preparing for everything.

The third pouch looked much emptier, and I expected a few stacks of bills in that, too.

But there weren't. There were passports.

Our birth certificates and other personal documents were kept in a fireproof safe in Mom's office upstairs. Maybe these were copies, for safekeeping. Or maybe these were the things from my mom's previous life, long ago—before she was taken.

I'd never had a passport. Where would I go? I was barely allowed the ten miles to my school. And I'd never had any interest in going any farther.

I opened the passport on top, saw my mother's picture staring back at me, with a plain white wall in the background. But this wasn't her old one from when she was a teenager. This was new. Her hair, long and straight, parted harshly down the middle. And that shirt—I knew that shirt. Plain black with a scalloped collar. I'd ordered it for her two Christmases ago. I checked the date, and sure enough, it was issued just over a year ago.

But then my eye caught a mistake. The name. *Amy Douglas.*

Maybe she'd had to change it before—before she became Mandy Thomas—and never told me. She'd changed it, after she escaped, so reporters would leave her alone. So we would be free from the horrors of her past: the infamous kidnapping, her abusive home, a life that had gone from bad to much worse. She'd given me the last name Thomas when I was born, and she changed hers to match it as soon as she could. I never knew her any other way. Maybe this was a mistake.

I pulled out the second passport, expecting a corrected version.

My fingers tingled. The face staring back was my own.

The girl looked happy in front of the white wall behind her—our own living room, the wall between the two curtained windows. This picture was taken the first day I went to high school. I remembered my mother making a big deal out of it—*All mothers have shots of their child's first day of school. Come on, let's do it!* Acting too cheerful—faking it, for both of our benefit. She'd stood close, snapped the photo, said, *Mug shot acquired,* and I'd never seen the picture again.

And now here it was, beside a girl's name that was not mine. *Lauren Douglas.* Born in late July, a few months before my own birthday. The passports trembled in my hand.

"What is it?" Ryan asked, searching through the boxes near the doorway.

"Nothing," I said, storing it all away. The room was buzzing again, but it looked like I was the only one who heard it. "Just our documents for safekeeping." I replaced the missing tile, smoothed the rug back over it.

Ryan went back to working methodically, his hands not shaking with fear. Like maybe there wasn't someone just outside the gates who had done something to my mother. Like we weren't trapped inside the house, a house set up to protect us because *she knew it would happen.*

And now there were passports in the floor—a version of us I didn't understand.

He repacked a box, slid it back my way. Opened another. "How about this?" he asked, holding the radio over his head in triumph.

It was old and brown, with a rabbit-ear antenna and a black dial that moved a red line between stations. He flipped the power switch, and static cut through the room at a loud volume. Static, and music, and radio stations. "It doesn't work both ways," he said.

"God, this is all *useless*," I said. When what I really meant was *I am useless*.

But Ryan was looking over my shoulder, his gaze fixed on the monitors with his head cocked to the side.

"What?" I asked, twisting around to see.

"I saw something," he said. He stood, his shoulders turned tense, and he stepped closer to the security screens. He reached a finger up, touching a dark corner. "There. I saw . . ."

He turned back around, and I saw his throat move. His eyes were wide, and I reached for his shoulder, like I had in the car—

And then I heard it. A dull thud. Something that seemed to reverberate through my bones. A sharp hiss, like air leaking from a balloon, and all the lights went dark.

CHAPTER 15

I groped for the flashlights that were somewhere between us on the cold basement floor. I couldn't see anything—not even Ryan's shape in the darkness. The static of the radio grew louder as all the electrical appliances in the house wound down to silence. No air circulating through the vents, or coolant in the refrigerator, or the faint buzz of the lights. Just the crackle of an out-of-tune station, Ryan's breathing, and my own.

My hand found Ryan's leg before the flashlight, and he gripped my arm, flicking on a flashlight with his other hand. He shined it in my face, and I held up my arm to block the light.

"What's happening?" he whispered.

But he had to already know. It's what my mother had always feared. It's what she prepared me for. "Someone's coming," I whispered.

I felt his breath, warm against my face, coming sharp and fast.

The power was off. And the alarm—the alarm was off, and the gates could be forced open, and there would be no sound—no cry for help.

"The generator," I said, moving closer to the light, keeping my voice low. "The backup electricity will turn on in a few minutes."

But without electricity, there was no current running through the wire atop the gate. The spikes didn't matter. The gate lock could be disengaged with a few tools, the doors forced apart. Whoever was out there could slip through the gap, and then all that remained were the walls of the house itself.

The generator had to kick in first. It had to kick in *soon*.

"How many?" Ryan said. The light jerked across the boxes of the basement as he stood. *"How many minutes?"*

"Three," I said, already counting down in my head from 180.

He swung the light to the stairs.

There were ways in; even I knew this. We had gates and locks and bars and cameras—but beyond that, there were window seals that could be broken. Latches that could be overcome.

We couldn't see what was happening out there, not until the generator kicked in.

The not knowing was the worst. My hands groped across the cold, dusty ground. The seconds slowly ticked down—*150*.

Come on, come on. My hand connected with the other flashlight, and I headed for the stairs.

"What are you doing?" Ryan asked, grabbing my hand. I felt my blood pulsing, my heart racing.

A hundred twenty. Two more minutes. Her voice in my ear, a lifetime of education. *You have to pay attention.* "I have to see," I said, weaving around a stack of boxes. Ryan was close on my heels. I spun around at the base of the stairs, realizing I'd left the safe room door open. It felt unnatural, and like it was calling to us—something that wasn't meant to be left exposed. Like it all might disintegrate in the fresh air, paper turned to ash.

A hundred ten. No time. The stairs creaked as we made our way to the first floor. I ran my flashlight quickly across the walls. Everything was still, and safe. The curtains were pulled tight, and there were no lights—not even from the clock over the stove or the glow of the alarm panel. *Eighty more seconds.*

I turned off my flashlight, crouching low and peering out from between the curtains—but it was impossible to see anything clearly from this distance. It was impossible to make out any shapes in the dark, other than the wall, the trees, darker than the night sky.

But then the shadows shifted, or something *moved*, and I saw the faintest light near the back gate. The beam from a penlight, maybe, as someone worked at the manual locks of the gate, trying to disengage the bars from the concrete base.

Sixty. One minute. "I'm going back down," I said. "To arm the gates as soon as the power turns back."

But Ryan didn't pull back from the window. "Ryan," I said. *Fifty-one, fifty . . .*

I put my arms around his waist and tugged him back. *"Ryan."* I knew how this could happen—how the fear could paralyze you if you let it. I'd sat at the kitchen table, immobilized, just moments earlier— and he'd been the one to pull me out of it. *Forty-three, forty-two . . .*

I gripped him tighter. "We have to *go*," I said. I felt his muscles trembling, his body on edge.

He spun around, the curtains dropping in a wave behind him. "Go," he said, pushing me ahead of him. "Go, go, go."

I ran. My hands brushed the furniture and the walls, my fingers finding the corners and the doorway. I turned the flashlight on once we were back within the basement.

Thirty-one, thirty, twenty-nine . . . I stood beside the alarm panel, and I waited.

The waiting was agony. Seconds, stretching out. Like Ryan in the car, after I'd seen the emptiness below us. Waiting for him to pull us up to safety. Waiting, and then falling . . .

Twenty, nineteen, eighteen . . .

I heard something click through the basement walls. Something hum. A motor revving, winding up—the generator underground, coming to life. My body uncoiling with relief.

The basement lights flickered once with the surge before turning back off, and the freezer in the corner kicked in with a whoosh. I hit the reset button, heard the alarm beep once—*Ready*—and hit the code to arm it. I tripped over the open boxes on the way to the safe room, turned the video feed back on, and stared at the black-and-white images. The gates were closed.

But had someone gotten in when we hadn't been looking?

"Why are the lights still out?" Ryan asked. They weren't on in the basement, and they weren't on in the yard any longer. The screen was mostly just a dark gray of shadows on shadows.

"The generator can't power the whole house indefinitely. There are gasoline containers in the front gate booth, but . . . it's still only connected to the essentials."

"What are the essentials?" Ryan asked, because it was obvious that our idea of *essential* was probably not the same as his.

"Refrigerator, freezer, heat, and surveillance," I said.

"There," said Ryan, pointing at the screen. A flash of light at the front gate. *Outside* the front gate. His finger was shaking, and he pulled it back, balled his hands into fists, like he was embarrassed by it.

Suddenly, on the back monitor, another flash of light swung in an arc, like a flashlight was rolling across the ground. It came to rest at the metal gate, illuminating a second shadow. He was using the light.

He was down low, near the ground. And he was digging.

My eyes kept darting from screen to screen—front gate, back gate, light to light. There were two people.

"They know we're in here," Ryan said. "And they don't care."

The outside lights I'd turned on, his car out front—yes, they knew.

He gritted his teeth. "Open the door."

"What?" I asked, wheeling on him. We'd both been staring at the screen, watching and waiting.

"The front door. Set off the alarm."

"It's not connected to the police," I said. It was a warning for us to get in the safe room and figure out what was happening first, before calling for help. My mother thought it wasn't safe to be on the police radar for a false alarm, not with our living situation so precarious. All it would take was a nudge and we might fall. Besides, right now without the phone lines, there was no way for the alarm system to call out, even if it had been connected.

"Yeah, but it'll be loud. How close are the neighbors?"

Not that close, I thought. But if Annika had gotten back home . . . would she hear a high-pitched alarm?

Would she try calling me, and then call the police? Or would she think this was just another odd thing about my life here?

"The friend I borrowed the car from," I said. "She might hear."

He held out his hand, and I took it, and I thought how ridiculous it was to be nervous of something like this in another circumstance, like before math class, earlier today. Now I held on to it and hoped it grounded me enough to keep me thinking, to keep me safe.

I followed him back up the stairs and went for the front door.

Ryan peered out the front window. His car was somewhere out there, around the bend, parked outside the gate on the side of the road. He glanced at me, and back to the gate, and I knew exactly what he was thinking.

If both people were at the back gate, could we make it?

Could we get through the gates undetected, start up his car, and make a run for it, leaving the abandoned house to them while we went for help? Or would they follow, drive us off the road before we could call for help—

My breath started coming too fast, and I steadied myself against the wall.

"We should've left, the second we thought something

was wrong," Ryan said. He balled up his fists again. "That's what I'm supposed to do. That's what I'm *trained* to do." I felt the tension leeching from his body, filling up the room.

Really he must've been thinking, *I should've stayed at the ceremony. I should've gone back with Emma and Holly and that other girl. I should've decided to call the police for myself,* before *we heard the car.*

Really he must've been thinking, *My life is in danger* again, *because of you.*

I stared at the windows, at the doors, at the black iron gates, and I saw them all through his eyes. They were not his protection, like they were for me. He was nothing more than trapped here. With me. For no reason.

Hanging from the car, tumbling past me, tethered by a rope—his fate tied to mine.

I had to get him out of here.

"What's that guy even doing out front?" he continued. "Why not help the other one, out back. It's like . . ." He swallowed. Shook his head. Changed his mind.

"Are you ready?" I asked, before he could give voice to the thing I realized too: *It's like they're watching for us. Making sure we don't leave.*

"Okay," Ryan said. "Yes. Open the door."

I flipped the lock and put my hand on the knob. Paused. *This house will keep us safe.*

No. We weren't safe. We were trapped.

I turned the knob and the front door cracked open, a cold gust of air pushing through.

I listened to the warning beep, and then, ten seconds later, the alarm started flashing. The light from the display flashed red, over and over, and there was a low, periodic buzz coming from the panel.

That's it?

It wasn't loud enough. It was only enough for us in this house—to wake us, or warn us. My alarm clock was more obnoxious than this.

It was only a warning—a call to action. But just for us.

And now I was wondering how safe an alarm truly kept us if it didn't call for help.

Ryan leaned into the door, shutting it, turning the locks, like he'd done it a thousand times before. "Turn it off," he said.

"Why?" I asked.

The buzzing of the alarm kept sounding, and we had to talk too loudly. "I don't think anyone can hear that," Ryan said.

But if I turned it off, it felt like we were doing nothing. "If someone drives by, they might hear it. Maybe someone out for a walk. I don't know, it's something, isn't it?"

He shook his head. "I can't think."

"Do you have a car alarm? Where are your keys? Do you have a panic button?"

"My car doesn't even have doors sometimes—it definitely doesn't have an alarm." He hit his palm against the door. "What do they want?"

I couldn't think, like he said, with the buzzing of the alarm. I couldn't concentrate.

Useless. Everything in this house was useless.

It couldn't save us. Only we could do that now.

My fingers shook as I entered the alarm code. Then silence . . . and something more. The sound of metal on metal—something happening in the backyard.

I had this image in my mind of men sneaking through my bedroom window, taking my mother—but to do that, they'd have to get through the gate first.

The alarm had been off. The alarm was *never* off. They could've disguised themselves as a delivery service, gotten buzzed in, snuck through the window, convincing her to disarm it, threatening her life, if they thought it could somehow trigger the police.

Or.

Or.

She could've let them in.

But no. She wouldn't. She'd *never*.

I remembered the day social services came for me. How she seemed to know, even before they rang the bell at the gate, what they were here for—so different from the first time they stopped by. She'd asked for their ID numbers, and she'd called the home station to double-check, to be sure of who they were first. And even then, there was a long moment when I thought she wouldn't do it. A moment where she turned around and pulled the curtains shut, her back to the door, a deep, steady breath. A moment where she grabbed my arm and pulled me down the hall— I'd said, "Mom?" because she was hurting me.

She stopped. Dropped my arm. Put a hand out to steady herself against the wall. And she didn't look at me when she said, "Kelsey, go let the nice people in."

Even then, she couldn't do it herself. Everything in her body screamed *no*.

I shook the thought. It didn't matter. Ryan was in the dark kitchen, banging cabinets around. Right now there were men outside, and we were inside, and we needed help.

Nothing about this house was set up to call for help. My mother had lied. We were not prepared for anything. We were not prepared for *this*.

The House of Horrors, Cole and Emma called this place. Steel-reinforced walls and spike-topped gates. And for what? For *what*?

It was as if we were an island. An island, cut off from the rest of the world.

I walked to the back window, pushed the curtain aside, and stared out into the darkness.

I felt the darkness staring back.

CHAPTER 16

Ryan was opening and closing kitchen drawers, rummaging through them with the flashlight gripped in his teeth, pulling out anything he could use. Knives, the fire extinguisher, an aerosol container that I thought probably only held olive oil.

He paused to look up at me, removing the flashlight from this mouth. "Is there *any* way out of here, other than through the gates, Kelsey? Anything you can think of?"

"No."

Think, Kelsey. We needed light. We couldn't call, and we couldn't run, but light could be seen for miles. . . .

"I have an idea," I said.

He placed his hands on the counter, and I could tell, even in the dark, they were pressing so hard into the marble that his knuckles were turning white. "I'm all ears," he said.

"I can make a smoke bomb. I can make it colored. It

will be bright. People will see it over the trees. People will come."

"You can make a smoke bomb?" He almost smiled before remembering where we were, why we had to do it.

I nodded. "Yeah, it's pretty simple, actually. My mom taught me a few years ago, in science. She used to homeschool me."

"I thought you moved here last year."

I shook my head. "No, I've always been here." I was just invisible. Trapped behind these walls without even realizing it. I could've disappeared and nobody would've noticed.

I started shaking, opening the pantry door, looking for the baking soda and sugar. "Everything else is downstairs," I said.

I spun to leave and he reached for me, just like my mom had earlier today in this very room. "Kelsey, please stop for a second."

I couldn't stop. If I stopped, I'd feel the momentum picking up, the air rushing by, like we were falling, and there was only one inevitable outcome. "What?" I asked, stripping the paper towels from the tube. I'd need that, too.

His arms went to my shoulders. "What do they want?"

"I don't know," I said.

He started to say something, but stopped. He was still staring into my eyes.

"I don't *know*, Ryan," I said. I thought my house was built out of paranoia. I thought it was because of what had happened, not what *might* happen.

"What are they after?" he asked. "Is there something here?"

I shook my head too fast. And Ryan kept staring, like there was something he wanted to say, but didn't. "What?" I asked.

I noticed his throat work as he swallowed. "Why do you live like this?"

I had to tell him. I had to explain—we lived like this for a reason. And now that reason had found us.

"My mother," I said on impulse, even though I knew that wasn't what he was asking. I blew out a slow breath, telling him the thing he was really asking. "My mother was taken years ago," I said. "Kidnapped. When she was my age. She was taken from her home, and she doesn't remember it." I shook my head again, clearing the thought of the similarities. Men at the house. Again. "She escaped a year later, and then she had me, changed her name, and moved here. And nobody's bothered us since."

He looked at me, like he was trying to work something out.

Don't ask, I thought.

Don't do it, I thought.

"Where's your dad?" he asked.

A dad. Like the man who stood beside him at the ceremony, straightening his tie. Like the person who taught you to ride bikes, who protected you. "I don't have one," I said. And from the wince in his expression, I knew my tone told him everything he was asking. The way his eyes snapped closed in impulsive response, as if he saw too much suddenly in my face—like my mom sometimes did.

His mouth opened, and I thought, *Don't say it. Don't.*

"I'm sorry," he said, but I'd already turned away, shrugging as I did. I knew nothing of it. I did not exist without this horror of my mother's life. Sometimes I thought she couldn't move past it, couldn't break free of the fear, because of me. Always here, always a reminder—look what happened. Look. *Look.*

I did not look like her.

But I could be like her.

I *needed* to be like her. Because if I was not, if I was the other half of me, what was I then? The half of me that could destroy her? I was either scared most of the time, or I was a monster. Those were my options.

"Ryan, I can make the smoke bomb, but it's going to take time, and we're running out of it. I need to keep moving." I needed to, before the fear caught up and worked the other way around, paralyzing me instead.

"Okay," he said. "Let's do it."

Down in the basement, I dragged two battery-powered lights into the corners, illuminating the room in a faint, uneven glow. I pointed to the boxes against the wall. "The chemicals we need are somewhere in the boxes for school stuff. Somewhere in that pile."

Ryan stood near the entrance to the safe room, eyes glued to the screen, his jaw moving slightly side to side, like he was having a conversation with himself.

"Anything?" I asked.

"They're still out there." He turned back to me, watching me like I was going to save us.

I could do this. I could get help for us.

There would be deliveries—Mom had scheduled the groceries for tomorrow. The mailman would come tomorrow. Help would eventually arrive.

But those things wouldn't happen in time.

We lived in the middle of nowhere. The entire night stretched in front of us, in empty silence, like the expanse of cliff below us. I felt us hanging once more—

"Won't your parents worry?" I asked.

"Eventually," Ryan said. "But maybe not."

"Is this something you do often?" I asked, and I felt a sting of jealousy, though I had no right.

"I spend a lot of time down at the station. They'll probably think I'm there—and like I said, they're practically family. The other firefighters will think I'm home. I'm eighteen. I kinda . . . fought my parents for some freedom. As long as I get my work done and I don't get into trouble . . . I'm an adult."

"Don't you live with them?"

"That was their argument, too," he mumbled.

But he won. I couldn't imagine trying that argument with my own mother. What she would say. What she would think. I couldn't even get her permission to go to Ryan's award ceremony.

The downside to independence—nobody came looking for you.

I grew frantic, trying to find the right box. But so far the boxes were mostly old school supplies, trinkets from my childhood, and pictures in albums, printed from the digital copies she stored on her computer, in case of a virus that wiped it clean. She didn't trust the Internet, didn't want our pictures anywhere that could be traced. I think she'd read an article about that once, too. How nothing was truly untraceable online. All this print was cluttering our lives. Like living with our own past, boxed up and waiting.

"Can I help?" he asked, just as I let out a breath of relief, finding the stack of boxes I'd been looking for.

"Here," I said, gesturing toward the collection of boxes in front of me, the ones we'd used for school experiments.

Ryan came closer as I pulled out the different chemicals—simple things, my mom had told me. Everyday things, from when she taught me. Textbooks and printed-from-the-Internet how-tos. She'd clear off the table upstairs and we'd cook at the kitchen stove, like we were making breakfast. Science was just a list of ingredients, she'd said. Science *creates*. I remembered dancing around purple smoke in the backyard, thrilled that we'd created this ourselves, watching until it fizzled and burned itself out.

I found my old notebooks, the recipes written in my own handwriting as I watched my mother.

"Kelsey? What the hell is all this stuff?" He was holding a container of one of the chemicals in his hand, frowning at the warning label.

"Chemicals," I said. "From when my mom taught me science."

He put it down, opened the box beside it, pulled out some wires. "And this?"

"Electronics. That was physics."

I started making a pile of everything I needed while keeping an eye on the security screens, searching for signs of movement.

"See if you can find something called potassium nitrate," I said. "That's the only thing I'm missing."

"Kelsey. This isn't normal. You get that, right?"

I shook my head. "I used to be homeschooled. We needed all this."

He shook his head again. "This isn't like making homemade play-dough. I didn't learn any of this in chemistry. Or physics."

"I know. That's why I tutor."

"Kelsey, stop. Look at me. *This isn't normal.*"

None of my life was normal, that was nothing new. I heard my mother's voice, standing over the kitchen table, materials spread over top. *You're trapped in a basement, and this is what you find. How do you get out?*

This was my education.

"This stuff isn't safe," Ryan said. He backed away from the boxes. "Your entire basement is combustible."

"What?" I stepped back from the boxes I'd been rummaging through so haphazardly just moments before.

"Flammable. Combustible. Take your pick. All of the above."

Like all it would need was a single spark and the whole house would go up in flames.

The lock at the top of the staircase made more sense now.

"Kelsey, they make us take hazardous materials courses as part of our training. This. Isn't. Safe. This shouldn't be in your basement."

This isn't safe. Surely my mother would've known that. Surely she wouldn't have let me play with this as a child if I was truly in danger.

"Well, right now it's our chance."

There were fire extinguishers throughout the house. A precaution. A fear. But maybe something more. How safe was I really, sleeping above this?

He nodded, "Okay. But careful. We have to be careful." And I heard an echo in the basement, my mother's words, warning me. Ryan started moving with purpose again, tearing open the tops of all the boxes in this section, taking things out, putting them back.

Finally, I pulled out a familiar container. "Potassium

nitrate," I said, heading back toward the steps. "Come on."

Ryan followed me out, but paused at the bottom of the steps to look behind him.

I didn't like the way Ryan was looking around the basement, like it was something to fear. This was my mother. *My mother.*

But now I was thinking about that hidden compartment under the floor of the safe room. The passports.

Her, but not her. Me, but not me. Both had felt like strangers.

Ryan checked the windows once again as I set the stove in the darkened kitchen. I heard the click of the gas, took out a pan, and started mixing the ingredients. Ryan watched me from across the room, looking at me like he wasn't quite sure what to make of me—the way Annika sometimes did, like our worlds were so far apart they almost circled all the way back around again.

"I'm sorry," I blurted.

"For what?"

"You shouldn't even be here. I'm so sorry."

He shook his head. Took a step closer. "I'm not."

I choked on tears. "You should be. I'll get you out, I promise."

"Us," he said.

"Right."

"You held us up with nothing but your fingers," he mumbled. "I have no doubt."

I looked up at him, at the way the light from the stove shone in his eyes, like a flame, and wondered what he saw in my own.

"I'm going to watch the monitors in the office," Ryan said. He backed away, the smallest smile on his face. "I can't believe your mother taught you to make a bomb," he said, like he was impressed.

"A smoke bomb," I corrected. A little lie. A white lie. The safest lie.

CHAPTER 17

I willed my hands to be still as I poured the contents into paper towel rolls and inserted the fuses—a length of my shoelace for each—my hands hot against the cooling mixture.

I moved on instinct. Muscle memory. Everything she taught me, second nature.

My mother taught me many things that I knew she didn't want me talking about. *Careful*, she'd tell me whenever I left the house—and I knew she wasn't just talking about staying safe. But it was all a symptom of her paranoia. See it on the news, teach me to evade it.

Know the exits, she'd instruct after a news report of a fire death. She'd have me stand in each room of our house, eyes closed, and she'd ask, "Where's the closest exit?" And I'd list them off—which window, which door. "Most deaths happen because you're still trying to get out the way you've always gotten out," she said, which was probably some warning fact she'd read on a website.

A news report of an armed intruder, and then came the lessons on *how to disarm someone*. Which joints to bend so that, muscle or no muscle, the wrist would cave, the weapon would fall. I wondered if things would've gone differently for her if she'd known this herself. If this was her way of making up for it.

Fear cannot hurt you, she'd promised. I learned *from* her fear, so I would not become a victim, as she had been.

If you are trapped inside a car trunk.

If you are kept in a basement.

If you are lost in the middle of the woods.

I grew up understanding all the horrible things that might happen to me. The things we could plan for and the things we could not.

I could be hurt.

I could be taken.

There were a thousand things that could kill me.

There were a million places I could be hidden.

But I thought I understood her biggest fear: I could leave one day as she had, disappear, and finally return—completely unrecognizable.

So. I never built anything more than a smoke bomb. But I did know how to create an explosion.

I was trying to remember the *if* that got us there, to trace it back. My mother sitting cross-legged on the basement floor, the materials spread out in front of her. "This is where the chemicals would go, and then all you need is a fuse. . . . And *voilà!*" Secrets passed down from mother to daughter, like the perfect way to apply liquid eyeliner.

"Kelsey!" A shout from my mother's office as I tested the material in the holder.

Ryan's face glowed a pale white from the glare of the monitors he was staring at.

He turned to face me, his eyes wide, like the moment we fell. "They're inside the gates," he said.

Something tightened around my throat, like a noose, and I gulped twice before I could get any air, my hand at the base of my throat.

"Where?" I finally said, moving to stand beside him. The screens were too grainy—I couldn't see anything. But then the clouds shifted outside, the moon shone, and a nondescript shadow passed in front of the camera—up against the house now. And then all the shadows felt too close, like spiders across my skin. I could feel them, just on the other side of the wall, searching for cracks. An involuntary noise escaped my throat.

My hand found Ryan's, and his fingers laced between mine, and I started moving us backward, until we were out of that room, in the open area in the middle of the house. He slowly turned to face me, and I held a finger to my lips, wondering if he could see me. I moved his hand to mine so he'd feel what I was doing.

His were trembling, along with mine.

I listened for any sounds in the stillness. In the dark, behind the walls, the shadows could be anywhere.

And then I heard it, my head whipping around to the front of the house. Someone pressed on the front door, tried to turn the handle, testing for weak spots. I felt the resistance of metal on metal all the way down to my bones as my eyes adjusted to the darkness.

If someone gets in . . . It was so outside of the realm of possibility to me growing up. Not this house. Not with the three layers of protection and the locks and the bars over the windows. Not with alarms and cell phones and landlines. Not with my mother always here, who would know exactly what to do.

"How much longer until it's ready?" he whispered.

"Soon," I said, testing the tops of the two different containers I'd poured. Almost dry.

He held up his hand, showing me the black object inside it. "I found your mom's phone."

I ran my hands along it, to make sure I was seeing it right. It was bigger than my cell, and bulkier, and it had a stubby rubber antenna on top and a thick button on the side. I shook my head. "My mom doesn't have a phone. Where did you find that?"

"In the back of a desk drawer," he said.

"Did you try it?"

"Yeah, I tried it." He shook his head. "Nothing. It's dead."

I ran my fingers along the side, where I felt a large button. I pressed it, but nothing happened. I ran my hand along the back and found a lever that opened a compartment.

My hands tightened around the device. "This isn't a phone. It's a walkie-talkie." I had the other half of the pair somewhere buried in my room, from childhood. Whenever I went outside alone back then I brought it with me. "Batteries," I said, pulling out the back square. I rummaged through the top kitchen drawer, feeling for the right-sized batteries. I grabbed an assortment and blindly started fitting them into the compartment, searching for the right one. I felt one click into place, and added another of the same size, flipping them around until the polarity lined up and the static faintly crackled.

I depressed the button on the side, and the device clicked once. I stared at Ryan.

"Do that again," he said.

I found a dial with my thumb and pushed it up, in case it was the volume.

I pressed the side button again and spoke quietly into the receiver: "Hello?" I released the button, listened to the static crackle back.

"Is anyone there?" I asked again.

That crackle again, like static, but, underneath,

something more—like there might be voices, straining to be heard.

I twisted another dial, and the stations switched with each click of the wheel—static, static, static. Higher pitched, lower pitched, the squeal of interference, the whispers underneath. I waited until I hit a station with silence, and tried again. "Please. If anyone's out there, please answer. I need help."

Dead air. Silence. Nothing.

I changed stations again. "Please. If anyone's there, my name is Kelsey Thomas, and I live on Blackbird Court in Sterling Cross, and I need help. *Please.* Call the police. There are men trying to break in, and we're trapped."

Ryan stepped closer. "It's a long shot," he said.

"Everything we're doing is a long shot," I whispered.

There was a sharp whistle from outside, like something cutting through air, and a dull thud behind the curtains in the living room—the impact vibrating in the stillness. "What was that?" Ryan asked.

"A rock?" I asked, mostly to myself. I pictured a man on the other side, hurling stones at the glass, testing for weaknesses. One of us was going to have to check. One of us was going to have to peel back the curtain. . . .

And of course it would be Ryan. He was already kneeling at the corner—he kept his head beside the wall and pulled the curtains back, then jerked himself away from the exposed window. He let them drop again, pulled his head away, and sat back on his knees, still staring at the spot.

"What?" I asked. "What is it?"

"I don't know," he said. "Come here."

I knelt beside him, and he moved the curtains in a wave again: the dark trees, the bright moon, and tiny fractures in the corner of the window, radiating outward like a spider web, frozen around—

"Is that a *bullet*?" I asked.

His wide eyes met mine. "That's what it looks like to me, too." He recoiled from the window. "You have bulletproof glass? Why the hell do you have bulletproof glass?"

"I don't know!" I said. "My mom . . ." *She's paranoid,* I wanted to say.

But I didn't know anymore. The power was cut. The window was shot. My mother was missing. Someone was attempting to break in. There was nothing paranoid about this house any longer. And there was no place safer.

"They can't get in," he said, his face incredulous. He started to laugh, unexpectedly, like I had when I was hanging in the car, realizing some kid from my math class intended to rescue me with nothing but a harness and some hope. He grabbed my hand, pulled me closer, so I could feel his heart racing against his rib cage. "They can't," he said.

A fortress, Ryan had said, and maybe he was right. Maybe my mom knew exactly what she was doing.

Maybe, all those years I felt like I had to hide and protect her, she was waiting, waiting for *this*, and she knew exactly how to keep me safe. Right now she was doing it.

I looked at the window again, at the bullet lodged in it. They were shooting at the corner. To break it. And they couldn't.

"Really," he said, and his arms tightened around me. "Nobody's getting in."

I heard someone at the back door, but this time my heart didn't end up in my throat. The door would hold, as my mother knew it would.

I felt close to her suddenly—like her fears weren't so hidden from me anymore. They were shadows, just outside the walls. And they were trying to get in.

Ryan was silent, and fixed in the middle of the room—away from the walls, away from the windows. But calmer. More confident. Maybe this was how it happened to my mother, too. These walls of concrete, these bulletproof windows, these bars and cameras—until she felt so safe that she became afraid to take a step beyond it.

"Come on," I said, making my way back to the kitchen. The packed material was dry, the fuse firmly in place. "It's ready," I said. "One at a time—they don't last that long."

Ryan stilled, thinking. "So, what do we do?" he said. "Throw them out a window?"

"Onto the roof," I said. "How's your arm?"

He smiled. "Good," he said. "I have a good arm."

I pictured the slope of the roof, the places it slanted and lay flat. "My mother's bedroom," I said. "Not until I say."

I held the backup lighter for the stove to the fuse—it ignited with a whoosh, and bright yellow tendrils of smoke started snaking over the counter, onto the floor.

"Someone will see this through the trees?" he asked.

"I hope so," I said. It would be bright. The moon was out. It would look wrong. It would, hopefully, make someone come. Make someone call. Make someone check.

He coughed, the smoke filling up the room.

"Go," I said.

And then I pulled open the back curtains, pounded my fist against the glass so they would see. So they would *look*. I felt both exposed and protected, and my heart was pounding against my ribs. "Now!" I called to Ryan.

I heard something hit the roof and roll slightly, coming to a stop. And then I saw faint wisps of smoke trailing over the side of the roof, over the windows, into the yard. I hoped some would go up instead. I hoped Annika would look at the sky and see.

By the time Ryan returned, the sound at the back door had stopped, and I wondered if this was enough. If they would leave.

I risked a glance out the curtains again. I was scared there'd be a face staring back, but the bulletproof glass made me bold. The smoke in the sky made me even bolder.

Like this was a game, and I had finally played a hand.

The phone continued to crackle. Ryan continued looking at me like he was seeing me for the first time. And my heart continued to beat, on and on, terrified and alive.

The room was still covered in a hazy layer of smoke and the scent of the chemical reaction. Ryan pressed his face between the gap in the curtains, and his face lit up in the glow. He stared at the bright smoke, as if he were making a wish on it.

I walked closer to the walkie-talkie to listen for a response—but it was all the same.

I picked it up and shifted from station to station, repeating the same message: "We're trapped in the house on Blackbird Court in Sterling Cross. There are armed intruders. Please send help."

The noises at the door had stopped. But something was happening on the roof.

A bang. A creak. Something rolling again—and the smoke no longer falling from above.

"Is someone up there?" I whispered.

"I can't see. . . . Oh. The wall. Kelsey, someone's there. Someone's on the wall."

I pulled the curtain farther aside and saw a shadow crouching on the back wall beyond the gate, leaning forward. The faint light from the house beyond lit up the profile—her hair, wild. She turned to the side and raised her hand, and I saw a phone held up to the sky.

"Annika," I gasped.

Go for help, I wanted to yell. But then I realized the reason she was holding her phone to the sky was because she couldn't get a signal, like us. *Go inside*, I wanted to shout. *Go. Call.*

But then there was a bright beam of light that traveled in a wide arc from the other side of the house, pulling her attention.

She stood up on top of the wall, arms out like it was a balance beam, and she walked toward the front. The lights stayed put, and I recognized the sound—an engine running.

I smiled, the hope almost painful in my chest as I gripped both of Ryan's hands in my own. His were cold, and faintly trembling, and he whispered, "We're okay."

I squeezed back reassuringly. Those were headlights in my driveway.

That was a car. Maybe the police. Maybe from Annika, or the message we'd sent on the walkie-talkie, or the fact there was a cloud of sparks flying from my rooftop. It didn't matter *why*.

Help was *here*.

And with it, relief, spilling out with a laugh, and Ryan smiling back as his hands gently stilled.

I imagined the men, fleeing.

I ran to the office so I could see both of them at once—Annika near the back, and the car near the front. It was hard to tell in the headlights, which were pulled all the way to the gate and pointing directly at the front door. The glare on the camera was too bright.

The lights cut off abruptly, and a shadow exited the driver's side. *Police*, I thought.

Annika was still toward the back, slowly walking forward. On the back camera, Annika was moving her hands, pointing to the roof—and then she froze. She turned. She looked like she was calling into the dark.

"Where are the men?" I asked. I scanned the screens for their shadows. "Where are they?"

Annika was frozen on the wall. And the person in front of the metal fence made their way closer to the gate. I couldn't see the intruders. Were they on the roof, watching? They didn't appear to be inside the gate anymore.

The person at the gate moved their hand to their face, shielding their eyes from the smoke—and their face caught the light of the moon.

Wide-eyed and confused, and familiar.

Cole.

Annika was making her way toward him, but kept stopping and looking over her shoulder.

Cole had one hand wrapped around the bars of the gate, staring up. He held out his phone, as Annika had just done, and pointed it up toward the sky.

Neither of them saw, as I did, the shadows moving just outside the gate, closing in on them.

Ryan and I had been watching the video monitors in the office, but now we ran to the front window, peering out a sliver of curtain beside the door. We couldn't see the shadows this way, but they were nearby.

"They're both outside of the gate now," I whispered, but Ryan didn't answer. He leaned closer to the window, his hands pressing against the wall.

Annika approached the front yard from the top of the wall, calling to Cole. I couldn't hear what they were saying, but they were both moving their hands, and then Annika froze again, like a deer caught in the headlights.

She held her phone out to Cole, and he did the same. They both shook their heads.

Annika hopped down off the wall, closer to Cole.

A shadow moved to Cole's left, and they both swiveled their heads in that direction. They saw it. Or it saw them.

Everyone froze.

Run, I mouthed.

A noise escaped Ryan's throat.

He stared at me—like the moment in the car before we fell. Like we were still falling.

It felt exactly like that—like fingers grasping for purchase, hands and nails reaching out for skin and bone. What each of us might do, taking the other with us.

"What do we do?" he asked.

There was the simple answer: open a window, tell them to run. Hope they made it to the car, made it out, before anyone else got to them, and close the windows back up, sealing us safely inside.

There was the simpler answer: nothing.

I took a deep breath, the air burning a path straight to my lungs. Ryan nodded at me. I nodded back.

We knew the answer already.

We knew.

Because what I was most afraid of in that moment—and what I believed Ryan was most afraid of—was not the men getting in. It was watching them on the camera as they harmed these other people because we were doing nothing.

I ran to the kitchen, grabbing the second container, and held the fuse to the flame. Tendrils of smoke began trailing behind through the house.

I hit the code to disarm the alarm, the faintest beep, and Ryan winced.

I pressed the button beside the front door to open the gate, and I took a deep breath, steeling my nerve.

And I thought I understood what Ryan meant about

not being brave for climbing into my car. How a bravery medal could feel cold and accusing, the jab of the pin over his heart, like a reminder, like the spiders I felt crawling across my skin—

Because it was not bravery that made me jerk open the front door to the chilled air, the endless possibilities. It was fear.

CHAPTER 18

Don't be afraid. *You're okay.*

Ryan stood beside me, both of us still tucked behind the front door, which was now cracked open. The metal gates continued to open, slowly and mechanically. *Faster*, I thought. *Please.* The cold night air poured in, and I sucked in a breath. The floor filled up with smoke—yellow and pungent and disorienting, rising up around us like a thick mist.

I hurled the smoke bomb toward the opening gate, as far as I could. And while it was still flipping through the air, smoke trailing as it flipped end over end, I yelled, "Run!"

And then I couldn't see Cole and Annika anymore, everything a fine haze in the dark, and I hoped the intruders had as hard a time picking them out as I did. The last I'd seen, the intruders were both outside the gate. Which meant Cole and Annika were closer. They could get here first.

My heart pounded against my ribs. Ryan's hands pulled hard on my shoulders, and I lost my balance, tumbling back into him.

"Get away from the door!" Ryan yelled, even as the back of my head collided with his mouth. "Someone has a *gun*!" Both of us were on the floor, buried in smoke, and I scrambled back to my feet, straining to see.

And then Cole was cutting through the smoke, heading straight for us, confused, but listening. He barreled into the house, where the yellow smoke still lingered around us, and before he had time to say anything, I screamed, "Where's Annika? The girl out there! Where is she?"

"Ran the other way," he said. "What—"

There was a bang as Cole kicked the door closed, but I was already turning around, racing for the living room windows. I yanked curtains apart at the side of the house, following Annika's shadow as it darted on top of the wall, racing toward the back of my house. "Dammit, Annika," I mumbled.

She was on top of the wall again, sprinting toward the back. And someone out there had a gun. *Shit*.

"Get in the basement!" I yelled toward Ryan as I headed for the back door.

I pressed the button to open the gate out back too—they had already dug another way in, what did it matter?—and pushed open the back door, terrified that the smoke over my house wouldn't be the call for help, but the thing that got my best friend killed.

She was a shadow on top of the wall, and I was a shadow hidden inside smoke and darker shadows.

"Annika!" I called her name as loudly as I dared. "Get off the wall!"

I took a step into the backyard, my foot crunching the grass and fallen leaves. I reached for her, even though she was across the yard and through a gate. "Annika," I called again, louder. "Please."

She caught sight of something, something *not expected* from the way she was backpedaling.

I watched her jump from the wall, and then her shadow disappeared, hidden by the tall weeds and the wall behind her. I took a few tentative steps farther from the wall of my house.

I kept in the shadows, breathing shallowly, listening for movement. Trying to remember where I'd last seen the others . . .

And then I saw her darting through the gate opening, practically *swinging* from it as her hand gripped the bar, trying to slam it closed behind her. "Run!" I yelled again. She peered over her shoulder as she approached, slowing down. We were surrounded by silence and the night. Her breathing, my breathing, a ribbon that had come uncoiled from her hair, dangling over her shoulder.

I grabbed her arm and dragged her toward the house. She was stumbling after me. There was a sour taste in the back of my throat, nearly choking me.

Something left over from the smoke, maybe. "Faster," I whispered, my lips turning cold.

She started moving faster, her breath coming in desperate pulls as we slipped inside the open back door.

I quickly closed the door and slid the lock, my hands shaking as I did. I leaned back against it, trying to steady my limbs, breathing in the lingering smoke. The house was silent, except for the walkie-talkie crackling with static on the kitchen counter. Annika's hands went to her face, covering her mouth in delayed shock.

I pulled her hand down from her face, my fingers linking with hers, and walked through the smoke, ready to arm the system again. But a cold gust of air blew the smoke inward, swirling against the floor.

And in the clearing as the smoke parted, I saw—the front door was slightly ajar.

No. *No.* Did I close that door? Did we lock it? Did Ryan?

No, wait, Cole must've— I'd heard the sound. *Did we lock it?* I froze, and Annika froze beside me, like my fear transferred straight to her. Either Ryan and Cole had made a run for it—*please, please, please*—or—

A shadow passed in front of the window, on the *inside*, heading down the hall toward my mother's room.

Someone else had gotten inside the house.

* * *

Annika sucked in a breath, and I gripped her hand tighter, willing her silent. We were closer to the basement door. We could make it, in the dark, if we ran. But not before they heard us.

The walkie-talkie was on the counter, and I took it, turning the volume down to silent. *Fight or flight, Kelsey.*

Flight.

I pressed my face into Annika's hair, her coarse waves tickling my cheek, and whispered, "We're going for the basement. Don't stop."

I inched down the hall toward the basement, and heard a creak as someone opened a door down the opposite hall. At least they were at the other side of the house. *Now or never.*

I twisted the knob, and in the silence, the gears echoed inside the handle.

The footsteps froze.

So did I.

We were listening for each other across the house.

Silence. Stillness. Shallow breaths. Annika's fingers were cold and clammy, and I felt my heartbeat vibrating through my skin. I willed myself to move, but my feet wouldn't obey. I didn't know what to do. Basement or front door? Hide below, or risk it out in the vastness?

Make a decision, Kelsey.

But it was made for me. A second man entered the front door, directly in front of me—separated only by open space and smoke. His wide eyes stared at me, and I stared back. He was dressed all in black, a hood pulled over his head—taller, bigger, everything about him in shadow, except for his eyes and the down-turned shape of his mouth. "Kel—"

I yanked the handle and flung open the basement door, pulling Annika behind me, slamming it after us. We'd made it halfway down the steps when it re-opened, and I yelled, "Go, go, go!" as both of us half tripped down the rest of the staircase.

There was a light in front of us—two people with a flashlight—and I caught Ryan's eye as he was push-ing Cole into the safe room. I barreled into Ryan, tak-ing him with me, skidding on the ground, pushing the door shut behind us all. It latched just as another body collided into it from the other side. We all jumped, and Annika let out a yelp. She was already crying.

The flashlight rolled across the floor, casting its beam across the room. The security monitors up above were the only other source of light.

Ryan leaned against the door, but it wasn't necessary. We were locked in. And they were locked out. Some-thing harder slammed against the door—something metal, pounding against us. I huddled with Annika against the shelves along the far wall, like that would make a difference. If they were saying anything out there, it didn't matter, we couldn't hear—not through the steel and the brick and the wood.

"We're safe," I said, like my mother would do—

starting with safety, working her way out from there. "They can't get in," I said. "They can't. They can't. We're safe."

Cole let out a grunt, and he pulled his hand away from his side. He stared at me, eyes too wide, face too gaunt.

"It's okay," I said.

But then his hand groped for the shelf behind him, and his body stumbled—a streak of blood where he'd grabbed for support.

I stood, my stomach in my throat. Grabbed his hand. Felt the warmth of the blood, and my gaze followed his, to his side.

I sucked in a sharp breath.

"Kelsey?" he said.

He spoke my name like it was laced with some deep, living history. Not like he hadn't even thought it in the past three years. Not like it could be wiped clean with a shrug, as it had been.

Like our connection was still fresh, somehow.

I reached for him as he stumbled, bracing myself as he fell into me.

"Oh my God," I said. I eased him to the ground, and I said, "You're okay, you're okay," and my voice echoed off the walls like a vicious taunt.

CHAPTER 19

I placed my hand over Cole's, which was pressed to his side, and I felt the quiver of his skin, the warmth of his blood. The whites of his eyes glowed from the monitor screens.

The rest was darkness.

"Cole," I whispered, though my words still seemed to echo. "You're *okay.*"

"Is he hurt?" Annika asked. She picked up the flashlight and shined it directly on Cole.

His gaze drifted down again, to the dark liquid coating our hands, the stain spreading through his shirt. I grabbed his chin, jerked his head back to face me. "Don't look," I said. "It's fine."

White lies. Simple lies. *Careful.*

The panic would make it worse. The fear would eat away until there was nothing left.

I looked over my shoulder, trying to get Ryan's

attention, but he already had his button-down shirt off, stripping it into pieces.

"Let me see," he said, crouching beside me in his white T-shirt and dress pants.

Cole propped himself against the shelves, and I pulled my hand away, lifting one side of his shirt in the process. Ryan's body tensed, and he quickly covered the wound back up, pressing down with the balled-up fabric in his hand.

"That noise I heard when we were upstairs," I said. "That wasn't the front door, was it?"

Ryan shook his head. He handed me a long stretch of fabric with his other hand. "Tie it around," he said.

"Oh my God," Annika said. "Is he shot? What the hell is going on?" She looked around the room. "And what the hell is *this*?"

"We don't know," I said, leaning Cole forward, keeping my hands busy to calm my nerves. "They showed up a little while ago, and our phones didn't work, and we were trying to get help. The smoke, that was me. And then you showed up, and you didn't notice that they were *coming* for you. . . ."

Ryan had his eyes squeezed shut. "You said 'basement,' and we ran, and I wasn't thinking. . . . The door. I panicked. I'm sorry. . . ."

"No, it's not—it's not your fault—"

"Yes, it is," he said, pressing harder at Cole's side.

I cinched the knot around Cole's waist, and he

sucked in a breath. I placed a hand on his shoulder, squeezed it reassuringly.

There was a crash on the outside of the door, and I imagined all the possible things it could be: a tool, a gun, an explosion. Annika let out a moan.

"It's okay," I said. "This is the safe room. Nobody can get in."

I wiped my hands against my jeans, but I couldn't get them clean of Cole's blood. They started trembling, and I balled them into fists. I stood, stepped closer to the monitors, blindly hoping. "Come on," I mumbled.

Annika stood beside me. "That's the view outside?"

"Yes," I said. "Somebody must've seen something. Or heard something. We can't be stuck here all alone." *We're not alone; we're not trapped; we're not dying.* I tallied off the list, trying to carve out our safety, but we *were* alone, and trapped, and Cole was bleeding on the floor. . . .

I looked back at Cole, and Ryan caught my eye, his face desperate, and I realized he must've understood something about Cole's injury that we didn't.

"Someone will come," Ryan said. But he squeezed his eyes shut when he thought no one was looking.

That taste had returned to the back of my mouth, sour, on the verge of sickness. I cleared my throat, swallowed air. The back of my neck broke out in a cold sweat. I was going to be sick, right here, in this safe room, right *now*—

Another crash from the outside, and Annika jumped. A noise escaped her throat, and she dropped her head into her hands. "We should've run for the car," she said, her voice cracking. "We're trapped. Oh God, we're trapped and they're . . ." Her voice trailed off. But the thought lingered:

They're inches away. Right on the other side of the wall. And there is nowhere else to go.

I took a breath, fought against whatever was rising in the back of my throat. Forced it down, closed my eyes. "I'm sorry, I didn't know what to do!" I said. I never did. Impossible choices, and I kept making the wrong ones. "Someone had a gun and you were on the wall, and this house is a fortress. I thought it was the safest choice."

But maybe she could've gotten away, gotten help, gotten us all out of here. Instead, I'd pulled her in. How many lives did I hold in my hands, dangling over that precipice?

I'd invited Ryan inside with me, dragged Annika, yelled for Cole. . . .

"What were you doing here, Cole?" I asked.

He winced as Ryan applied more pressure. "What do you think? My mother sent me to check on you. Apparently she'd been trying to call after you sent her some message." He coughed, and Ryan murmured something to him. Cole continued. " *'Just swing by,'* she says. *'Get her to call,'* she says. *'I'm worried,'* she says." He spoke slowly and deliberately through his clenched teeth.

I heard the bitterness in his voice, but instead I felt a surge of hope. "If she doesn't hear from you, she'll send help," I said, grasping onto the idea.

Cole laughed, and it reminded me of how he used to cry instead, as a kid who'd just fallen backward off the swing set. "I wasn't going to come," he said.

I thought that was the end of it. That he was mad at himself for being here. But he continued. "So I sent her a message." He slid his phone across the floor in my direction.

His text read: **All okay at House of Horrors.**

"I told her I did it. I told her before I came here. I lied, because I didn't feel like coming to help you again when you so obviously didn't want it." I flinched, but he continued as if he hadn't noticed. "But then I felt guilty, *of course*, because if something *did* happen to you, we would be so screwed. So I drove by, for my own peace of mind." He tried to laugh, cringed. Gestured to his side. "And this is what I get."

"I'm sorry. . . ."

Something crashed against the door again, and Ryan's eyes widened.

"Someone will come, right?" Annika asked.

I stared at Ryan. He stared back.

"Of course," he said.

I pulled out the walkie-talkie, turned it on, depressed

the side button, holding it to my mouth. "We're trapped inside the basement of the house on Blackbird Court in Sterling Cross. There are armed men. Please send help." Only the static echoed back. I changed stations, found the clearest channel, and repeated the message.

"There are better houses than this one to rob," Annika said, her voice wavering along with the flashlight in her hand. "I mean, no offense."

Cole swallowed, tipped his head toward the door. "This isn't just a break-in. They're right there."

They were all watching me, and something crashed into the door once more. Everyone jumped.

Annika looked straight at me. "Did you know that man upstairs?" she asked.

I thought of the man at the front door, the way he'd started to speak. Started to say my name . . .

"No," I said. She pursed her lips together, and I repeated, "No, Annika. No."

"Then why are they *trying to get in?*" She sucked in a breath, held her hand to her mouth. She was going to crack, I could feel it. The whole room tingled with fear, like chemicals waiting for a spark.

Because my mother escaped. Because they've come back for us. Because there's no such thing as safe, not really.

But I grasped for anything else to tell Annika. Any other possible explanation. Like I was falling, and desperately reaching out an arm on the way down.

"There's money," I said. I yanked back the carpet,

exposing the square tile that could be removed. I lifted the lid and pulled out the envelopes of cash, one in each hand. Cole's eyes went wide, and Annika took one of the bags from my hand.

She unzipped the pouch and peered inside. "Holy shit. You're not kidding."

Ryan shook his head. "You think they're here for money? Really?" His eyes bored into mine, like he thought I knew better. Of course I did.

Annika took the other bag, ran her fingers over the edges, fanning the money.

Cole stared at the door. No code on this side. Just a lever and a wheel. Just a little bit of muscle.

"I don't want to die for a couple grand," he whispered.

"You're not going to die," I said. But I looked at Ryan, asking. I looked at the monitors, waiting. The longer nobody came, the less of a chance they would at all. Ryan swapped out the fabric he was holding against Cole's side for another piece, and I could see it was soaked through. Ryan didn't meet my eye.

Annika let out a low laugh. "This isn't just *a couple grand*. Try *twenty*."

My shoulders stiffened as all eyes turned to me.

I shrugged. "My mother doesn't trust anything on-line," I said, hoping it was true.

Cole narrowed his eyes, coughed, winced. "Your mother is batshit."

"My mother is *gone*!" I said, my hand to my mouth.

Everything trembling, everything wrong. I pointed at the door. "They—"

"Okay," Ryan said, placing a hand on my own, pushing it back down. "It's okay."

I stared back at him. Shook my head. No, it wasn't, and he knew it, too.

He knelt beside Cole again. "Enough," he said. "You need to stay calm. You need to stay *still*. Keep pressure on this."

Cole moved his hand to his side, pressing down, and flinched. "I'm just saying, that's a lot of money to have just sitting in your floor. Maybe not for you guys," he said, looking between Annika and me. "But for me and Baker here . . ."

I didn't think they really knew each other. They were both seniors in my school, but they ran in different crowds. But now that I thought of it, they must've overlapped at parties or classes. Now I wondered how much they really knew about each other. Cole's house wasn't small by any stretch of the imagination. It was bigger than this one, probably. But his wasn't turned into a fortress. It was typical, a middle-America two-story cookie-cutter house, on a street of similar homes that reminded me of the neighborhood my mother was taken from, years earlier. I had no idea where Ryan lived. The article in the paper said Pine View, but I'd never heard of it. All I knew of his upbringing was that he came from a long line of firefighters. It was in his blood, he'd said.

They were both eyeing the money. Even Annika was staring at it, appreciatively.

"You really think they're here for this?" Annika asked.

Ryan was watching, and I didn't answer.

"Offer it," Cole said. "Either way, offer it."

I tilted my head to the side, looked to Ryan—waiting for him to come up with a better idea. Trying to read the expression on his face.

He leaned his head back against the wall as he sat beside Cole. Seemed to concede something, either to me or to them. He did not say a word.

"He's right," Annika said. "That's a lot of money. Even if they're not here for it, maybe it will change their mind." She held the pouches out to me.

Did this amount of money have the power to do that? To change someone's plans? It must, if they were all looking at it like this. I took the money from Annika. "Okay, right. And how exactly am I supposed to do that?" I asked. "Slip a note under the door? *Dear Intruders: Take this and leave us alone. Signed, the people stuck inside the safe room.*"

Ryan choked on a laugh.

Annika gasped, and I thought she was close to tears again. "It's not *funny.* Kelsey, really?" She looked at me as if she wasn't sure exactly who I was.

Ryan shook his head back and forth, his eyes now focused on me, his lips curling into a grin. "She is really funny, though."

"There's something wrong with the both of you," Cole said. "Snap the hell out of it. Look where we are! Someone *shot* me!"

I bit the inside of my cheek, couldn't help myself. Folded in two, clutching twenty thousand dollars and trying not to cry all over it. My mother was gone, and we were trapped in a room, and her nightmare was literally standing on the other side of this wall.

I thought of Ryan's face when he noticed the bullet lodged in the window. And me laughing when he brought out the harness in the car. Because something cracks inside you, short-circuits your emotional grid, your body saying *Enough, enough.*

Turned out there had been nothing wrong with us. With my mother. With me. Turned out we had reason to live the way we were living. All the fears: legitimate. Everything had been for a reason.

You're not paranoid if they're really after you.

Ryan and I were forgetting the room we were in now, and I could see how my mother could forget her entire captivity, too. You disconnect. You go somewhere else.

I drifted across the room, reached my hand down for Ryan. He used me for leverage and stood up beside me, and I stopped thinking of the walls, the blood, the men.

Enough, enough.

I wanted to make Ryan smile again. Even if it was

because I was being completely ridiculous. I felt the delirious laughter bubbling up and over, urging me on.

I depressed the key on the walkie-talkie again, listened to it beep, and said, "Hello, intruders," and Ryan tipped his head down, grinning with half his mouth. We were somewhere else. Anywhere else. Sending text messages to each other, captions of moments frozen in time, meaning layered under meaning. "I'd like to make you an offer you cannot refuse."

I let go of the button, dropped my arm beside me, Ryan smiling in a way that made my heart squeeze, shaking his head at me. He wasn't trapped in a room with no escape. I wasn't responsible for the lives of three other people.

He took a step closer—and the walkie-talkie beeped in my hand, cutting through the static.

"We're listening," a low voice replied.

CHAPTER 20

It was suddenly so quiet I was sure I could make out four distinct heartbeats fluttering through the room. My hands tingled. The room sparked. Shadows and fears, come to life.

A chill ran through the room, and I expected to see the cold puffs of breath from everyone else as they stared at the device in my hand. Ryan placed a hand on my elbow, like he was offering to take the walkie-talkie from me. But this was *my* house.

I raised the phone to my mouth, pressed the button. "Hello," I said. Not quite a question. Not quite a statement.

A pause of static filled the room, and then, "What's the offer?" The words were clipped and deliberate, emotionless.

I stared at Ryan, at Annika, at Cole.

"Do it," Cole said.

"And then what?" Ryan asked. "We give it to them, and trust they're going to walk away? Leave us alone?"

"And how do we just *give* it to them," I asked, "without opening the door?"

"Do you have any better ideas?" Cole asked. There was a small puddle of blood forming below him, but he didn't seem to notice. I wondered if he'd gone numb, into shock.

Annika was chewing on her thumbnail, staring at the door.

I did not, as it turned out, have any better ideas.

I squeezed my eyes shut, pressed the button on the phone. "We have money," I said. "Around twenty thousand. It's yours, if you leave. We'll leave it outside the door, but you have to wait upstairs. We have to see you on the cameras. Outside. Before we open the door."

The static continued as we waited. No response. The silence stretched out, becoming something real, filling up the empty crevices, turning my muscles tense and putting my nerves on edge.

"Maybe they're deciding," Annika said, shifting from foot to foot, scraping her heel against the concrete as she did. "Maybe they're talking about the split."

Ryan shook his head. "No, this was a stupid idea. This isn't how things work—"

"Oh yeah?" Cole said. "Then how do *things* work, Baker? Enlighten us. Please."

"Okay," Ryan said, his voice rising. "For one thing, you don't get to bribe intruders out of your house. Because they have so much honor, right? *Fair trade*, they'll say. *Let's shake on it.*"

I didn't like seeing this version of Ryan, who wasn't hoping for the best anymore. He'd moved past it, into reality: There were men outside, and we were inside, and Cole was bleeding, and they weren't leaving. They had guns, and we had nothing.

"Right, you know what's stupid?" Cole said, staring at me. "Telling them they had to wait outside, Kelsey. They probably think we're planning how to escape. You don't get to make demands when we're the ones trapped!" I could feel the desperation in his voice. He was starting to panic. His breath coming too fast, his arm shaking, pressed against his side.

"He's right," Annika said. "We're stuck in a cellar. I don't see how we have that many options."

"It's not a cellar," Cole said, trying to twist in her direction. "You know what this is? This is the *panic* room. My mom told me about this."

"Stop it," I said. And his gaze: *I know, I know, I know what you are.*

Annika tilted her head. Picked at the polish on her nails, which I knew was a nervous twitch. Looked at Cole from under the mess of hair that had fallen in her face. Looked my way again, as if she were seeing me for the first time. There was a look she gave to people she didn't know: slightly pursed mouth, eyes roaming, as if she wanted them to know she was mentally assessing them. It used to make me smile, make me feel like I was on the inside of her world. But now that look was turned on me, and I didn't know what she would see.

The walkie-talkie chirped, interrupting the argument. "We have a counter-offer."

That voice again. Low, deliberate. I pictured his mouth moving, the way he began to say my name. . . .

"Say something," Cole said.

I waited for someone to agree or disagree. I wanted to be sure, but there was only the silence and the waiting and the phone in my hand. Everyone's faces flickered from the glare of the screens and the solitary flashlight. I raised the device to my mouth. "What is it?" I answered.

There was a long gap of silence again, and I was halfway to repeating the question when the receiver beeped once.

"Give us the money. And give us Kelsey Thomas. Then we'll leave."

My name sounded like poison in his voice. I felt everyone's eyes on me, even as the room filtered and narrowed to a point—*me*, they wanted *me*—because now they all knew what Ryan must've already suspected. They weren't here for the money, or a burglary at all. Someone spoke my name at the front door because they were looking for me. All of this was because of me.

Ryan was on his feet in the middle of the room, like he was waiting for a fire about to ignite, but wasn't sure which corner it would spring from. But my focus was on Cole—staring at me, staring at the device, now fizzling with static in my hand.

"No," Ryan said. "Tell them no."

Annika shook her head too fast. "No way, Kelsey. No way. If we open that door, they'll kill us. Look at him," she said, pointing to Cole.

But I was already staring at him. At the blood soaking through the makeshift bandage and his shirt. At the life dripping onto the cold basement floor.

His eyes were locked onto mine, and I knew he was thinking the same thing.

"One life for three," I said.

"No," Ryan repeated, and Annika was still shaking her head.

I pulled Ryan into the corner, turned so I couldn't see Cole and Cole couldn't see me, lowered my voice. "Is he going to die?" I asked.

He closed his eyes. Didn't answer at first. "I don't know," he said. "I'm not a medic."

"Best guess then."

He set his jaw. "I really don't know. Eventually, if he doesn't stop bleeding, I guess."

"Can you stop the bleeding?"

"I'm *trying*," he said.

I touched his arm. "Look at him." But he didn't. He looked at me instead.

Cole raised his voice from across the room. "We can get help, Kelsey. If they let us go, we can get help."

"No," Ryan said. Hands up. "Final answer."

"I'm sorry," Cole said, "I didn't realize this was a dictatorship." And for a moment, I was surprised that Cole even knew the term.

"No, it *is* stupid," Ryan said, and I saw the calm facade crumbling down. His voice rose; the air filled with tension. "You think they're not going to hurt her? That we'll have time to get help? You don't *trade people's lives*!"

"Except you already are." Cole lifted his hand to Ryan, palm out, and even in the dark, we could see it covered in blood.

Annika was looking from the door, to me, to Cole. She seemed on the verge of speaking, and I was scared. Scared because I had thought Emma was my best friend too, and I had thought Cole had liked me, and they both had traded me in for nothing, in a heartbeat.

And now we were bargaining with people's lives. We were inside a panic room. We were panicking.

Will you trade money? Your word?

Will you trade another person?

Turned out I didn't want to see. Like looking down when you're already hanging from a cliff.

Her breath hitched. Her hands shook. Annika was unraveling, and I pictured her hopping down from the stone wall into the tall weeds even though *there might be snakes, darling,* then pulling me close and making sure I was okay.

I placed a hand on her shoulder, and everything inside of her stiffened.

"It's okay," I said. And I meant it. It was okay to want to be safe. To be willing to do anything for it. I understood how my mother would start with safety and go from there. At the sacrifice of everything else. I wanted her to know, I, of all people, understood: *it was okay.*

"No, Kelsey," she said. "No."

And why was Ryan on my side? *Just doing what I'm trained to do.* It's an oath. A responsibility. It's his *job.* He can't choose to give me up. He literally can't. But deep down, I wondered if he wanted to. That's human nature. Self-preservation.

I handed Cole the device, because he was the only one who would do it. Then I turned around, hoping no one would notice the tears starting to come in the dark. *Enough, enough.*

I wondered if this was what falling felt like. Giving over. The fear in the lead-up, and then a long calm. Your finger muscles failing, the cut too sharp, the will giving out, your whole body saying *Enough.* And letting go.

"Don't," Ryan said, but I heard the beep of the walkie-talkie as Cole prepared to relay the message, sending me to my fate.

"Okay, so how do we do that?" Cole asked the

people on the other end. "Hypothetically. How do we know you'll let the rest of us go?"

The static filled the room.

"Put down the device," Ryan said.

"No," Cole said.

"I thought this wasn't a dictatorship," Ryan said.

"No, I just don't care about the opinion of the guy trying to get in her pants at the moment."

"That's not what I'm—"

"No? Tell me, Baker, what *were* you doing here this evening? Nobody's allowed in here, isn't that right, Kelsey? Nobody sets foot inside the House of Horrors, and yet here you are."

What are you doing here? The same question I'd asked Cole.

"I came to talk to her," Ryan said. It made sense, and it sounded nice, and *he had*. He did come here to talk to me. Except. Except there was something in the slant of his face, the cut of his eyes away from me, which made me second-guess him. Or maybe that was just this room, twisting us all around.

Like my mother, seeing the danger in everything first, instead of all the ways we could be safe. It was all in the perspective.

Cole started laughing. "Of course you did. Talk your way right into the house, did you?"

"He was leaving," I said. "And then I noticed something was wrong, and he stayed."

"To be the hero, I bet," Cole said. "And why do you think that is, Kelsey?"

I thought everything was straightforward. Ryan followed me home because he wanted to ask me out. My mother acted the way she did because she was afraid for no reason.

But nothing was that simple anymore. Not even this.

"It's not like that, Kelsey," Ryan said, his voice low— but I didn't know what to believe anymore. *I want to talk to you*, he'd said.

The walkie-talkie crackled. "Send her out. You have our word."

"No," Ryan said to Cole.

"You don't get to decide my fate," Cole said.

"And yet you can decide ours?"

"You want us all to *die* alongside her?"

Annika moaned again, hands over her face, and my fingers started shaking, my spine tingling, as Cole's words echoed through the room, through all of us.

Die. They thought we were going to die in this house.

We were trapped in a room, and there were men outside, and they were trying to get in. How many ways could this possibly end?

I should do something. I *should*. But all I felt was the dread in my stomach, and all I could hear were my mother's fearful words, and all I wanted was the safety of walls and stillness.

This was the danger. Right here. In *this* room.

Everyone turns on you.

This was the truth that could paralyze you, devastate you.

This was why we needed the house. The four walls, the gate, the locks, keeping us safe. This was why nobody should be allowed inside. They push you out.

Out there, anything can happen.

But in here, they could rip your heart out clean.

CHAPTER 21

Annika grabbed my hand, as if she wanted me to be sure. *Not her.*

"No," Annika said. "If you open that door, we are *all* dead."

Then she started moving boxes again, slamming them around. "Come *on*," she said to the others. And then, throwing her hands up in exasperation, she asked, "How are there no weapons? *Seriously.* If this place was meant to keep you safe, shouldn't there be some sort of weapon? Is there no *gun?*"

I winced. "No guns," I said, repeating what I'd told Ryan.

"Why?" she asked. "If this is supposed to protect you, then why?"

"Don't ask why," Cole said. "Nothing makes sense. Really, Kelsey shouldn't even be allowed to live here. Did you know that? That's what I used to hear over dinner, night after night. But my mom can't bring herself to take her away. To, quote, 'be responsible for taking a child from a mother who obviously loves her so much, despite her faults.'" He shifted positions and winced. "I read through my mom's notes years ago, Kelsey. You know what it is? *Nonsense.* All those sessions, year after year, they don't make any sense. Your mother is lying," he said.

Cole had access to our secrets, and suddenly I was frightened of him. Of what he knew, and what he was saying . . .

I couldn't stop my limbs from shaking, but I didn't think it was from the fear. "Really, Cole? Really? She's scared *for no reason?* Then please, explain to me *this.*" I pointed to the door, but my finger wasn't steady. "She just doesn't *remember.*"

He shook his head, contorted his face into something between a grimace and a grin. "There's nothing wrong with her memory. Haven't you figured that out by now? When I said it's *nonsense,* I meant just that. She makes shit up. She *pretends.* My mom realized that, you know. It's the one thing she's sure of."

I had started shaking my head as soon as he began speaking, and I didn't stop. "You can't fake what happened to her. You can't fake this house."

"I didn't say she wasn't afraid," Cole said. "I just said it's obvious she knows exactly what she's afraid of. She just chooses not to tell. And now *look what happened.*"

He was lying. This was a lie, and so he was a liar. "Shut up," I said.

Her, but not her.

Me, but not me.

This other version of us, just underneath my feet. Pull the carpet aside, lift the square, unzip the pouch, and meet someone new.

Ryan touched my shoulder, grounding me. "Nothing in this house calls out for help," he said. "It's only for safety on the inside."

Even Ryan, now. Even him.

See it, Kelsey.

She didn't want anyone else to come. She didn't want anyone else to know she was here.

She didn't want the police here.

The passports with the wrong names, and her fear of our names in the paper. The birth date from school not matching up with the one on the police report, the date I'd given them myself.

The nightmares with the spiders. *She remembered.*

We were hiding. And she knew exactly what we were hiding from.

Cole looked at me as I slid to the floor across the room. *I know. I know who you are.*

Who was I? The truth was, I wasn't sure anymore. A girl who sprang from the earth with no understanding of her mother. With no father. Raised on fear and lies and stories that came tumbling down when you pushed too hard. Names and faces that didn't match, dates that didn't line up.

This was not the Kelsey Thomas I thought existed.

This was something dangerous—like something in the corner of my eye, taking shape. The edges of a shadow, sharpening and turning solid.

"The papers," I said. "They found us again from the papers."

"Who? Who found you again?" Annika asked.

"Whoever took my mother. She was kidnapped, when she was our age. And now they're back for us."

Annika's mouth formed a perfect circle, and I thought, *I should've told her.* This was my best friend, and I should've told her years ago about who my mother was, why we lived this way. But I had been taught not to. I had been raised inside the secret. Inside the lies.

"They found you from the papers?" Ryan asked, turning pale.

"We have to do it," I said, ignoring him. "If they've waited this long, they're not going to just leave. They might have my mother. I have to go with them." Out there was danger. But out there were *answers.* Out there, somewhere, was my mother. Through that door was the only way to find her.

"I'm not letting that happen, either way," Ryan said. He looked at Cole, at Annika. "She saved my life, did you know that? Held us up with nothing but her fingers. Nobody hands her over."

Can you do one thing that defines who you are? Ryan placed too much emphasis on that moment—the one where we were falling. The one where I held us up with the joint of my fingers, as if there had been any other option.

But there was, I realized. To let go. To find out what waited on the other side. But to do that, Ryan would have to let *me* go, too.

"I'm not the girl who held us up," I said. "You can't base everything you think you know about me on that one thing. You can't *like* me because of that. It wasn't me. The girl in the car, that was somebody else."

"It was the Lodge," he said, voice low, attempting to have a private conversation in a public place. "Not the car."

"What?"

He stepped closer, talked closer. "Why I liked you. Why I *like* you. It's not because of the car. It was from before, back at the Lodge. I thought you were fearless."

I started to laugh. "You're insane. And wrong." The Lodge had two functions: as a food and hang-out place for people with year-round passes, and as a hotel that, in the summer, remained half-empty. We rotated between checking people in, answering questions at the information station, and cleaning tables during the busy hours. The strangers, the uncertainty, the way things changed every day—all of it made me nervous. Ryan was the constant that kept me grounded.

He stepped closer, hands held between us, like he wasn't sure what to do with them. "You always did whatever you wanted. Ignored the assholes. Didn't fake it, or smile when you didn't mean it. Smiled, and laughed, whenever you *did* mean it. And when you smiled at *me*—" He dipped his head, like he was remembering. "You're not afraid to just stand there, be yourself. And then I finally got up the nerve to ask you out, and you kind of said yes, but then changed your mind, so I was confused. I figured you were just trying to be nice, but didn't *really* want to."

"No, I acted that way because I was terrified," I said. "It was all so overwhelming, I couldn't even think about how I was *supposed* to act. Fearless is the exact opposite of what I was. I'm scared all the time," I said.

"Are you sure?"

I opened my mouth to respond, but I wasn't sure anymore. Maybe the feeling I had was not exactly fear—maybe I'd spent too long looking at it from a single perspective. Maybe I couldn't tell the two apart: the will for something to change, the fear of the unknown. Possibly it was both.

The walkie-talkie crackled on the floor beside Cole.

"Well, this is sweet," Cole mumbled. "And possibly not the best time, you think?"

But Ryan ignored him. "Kelsey, I'm not who you think. I'm not some hero."

Why are you here? Cole had asked him. And suddenly, I didn't want to know the truth. I could see on his face—he was about to become someone else. I could feel him shifting, his face cracking and rearranging even as he spoke, and I didn't want him to. Like the picture of my mother on the passport. Like my own. Another side, another possibility, something meant to stay hidden that would become overexposed in the light.

"It doesn't matter," I said.

"I did it," he said, before I could stop him. But his words made no sense. *Did what?*

He cringed, ran a hand down his face. "It was me. *My* car. I was on my way to the station, and I was late, and I took the turn too fast—and I was on the wrong side, just for a moment."

My heart stopped, my mind shifted.

The headlights. I took the shattered memory, filled in the gaps: A green Jeep. A boy in the seat, a shock of light brown hair, eyes wide in terror—

"I got back over in time, but it was too late. The lights must've scared you and you cut the wheel and—"

And I fell.

How had I not seen it? His need to come after me, to save me, to keep on saving me, to make sure I was okay . . . motivated by his own guilt. Not because of me.

"Oh my God," Annika said.

My mouth must have been open, my face twisted and unsure, because Ryan winced, letting out a long exhale. "Yeah," he said. "That's what I thought."

His fault, and yet. "And then you came after me," I said. "You made a mistake, and you were scared, and you took the risk to come after me."

He shook his head. "I lied to you. To everyone. I

didn't say anything, and people started thinking what they wanted, and it all got out of control. And now they think I'm something I'm not. I was so scared I was too late. . . ."

Because I was his mistake. His wrong to right. The guilt he could not live with.

He insisted, the mayor had said. *He was already climbing down into the car. He insisted it be him.*

And he was still coming after me. Except. It wasn't *me* he was after, it was himself he was trying to fix. A guilt to work off, for his own redemption.

I put up my hand, to keep him back. "Enough. Okay," I said.

"I'm trying to apologize here," he said.

"I already said. *It's okay.*"

Cole coughed. "Are you kidding me right now? Can we maybe *not* do this right this second?" He cursed, and Annika sank to the ground next to him, pressed her hands with electric-blue nails into his side.

But Ryan continued. "It's not okay. I ran you off the road and called nine-one-one and never said it was me. Never took responsibility. Didn't want to lose my license and get kicked out of the department. And I let them treat me like a hero, and never said anything. I *wanted* to. I just couldn't. Partly because it was you, and I already liked you, and I didn't want you to see me any other way. Mostly, though, I'm a coward. It got out of control, took on a life of its own. I just wanted it to go away." The words poured out as if he couldn't stop them. As if this were a last confession, because he might not get another chance. He paused, looked down. "I thought it would. I thought everyone would just forget."

"Okay. You're forgiven. Just stop." I turned around. Because what Ryan didn't understand was that as soon as he shifted, so did I. I became nothing more than a debt to fulfill. A regret to undo.

"Just like that?" he asked.

As if he thought this conversation was simple. "Yes, just like that," I said. "You're forgiven. And you don't have to do this anymore. You *didn't* have to do this. Your slate is clear."

"That's what I'm trying to explain," he said, and his hand was on my elbow, turning me back around. "That's why I couldn't say it before. Kelsey, I didn't follow you home to wipe my slate clear. I wanted to tell you, but not for my conscience."

"Kelsey . . . ," Annika said in warning. She had picked up the walkie-talkie, which had wound down to silence. "What are they doing out there?"

But Ryan was staring at my mouth, and we were in a dark corner of the room. And Cole and Annika were right there, right behind us, and there was blood on the floor and my hands. There was a nightmare on the other side of that wall. "Something's going to happen," I whispered.

"Hey, we're going to be okay, right?" The side of

Ryan's mouth quirked up as he reached for me, and that's when I knew he was lying for the both of us.

Carve out a piece of your world, and live inside it.

I cut my eyes to the side, as in *We have an audience.*

And the side of Ryan's mouth quirked up, as in *I don't care.*

Unafraid to just stand there in front of me, as himself.

Somebody mumbled under their breath, but I didn't care. I didn't listen. *We're going to be okay.*

My pulse kicked up another notch.

Ryan pulled me closer, into the corner, and he kissed me, his lips soft on mine, his arms looped around my waist. Everything else fell away—the walls, the people, the versions of us hidden under floorboards and lies.

We were safe, and whoever we wanted to be, as long as we stayed inside this room. I wanted to stay and never leave. My hands made their way to his back, and then his shoulders, and then his hair, and I felt him pull me impossibly closer. But it was starting to feel like the type of kiss we were scared to break.

Prepare for anything, but know you're always safe here.

I gasped, and Ryan pulled back.

"We're missing something," I said. "There's another way."

There was a way out. A way out without guns or weapons or bribery money. Without having to make that choice to trade my life for theirs.

This room, this house, was not meant to call for help. It was not meant to be a last stand. It was meant to protect, until we could find another way.

If my mom didn't want the outside world to come for us, then there was another way out, for ourselves.

I smiled, a hand to my mouth, because I was sure of it. There was a way out of this room.

CHAPTER 22

Ryan looked like he was still trying to regain his bearings after the kiss. I watched his face as everything shifted back—the walls becoming walls again, the people becoming people, the outside trying to get in.

"No, listen," I said, his arms still linked around my waist. "There's a way out. There has to be."

"The way out is right through there," Cole said, tipping his head toward the exit, just as something collided against the door once more. They had started up again, and they were in a room full of chemicals; if they decided to look around. . . . *Faster, we would need to be faster.*

"The alarm doesn't call the police. There are no weapons here to defend us. She didn't think the police would ever come if she needed them—she didn't want them to, for whatever reason. But she wouldn't just . . . leave us here," I said. "She was scared, but she was also smart. Look at this place. She would not leave us to be sitting ducks inside this room."

"Well, there was that walkie-talkie," Annika said.

I shook my head. "It wasn't in here. It was up in her office. There's something *here*. There has to be."

Don't let me down, Mom.

The others looked at me curiously, disbelievingly, hopefully, in turn.

"This door," Ryan said, pointing. "I didn't notice it from the outside the first time we were in the basement."

I nodded. "Things are meant to be hidden here," I said. *And so were we.*

"Did she ever show you? Tell you something?" Cole asked. "I know you've been in this room before."

But that's the thing. She never told me about the passports, either. Or whatever she was hiding in her past. She never expected to leave this house.

What to do if men got inside.

She'd never told me, because she always expected to be here to help.

I placed my hand on the shelves, on the metal bars lining the walls from floor to ceiling, and looked at the metal base. I shook, and they *gave*. "These aren't connected to the walls," I said. And now the boxes were scattered around the floor, no longer weighing them down. "Help me."

But Ryan already had the other side, trying to force the shelf away from the wall. Annika was working on the one against the opposite wall. Ours started to tip, and we only had a second to yell "Watch it!" before it came crashing down. The remaining boxes slid off the shelves, and everything scattered. Behind it, only thick concrete remained. I ran my hands over the cold wall, feeling for any seams, any hollows. I knocked on the spaces, and Ryan did the same. Ryan helped Annika pull her shelf unit away from the wall as well. I moved on to the third unit, pulled it out from the corners, inch by inch, as the metal feet scraped against the floor.

"Nothing," Annika said as she kicked the wall. She was staring at the door again. The only exit we could find.

"Nothing here either," Ryan said.

Cole was resting with his back against the door, staring at the mess. Annika shined the flashlight over everything, looking for any deviations in the walls.

What had my mother taught me? She had prepared me for this.

Look for the exits. The ones besides the obvious. Windows. Ceiling. Floor. There were no windows in this room. I looked up at the ceiling—there was a single vent, but it was too small for anyone to fit inside. And the floor was a floor.

Except.

That tile. "Check the other tiles," I told Ryan. I kicked the debris aside and rolled the rug completely out of the way.

Annika dug her fingers into the edges next to the hole, trying to pry the tiles away, but nothing gave. "It's all one big slab," she said. "They're not tiles. It's just the design."

We were stuck inside a concrete box. But *someone* had cut away this square in the middle of the floor. Someone had *dug* to make room for this hole, for this compartment to hide things inside.

Passports. Money. New names. Things you would need *on the way out*. A go-bag, for when you ran. *Where, Mom?* I thought, rocking back on my heels. *How do we get out?*

I crawled back to the hole, nudging Annika aside with my shoulder, and pointed the flashlight inside the hidden compartment. Inside the floor. Under the rug. It made no sense to dig a single hole to hide passports. Unless there was something more. Something already there . . .

A safe room within a safe room, Ryan had said, and then I was running my hands around the seams, tapping at the sides and the wooden bottom. I took the base of the flashlight and hit it against the walls. The sides were dull and unforgiving against the concrete. But when I hit the bottom—it echoed. It echoed because it was hollow underneath. Because there was a way out.

I dropped the flashlight, and Ryan picked it up, shined it into the gap again.

My fingers shook as I used my nails to pry the

bottom lining up, a piece of plywood, and my entire body trembled with adrenaline as I saw what lay underneath: hinges along the seam, a lever in the middle. A way out.

Ryan and Annika hovered around me, watching. Cole made his way closer, dragging himself across the floor. I moved the lever, and the bottom dropped open—revealing a cold, dark tunnel below.

Annika shined the other flashlight. "It's a tube," she said.

"A drainage pipe maybe," Ryan said. "Not a lot of room," he mumbled.

"But enough," I said. "Enough room."

"Where does it go? What if it stops?" Cole asked. "What if we just get trapped somewhere else?"

"No," I said, "it wouldn't be here if it didn't go somewhere. It's a way out. It's hidden. It has to be."

Of course there was a way out. There were many ways out.

There were the passports under the floor. There was the door, right in front of me. And there was the pipe below us.

There's always a way out. The problem was deciding which one to take—and taking it.

From the floor, the air felt colder—I imagined dropping down inside, an endless fall, and hoping for the bottom.

"How deep is it?" Annika asked, positioning the flashlight directly over top, the light cutting straight through the shadow. I could see the bottom, but there were no steps to get back up, and it was deeper than I was tall. Maybe if someone stood on someone else's shoulders? Maybe.

Ryan backed away, shook out his arms. "Someone has to go first," he said. And that someone would be him. He ran his teeth along his bottom lip. "And then you need to help Cole get down." He shook his head. "I can't believe there's really a way out. Where does it go?"

"I don't know," I said. "But it's somewhere *other than here.*"

Annika started laughing, "Holy shit, Kels. Holy shit."

Goose bumps rose on my arms and legs, and there was a feeling of something sizzling in the air. Fear, or something else. Like water starting to boil. Like Ryan said, maybe it wasn't just the fear.

We heard something pound against the door again. "Let's do this," Cole said. He pushed himself to standing, leaning to one side, a hand pressed into his side. Annika grabbed on to his other arm for support.

"Okay," Ryan said. "I'll go first, to help you all down."

He eased his body to the edge of the hole. I knelt on the other side, holding the flashlight. "So," he said, the slightest smile. "This has been fun."

"Next time," I said, "we'll pick something better. Safer."

"Like a padded room?" he asked.

"Ha." I leaned across the gap and kissed him quickly, and when I moved back, he pushed himself off the edge and was gone.

He put his arms over his head as he descended, his feet scraping against the sides to slow his fall. When he reached the bottom, he shined the light back up toward us. "It opens up," he called. "A little at least. It's a tunnel. And I can hear some water."

Which meant it went somewhere, and so would the tunnel. And so would they.

"Come on," he said. "There's enough space for all of us here, but we'll have to crawl the rest of the way."

Annika and I helped Cole sit on the edge, and Ryan waited at the bottom. Cole slowly scooted off the edge, and he grunted as he fell, Ryan bracing for impact at the bottom.

Annika pulled me close, whispered in my ear, "I'm sorry."

As if she knew I could sense her wavering earlier, that I knew she had thought it, even if she hadn't done it. But I understood fear. I was *raised* on it—I knew what it could do to a person, what it could turn you into, if you let it. I held her tight.

"Me too," I said, and then she took herself to the edge and pushed herself over.

"Come on!" I heard Annika whisper-yell from the tunnel below.

I peered over the edge, and Ryan was looking back up, like he could read the indecision on my face. The door behind me, the pipe below. Out there were answers. On the other side of the wall were the only people who knew what had happened to my mother. The only constant in my life. The person who had promised to keep me safe—and always had.

He reached up a hand, like he understood. "Kelsey," he said, and his voice wavered. "I would never forgive myself. Please."

Impossible choices, and I had to start making them.

Little trades, like chips at your morality—strip away what you think you're supposed to do, what you're told you're supposed to do—and keep chipping in the dark, until all that's left is you.

I wanted my mother, I wanted to help her. But more than that, I wanted to be free.

"I'm sorry," I whispered to the empty room.

I lowered my two feet into the hole, and I fell.

Ryan caught me around the waist as I slid to the bottom. His arms shaking, his mouth slightly open, he was staring into my eyes like he knew exactly what I had been thinking.

"I'm here," I said. But I had to say it again before he released me.

It was dark and cold and musty, and the tunnel before us was darker and colder. We'd have to crawl. Cole was leaning against Annika in the space beyond.

Ryan shined the flashlight down the pipe, but all we

could see were a few areas of standing water—no light at the end.

Annika put a hand to her mouth. "I can't do it," she said.

It was narrow, and we didn't know where it ended, but it was better than standing still and waiting again. *Act before the fear.*

"I'll go first," I said. "Just follow me. Close your eyes if you need to."

Ryan handed me the flashlight, but it clanged off the base of the pipe as I crawled, and I worried someone would hear us. So I tucked it into my waistband and moved in the dark. I felt Annika periodically brush against my leg, and I heard breathing, but I didn't call out or check in on anyone. Didn't want our voices to carry. Didn't want to be found.

We kept moving. We could've been crawling deeper into the earth, or through the mountains, but we kept going. And then I heard a steady drip, just before I saw a faint light. I started moving faster, and eventually when I looked up, I saw the moon through the sewer grate bars above. Like the black iron gates at home, shadows against the night.

I waited for everyone to catch up. "We're at a road," I said, my body trembling, from the cold and the wet and the fear. We were caged animals. Savage creatures living in darkness. With the water and the dark, the blood and the sweat, we were unrecognizable.

And then I climbed, pushing open the grate,

stumbling into the ditch on the side of the dark mountain road.

The mountains seemed closer in the night, their shadows stretching ominously in the moonlight. The dying leaves rustling on the tree branches. I pictured that leaf in my lap, from when we were hanging over the car. Slowly curling, slowly dying. And I felt the vastness, as my mother called it. Everything and anything that could possibly happen, just a blink away.

I felt it like a rush of air, coming from nowhere. Felt it like me, running full-speed and free through the cold night.

CHAPTER 23

The four of us lay flat in a ditch on the side of the road as Ryan made contact with his cell. "Help," he said. "We need help. This is Ryan Baker, and there's a home invasion going on at Blackbird Court in Sterling Cross. They're armed, and we've escaped. There's a gunshot injury." The words poured out of him, and I knew there was finally, *finally* someone on the other end.

I crawled across Annika to get to Cole, who was lying too still, no longer pressing a hand to his side, and I listened to our breathing as Ryan continued. "I don't know where we are. We're on the side of a road somewhere near Blackbird Court. I think." A pause. "I see trees. Just trees."

I heard wheels on the road, saw him debating standing up, gripping the grass. Saw him change his mind, lowering his head out of sight. The headlights lit up the trees behind us as they passed, and I squinted from the sudden brightness.

"We're not moving," he said. "Not until the police arrive."

He joined me in the grass beside Cole, nodded as he saw that I already had my hands over his side, pressing on his bandage. The movement and adrenaline had made him worse. His skin was cold, his eyes unfocused, staring off into the night sky.

"Hey, we made it," I said.

His chest rose and fell, and he placed a hand over mine, on his side. But it was weak and cold, and it slid off just as quickly as it had appeared.

"They're coming," I said. I pressed myself close to his body, my mouth to his ear. "We're okay," I said as I rested my forehead against his shoulder. And I thought how unlikely that I should feel closer than ever to someone only as they were slipping. That it was only as they were drifting away that I wanted them to stay.

We lay that way until we heard sirens, and Ryan spoke into the phone, and then he stood on the edge of the road, his arms waving, until red and blue lit up the sky and the road and our faces.

The EMTs pushed me aside and took over, assessing Cole's injuries. Cole winced as they moved him, which I took as a good sign.

"My mother," I told them, gasping. "My mother was taken."

One of them swung a head in my direction. "By who?" he asked.

I shook my head. "I don't know, she's just *gone*."

"We've got officers heading to the house now." He looked me over, blocking my view of Cole. "Where are you hurt?" he asked.

I arched my neck to see over his shoulder. "I'm not," I said.

His gaze lingered on my arms. "You're covered in blood."

I looked down, saw it crusted into my jeans and my shirt. Felt it under my nails, thick and congealed. "Not mine," I whispered.

I wiped my hands on my pants, but nothing happened. It clung to the creases of my palm, the ridges of my fingerprints. *Blood on my hands.* "He's going to be okay, right?"

He placed a hand on my upper back, led me toward the road. "Come on," he said.

Ryan and Annika were up on the road, speaking to a police officer. But all the words sounded too far away, out in the vastness. The flashing lights turned our faces garish and unnatural. So when the police officer gestured to the back of his vehicle, I happily obeyed. I wanted to crawl inside his car and never leave. Annika climbed in after me, followed by Ryan, and we were silent and stiff the whole way to the station. I imagined we were all repeating the same type of thing in our heads, like a prayer: *This is over, this is over, you're safe. You're safe.*

An hour later, and Ryan, Annika, and I still sat in an office across from two plainclothes officers—one sitting at the desk, the other standing behind it. "Once more," the one sitting said. His desk plaque said DETECTIVE MAHONEY. "From the beginning."

Ryan let out an annoyed breath. Annika checked over her shoulder out the glass office windows again. The man standing behind the desk looked at me with a mixture of sympathy and compassion, but Detective Mahoney was all business.

Detective Mahoney held out his hands, palms up. "I know, I'm sorry. The more we can get right now, the more help this will be going forward. Even by tomorrow, things will start to fade."

I thought of my mother, fading away too.

I closed my eyes, started again. "We got there, and the alarms were turned off," I said.

"And what did you first notice that let you know your mother was missing?"

I thought of the feeling in the house. The emptiness. "I knew right away," I said. "The door was unlocked, and the lights were on, and I heard the emptiness."

"You heard the emptiness?" he said.

Apparently that wasn't a normal response. But the

house was never empty. It had a *feeling*, a stillness that resounded.

"And you decided not to call the police?" he asked.

Ryan groaned. "I should've," he said.

"I called Annika," I said. "I called her first. And then I sent a text to Jan."

He consulted his notes. "This would be Janice Murray, then?"

I nodded.

He flipped through pages and pages of everything we'd given him. "Other than this *emptiness* you speak of, what else was there that made you think your mother had been taken?" he asked.

Ryan stood, pushing the chair back. "Is the fact that there were two men with a gun who forced their way into her house not enough?"

Detective Mahoney raised his hands again, as if he was used to calming people. He waited for Ryan to sit down before speaking again. "Okay. Here's what we know, and what we're trying to figure out. The house was empty when we arrived. We saw where the gate had been tampered with out back, and the bullet in the window, which all happened *after* you returned home, yes?"

I nodded.

He continued. "Nothing seems disturbed inside. Other than the smoke, which you yourselves admitted to."

He paused, waiting for it to sink in. "You've heard

the saying that the simplest explanation is most likely the right one?" he asked.

I leaned forward. "Yes. The simplest explanation is that the people who were in my house took my mother."

He leaned forward as well. Folding his hands on top of his desk. "We have people looking. I promise. But here's what the simplest explanation looks like to me: it looks like someone noticed your mother left, and they thought the house was empty, and they tried to rob it, and you were caught up in it."

I shook my head, felt the need to rise from my chair like Ryan had, made myself speak calmly, rationally. "She's agoraphobic. She can't leave the house."

Annika caught my eye. She kept staring over his shoulder, or at the blank wall, and every time someone spoke, she looked surprised. "Someone said her name," she said. "Someone asked for Kelsey Thomas by name."

The detective leaned forward again, and Annika slouched lower in her chair. "There's another option, of course," he said, "and I don't want to worry you. But your name was just in the paper, along with your picture. And the timing makes sense. Look, you're a pretty girl. It's possible someone became fixated with you after the story. It's possible."

As if being a girl was a reason in and of itself not to feel safe. My mother did not cast her net wide enough, it seemed. The dangers were everywhere.

Ryan straightened his back, looked at me. I knew what he was thinking—my name in the paper still came back to him. But the police were grasping. They were finding a story that made sense. "And my mother, then? What happened to my mother?"

"We will need to talk some more to Janice Murray before making any conclusions. But we have a bulletin out to all departments. We have people at the house, searching for evidence. We're going through your mother's computer and her phone records. We're interviewing neighbors." He leaned forward, placed a hand over mine. "If she was taken, we will find her."

"If? *If?*" My voice was rising, my frustration was rising, and something was rising in the back of my throat.

"Just a few more questions. You say you got out from a tunnel under the floor in the safe room of the basement?"

For the third time, I didn't answer.

Detective Mahoney didn't speak, but the man behind him took a step forward. "The house is a crime scene, Kelsey. We're still processing, trying to piece together the story. We're going to need that code."

And I hadn't given it yet. Kept saying I didn't remember, but that was a lie, and Ryan knew it. I thought of the fact I wasn't supposed to give the code to anyone. *Ever*, my mother had said. But she had also promised to always be there. She had been taken. And they didn't believe it.

"Twenty-three, twelve, thirty-seven," I said. The numbers felt like sandpaper in my mouth.

The other detective wrote it down, excused himself from the room, already reaching for his phone. "Yeah, this is Conrad. . . ." His voice faded out in the hall. Ryan reached a hand down for mine.

"We've spoken briefly with Janice Murray, and she said she has power of attorney over you," Detective Mahoney said.

"Right," I said.

"You'll stay with her?"

I hadn't thought of the logistics of where I'd stay, who would take me in. Hadn't realized yet that I'd have to keep moving, even as my life had seemingly halted. "Yes," I whispered.

"I'll arrange for someone to bring you to her house, then."

"Not necessary," Ryan said, and the detective looked to me for confirmation.

He turned to Annika. "Your mother should be here within the hour. Do you want to wait for her here or at home?"

Annika didn't look me in the eye. "Here," she said, and my heart sank. She was scared. She was scared of home, the one place that should keep us safe.

"Annika," I said, reaching for her. But she didn't look up. Just flinched at the sound of my voice. "I'm sorry," I said.

"Come on," Ryan said, a hand on my back. Once we

were out of the room, he said, "She'll come around. Give her some time."

When we rounded the corner to the lobby, Ryan stopped in his tracks. A man faced him—same height, same hair, broader-shouldered and softer all around. "Dad," Ryan said.

"Son." His face was impassive, and then he reached for Ryan, pulled him closer, brought Ryan's head down to his shoulder, his large hand around the back of his head. The distress on his face broke through only when Ryan couldn't see. He took a shuddering breath before releasing him. "You *call* me—"

"Dad, I'm—"

"Oh, I know. You're an adult. You're part of the company. It's part of the job. *I know.* But I'm your father, and I got a call from the captain, and I had to pretend that it was no big deal in front of your mother so she wouldn't lose it. So don't *'Dad, I'm an adult'* me, okay? I know the game. I know it."

Ryan swallowed. "Okay."

"Okay," his dad said. He rolled his shoulders, let out a long breath. "You guys okay, then?" He looked between the both of us.

Ryan looked at me, then his dad. "We're okay," he said.

"They had Kent bring your car down. If you're all done here, follow me home. Your mother has insisted that she see you in the flesh."

And then I felt it. The emptiness. That Annika's

mother was coming, and Ryan's father was here, and Cole was at the hospital with his parents and Emma—and who did I have? Where was my mother? The room tilted and spun, and I couldn't ground myself. I grabbed on to Ryan's sleeve, as if I might slip through the cracks otherwise.

"I will, Dad. I'll be right home. But I'm driving Kelsey to where she's staying first."

A muscle in his dad's jaw twitched. "All right. We'll see you at home, then." We were almost out of earshot when he called, "And, Ryan?" Ryan paused, turned back. "Drive safe, son."

It felt like déjà vu, getting into Ryan's car, directing him to the house I'd be staying at. That same silence sat between us, because there was too much to say and not enough to make sense of. I couldn't give voice to any of the terrible things I was thinking: my mother was gone, and there were no witnesses. And wondering . . . what if the same had happened to me? Could I just disappear like that? Would people give explanations and let me fade away in their memories? Would anyone even notice?

Ryan stopped in front of Jan's two-story blue house. The street was dark, except for a few porch lights on the block. Jan's house was closed up and completely dark.

"No one's home," he said.

"I know. They're all at the hospital." She had told me to let myself in. That someone would be bringing Emma back soon. "I know where they keep the spare key."

I reached for the seat belt, and his hand covered mine. "Yeah, not going to happen," he said.

"I'm sorry, what?"

"You're not staying here."

"It's Jan's house."

"It's empty," he said.

"They'll be home later."

"Tell her you're staying with a friend," he said.

He shifted the car into drive, and I tried to find the words to explain that I had nowhere else to go. Nobody else who would take me in.

"Me, Kelsey. You're staying with me."

I pictured his father at the station, his worried mother at home. "Your parents will let me?"

He kept driving, didn't look at me when he answered. "I find it's sometimes better not to bother them with such questions."

I discovered how this was possible when we arrived at his place—a ranch set pretty far back from the road—and pulled into the detached garage at the end of a winding driveway. He held a finger to his lips and opened a door at the back of the garage, leading me up the stairs to an apartment over the top.

"Ryan? Is that you?" a voice called from down below.

"Stay here," he whispered.

He jogged down the steps, and I heard him talking to a woman. His mother, I assumed. "Yes, I'm fine, I'm fine," he said, and I smiled—my mother would be the same way. There were some similarities in our family after all.

I stood in the middle of the room. There was an unmade bed in the corner, just under the window. A couch against the other wall, a small television across the way, and a low table in between. A bathroom behind me, and slanted roofs on either side, so you could stand upright only in the middle third of the room.

When I turned back around, Ryan was standing at the top of the steps, watching me. He didn't come any closer.

"So," I said, "this is where you live."

"Sorry, I know it's not much. But there are people here, and my dad is kind of a badass for an old guy. I promise you'll be safe."

As if he could see straight through me.

"Thank you," I said.

He was still watching me from across the way. "Um. I'm gonna, um." He went for his dresser, pulled it open, reached a hand in, and froze. He raised his hands and backed away. "No, you do it. I don't want to be creepy. This is the T-shirt drawer. And there are sweats below but I don't know if they'll fit, but you can try, and I'll just . . . run to the kitchen. . . ."

I looked down. I was covered in blood still. As soon as he left, I stripped off my jeans and purple shirt, and threw on the top shirt from his drawer, which fell almost to my knees and, honestly, probably covered more skin than most of what I'd wear all summer. I used his bathroom and scrubbed at my hands and nails with the bar of soap, watching as the pink water swirled down the drain. The tips of my fingers were cold, and no amount of hot water was able to change that.

Ryan still wasn't back, so I sat on his couch and tucked my legs up inside the long shirt, trying to calm the ever-present nerves.

I heard a door from somewhere in the garage, another at the bottom for the steps, and my spine stiffened until I heard his voice from just out of sight. "Okay if I come in?"

"Yes," I called. He came through the open doorway with two bottles of water and a bag of chips, which he placed on the table in front of me.

Then he dragged a canvas bag from his closet. "Here," he said. He opened the bag, which was full to the top. "I'll put in a load of laundry, so you have something to wear tomorrow. Before we can see if we can get into your house."

I crammed my ruined clothes into the bag. "You do your own laundry?" I asked, and then I blushed.

He almost smiled. "Part of the arrangement. If I'm going to claim to be an adult, I kind of have to do the adult stuff."

I thought of all the firsts that were supposed to be so important. Realized nothing had prepared me for this one: *First time a guy does your laundry.* It suddenly felt bigger than all the rest. More intimate, more meaningful. Everything within me warmed.

Ryan headed back down the stairs with the laundry sack, and I stared at my phone on the coffee table. Jan hadn't called. There was no sign of my mother. And the people who had come—who had tried to take me—were out there still.

There was a window into the night, and people that could be watching. There were no alarms, or bars, or gates. No first or second or third line of defense. Just me and the empty night, every possibility on the other side of the thinnest window.

I stood across from the glass, but all I saw was my face in the reflection. My hair that was falling in a mess past my shoulders. A girl disappearing in a too-large shirt, with too-wide eyes staring back.

Ryan's reflection appeared behind me, and I felt his hands move to my arms. "Hey," he said. "I got you."

His eyes met mine in the window reflection, and I sank back into his chest, let him wrap his arms around me, felt his breath on the side of my face, his fingers trailing down my arms.

I shivered, and he stepped back.

"Sorry," he said. He took another step, cleared his throat. "I'm gonna watch some TV. Over there. On the other side of the room. And you can take the bed. And try to sleep."

"I can't sleep," I said. "I can't close my eyes."

"You can," he said. "I'll be right there. Nobody knows you're here. Nobody."

I wasn't sure whether I should take that as a comfort or not.

In my dream, I saw his face. The shape of his mouth, his eyes, the way he looked straight into me. In my dream, like in reality, I knew exactly who he was. The poison in his voice, my name dripping from his lips.

He was the mirror from which I came.

I woke gasping for breath. There was a hand on my arm, and I jerked back.

"Hey, hey," Ryan said, hands held up. "You were having a nightmare."

I stared at the walls, the shadowed corners. The dark window, the sloped ceiling, trying to orient myself. *You are sleeping in Ryan Baker's bed, because you have nowhere else to go.*

"You're safe," he said. "We're safe."

I stared into his eyes, trying to latch on to his compassion. But I felt a tear roll down my cheek, and he pulled me closer. The nightmare existed whether I was sleeping or awake. My mother was gone, and I was alone.

No gates or bars or alarms would change it. No words or promises.

He repeated the words "We're safe" until I felt them in my head and in my body, but what he didn't know, what he couldn't know, was that the words weren't real. It was a temporary sentiment. All pretend. Nothing more than a beautiful illusion.

CHAPTER 24

I woke before Ryan, who was sprawled on the bed beside me. I wasn't sure exactly how that happened, or what that meant, but he was here, and I was okay, and the world kept turning, despite the fact that my life would never be the same.

The first thing I thought was: *My mother.* But what could I do, except wait to hear? Who could I call, and where could I look? I had never felt so helpless—not when I was trapped in the safe room, and not when I was hanging over the edge of the cliff in my car.

There was a bird on a branch outside the window, and it quickly took flight—a beating of wings in the crisp air. My body shuddered as it disappeared from view.

I stared out the window, the glass cold against my bare hands, and wondered if anyone was out there. If they knew where I was. If they were watching me back. From Ryan's window, I had a good view down the driveway, and I could see the top of a house some-where next door, but much of the yard was hidden in trees.

Surely the fact that nobody had come for me in the middle of the night was a good sign. Surely there would be answers today. Jan would know what to do and would convince the police how to find my mother, and we would be okay. *We would be okay.*

An alarm began faintly buzzing beside the bed, and Ryan stirred beside me. I felt my face heating up as he reached an arm over to the bedside table to hit the clock. He was slow to wake, which surprised me, based on how much energy he seemed to have in class and at the Lodge.

He rolled over, grabbed a pillow, placed it over his head and moaned. Then he froze. He slowly lowered the pillow and tilted his head to my side, staring di-rectly at me. "Hey," he said.

"Hi."

I decided Ryan-in-the-morning was my new favorite kind of Ryan. Vulnerable and unsure, a small smile as he reached a hand over to mine, on top of his com-forter.

We heard a noise downstairs, and my first thought was, *Them. They're here. They've found me.* I searched for alternate exit strategies: the bathroom, the phone, this window—

But Ryan cursed, bolted out of bed, and was run-ning *toward* the stairs.

I heard the door at the bottom open just as a woman's voice said, "Oh, I was just coming to see if you wanted breakfast before school."

School. As if I could do something that normal. As if my life would ever be that simple again.

"I'm not feeling so hot," Ryan said. "I was coming down to tell you."

"Okay," she said. "I wasn't sure if . . . Well, I'll be home after dropping Jay at school, so if you need anything . . ."

When I heard the door for the garage close, I crept out of bed and checked my phone, but nothing. Nothing from the police, or Jan. No news of my mother.

Ryan stood just at the entrance to his room. He didn't come any closer. "You can go ahead and use the shower," he said. "She's taking my brother to the middle school. She'll be gone for a while."

"Okay."

I was standing in Ryan Baker's bedroom in his T-shirt and nothing else, and he was looking at me like . . .

"Hey, Ryan?"

"Yes, Kelsey?"

"I'm not going to break."

"I know you're not," he said.

"So you can stop looking at me like I might."

"That is definitely not why I'm looking at you." He gave me that same small morning smile, and continued, "You're in *my clothes* and you're in *my room* and I'm thinking, *Don't be a dick, Ryan, she's having the* absolute worst day of her life and this isn't the best time to tell her you like the way she looks in your clothes, in your room."

My face heated up. "You're thinking all of that?"

"I am."

"Oh." *Oh.* "Well, I'm thinking, *You're standing in Ryan Baker's room, wearing Ryan Baker's clothes, and you really shouldn't be thinking about anything other than the fact that your life has gone to shit and you don't know where your mother is, but Ryan is there and he's making it better.*"

He tilted his head, took a step closer. "You're thinking all of that?" he asked.

"I am."

"I'm thinking I want to kiss you now," and I was nodding, but he was already walking toward me, and he backed us straight through the bathroom doorway until I was pressed against the sink, with both his hands cupped around the base of my neck, his fingers stretching up into my hair. And then he used one arm to help lift me onto the counter, his palm lingering where the fabric of the shirt met my bare leg, his hand circling the outside of my thigh.

"Oh," I said when he pulled back.

"Oh," he said, and then he kissed me again.

And then the buzzing of my phone on the table slammed me back to reality, his hands slipping, the distance growing as I skirted past him for the cell: Jan.

"Hello?" I picked up, my hand over my heart, my pulse already too fast.

"Kelsey, where are you? Emma said you're not at home."

"I sent you a message last night. I'm at a friend's. Is Cole okay?"

"What? Yes, Cole will be okay. We're on our way home with him as soon as the paperwork goes through. The police just called to let me know we've been cleared to go back into your house to pick up what you need."

"Thanks, Jan."

"Kelsey, come back," she said. "We need to talk."

I hung up the phone.

Ryan looked at me from the doorway of the bathroom.

"That was Jan. Still no word on my mom. But I can get back in the house."

"I'll take you," he said. Then he grinned. "I'm just gonna take a nice, cold shower first."

There was a police cruiser at the start of my driveway, blocking it off to traffic. And there were two other cars—no, *reporter vans*—hovering around outside.

"Oh God," I said.

"Yeah." Ryan reached out and grabbed my hand as he rolled down the window.

The police officer asked for our IDs, and Ryan held

out his driver's license. The cop looked from him to me.

"I left it in the house," I said. And then I pointed for emphasis. "That one."

He looked closely from me to Ryan and waved us through. I wondered if they had men stationed outside Annika's place, too.

I tried calling Annika as Ryan navigated the driveway, but her cell went straight to voice mail. I sent her a text, in case she was grounded and couldn't keep her phone on. Just checking in, I wrote. You okay?

There was another cruiser at the end of the driveway, and we parked behind it. The black iron gates were ajar, the light overhead still out, the system still down. Even the front door remained unlocked. The house smelled faintly of smoke, of chemical reaction, and there was a fine haze clinging to the walls, like we were inside a dream.

Everything served as a reminder: the pan on the stovetop; the curtains pulled back, revealing the bullet hole; batteries scattered on the kitchen counter. I saw shadows in my peripheral vision, something that didn't belong, but when I turned to look, they disappeared.

There was nothing familiar about this house anymore. Nothing safe, everything ruined.

I walked down the hall toward my room, seeing everything anew, as an outsider might. Bars over windows, thick, tinted glass, cameras pointing at the outside, and a basement full of chemicals.

This was the home of someone mentally unstable. Someone who needed to agree to weekly visits with Jan in order to keep custody of her child. A person who was unpredictable. Someone the police could not begin to understand. I felt her slipping even further away.

Someone else had been through my room, my desk, and everything felt tainted and wrong. I pulled open the dresser drawers and threw piles of my clothes onto the bed. Ryan got a garbage bag from the kitchen, and he held it open as I randomly tossed clothes and toiletries and a toothbrush inside. And then I thought of the basement, the money, the passports. The things that were hidden—and that should be kept hidden. The police wouldn't understand them—they *couldn't*—if they didn't understand my mother.

"Will you wait up here for me?" I asked.

"I can come with you," he said.

But I shook my head. "I'll just be a second."

He didn't argue, but he stood in the foyer with the garbage bag beside him, looking at that family picture again, of me and my mother with the light streaming through behind us, big smiles. Perfectly normal.

The stairwell was dark. The main power hadn't been turned back on, but the generator was still running, and the battery-powered lights were still set up in the corner. The boxes that Ryan and I had searched through were still open and scattered haphazardly, in disarray. The door to the safe room was now open as well, and darkness beckoned. I stayed near the entrance, saw the shelves pushed back to their upright positions, the boxes and supplies now stacked into some semblance of order. The hole in the floor that we'd escaped through. And the darker spot on the floor, where Cole had bled and kept bleeding, until we'd found a way out.

I pushed a box aside with my toe, crouched down to search for the plastic envelopes, then heard footsteps on the stairs. "I'm almost done," I called.

I looked over my shoulder, but it wasn't Ryan. It was that other officer from yesterday—Detective Conrad, I thought—and he held the plastic envelopes in his hand. "Looking for something?" he asked.

He no longer looked at me as if I was the victim, with an expression full of sympathy and compassion. Something had shifted.

I was never supposed to give out the code, because it wasn't safe. *Careful.* I was supposed to be careful. I was supposed to keep things hidden—and this, I now understood, was one of those things.

I was in the basement again, and I was trapped. I felt the walls closing in, his voice echoing against the walls as he gestured for me to follow him back upstairs.

This too was an ambush of sorts. And I could already tell—it was going to hurt.

"That's not yours," I said. I stood in the kitchen across the island from him, the envelopes on the counter between us.

"I know that. Is it yours? Why were you downstairs looking for it?"

"It's my mother's," I said. "And it's not safe just sitting here in a house with no locks."

He drummed his fingers on one of the envelopes. "This is a lot of money," he said.

Ryan stood beside me, joined by a second officer, this one in uniform. "She didn't trust anyone, let alone online banks," he said, repeating what I had told him earlier. Believing me.

"Who is she, Kelsey?" Detective Conrad asked.

"Excuse me?"

He pressed his lips together. "We want to talk to you some more about your mother." He slid the fake passport across the table, opened to the familiar photo. The one with my mother, and the wrong name, and I knew he had me.

"Call Jan," Ryan said, his body tensing beside me.

"You're not in any trouble. We're trying to find her," Conrad said.

"Someone *took* her," I said. "I don't know why she has this. Until yesterday, I'd never seen it before. But I know she was terrified, and she was ready to run if they found her again." My hand lingered over the picture, the image seared into my mind. "That must be why."

"If *who* found her again?" the second cop asked.

"Whoever took her the first time! She was kidnapped when she was a teenager. Maybe you remember it? Amanda Silviano?"

Detective Conrad narrowed his eyes. "Yeah, wait, wasn't that the one where everyone suspected the dad, and then he killed himself, and then she reappeared?"

The horror of her entire life reduced to a single sentence. "That's the one," I said.

"Was it ever solved?"

"No," I said.

"Wow," the uniformed officer said. "So that's why she's living like this? She was terrified it would happen again?"

"It *did* happen again!"

There was a long pause, and they looked at each other in the gap. Detective Conrad lowered his voice, going for calm and compassionate once more. "We've spoken to Jan. We know that your mother has been living with this fear. We know she brought you up like this. This was what you've been raised to see, Kelsey."

I shook my head, eyes wide, disbelieving. "There were men here, and she's *gone*."

He nodded. "She turned off the alarm, isn't that right? All signs of forced entry happened *after*, correct? That's what you told us yesterday. I think we need to consider the possibility that she left willingly."

"She couldn't," I said. "There's no way."

"But she had passports. She was *planning* to one day."

Or she was hoping to, and she couldn't.

"Listen, we'll be in contact with the cops from Atlanta," the officer said. "See if we can't dig anything else up. But it's an old case, Kelsey. I'm not holding my breath."

"Oh, one more thing," the detective said. He tapped the envelopes on the table. "Where'd she get the money?"

"Inheritance," I said.

"From who?"

"Her father?"

That pause again, and my heart sank. The men shared a look before the officer spoke, and I realized they already knew. They knew my mother's story. They knew before I got here and told them. "I remember that case," the officer said. "It bled him dry before he killed himself, isn't that right?"

I crossed my arms over my chest. "I don't know, I wasn't alive."

My feet itched to move, to leave. I didn't like where this was going. Everything about this conversation whispering *Wrong*.

"So let me ask you again," the detective said. "Where'd she get the money?"

"She works. From home. She does bookkeeping, you know."

He looked around the house. "Pretty nice setup you've got going on here. How much do you think it costs to set something like this place up?"

I didn't answer. I had no idea. But they didn't seem to care. It was as if they were playing a part, and were working themselves up to something.

The detective turned to the officer. "What do you think?"

The officer whistled. "A lot," he said. "A lot of money."

"Is it possible she stole it?" Detective Conrad asked. He was looking at the officer, but he was really asking me.

"Kelsey," Ryan warned. "Let's go."

"We'd like you to come down to the station, talk some more. But first, did you know about this?" Detective Conrad slid the other passport open in front of me, and I heard Ryan suck in a breath.

It was my face. With a name that was not mine.

I closed my eyes, willing it to disappear.

"No," I said. "I didn't know. I swear."

Me, but not me.

Ryan's face was caught between surprise and something more. He was scared of me, that girl in the picture that he didn't know.

And how could I explain? I was scared of that girl, too.

Ryan picked up the bag, and I stumbled after him. I

was disappearing, my life in a plastic garbage bag, and the woman I thought I knew better than anyone was shifting before my eyes.

Ryan stopped just outside his car. He threw the bag into the backseat, had his hands on the hood of the car, leaning forward. He took a deep breath, turned around. "Who is she, Kelsey?"

I took a step back. Because he was staring at me like he was asking something more—not just who she was, but who *I* was.

"I don't know," I whispered. I shook my head, fighting back the tears. "I don't know how she got the money, or what she was hiding from, or why there are passports . . . or why Cole says she remembers what happened. And I don't know where she is. But I know, I *know* she's not okay."

"Okay," he said, and his hands hovered between us, like he was debating. No, like he was waiting for a sign from me. I stepped forward, and he pulled me toward him. And I tried to keep my word to him. That I would not break.

But a new thought had lodged in my head, circling and digging, refusing to let go: *Who is she, who is she, who is she—*

This went to seventeen years of lies, not just to me, but to the world. She had to have a reason. The woman who'd stood in front of me, who raised me, who had nightmares and feared the world: she was real. But so was this other one.

Can you love someone if you don't really know them? My heart was in a vise.

Who am I? I do not know.

CHAPTER 25

Ryan parked in front of Jan's house and grabbed my bag from the backseat. I stood in front of the door, not sure what to do. Too much time had passed to just walk in or use the spare key like I used to. I rang the bell, heard the footfall of someone heading down the steps.

Emma flinched when she opened the door, her eyes darting between me and Ryan. She shrank behind the open door when she realized she was standing in front of Ryan wearing pajamas and no makeup.

"Is your brother okay?" Ryan asked.

She hung on the side of the door, moving it back and forth. "Lost a lot of blood, but the bullet missed all the organs. Guess we have you to thank," she said.

Ryan shook his head. "Kelsey got us out of there."

"Right," she said. She opened the door wider, and I heard her mumble, "But she also got him *in* there."

The house was otherwise quiet, but I saw Jan's car out front.

"Everyone's sleeping," Emma said, by way of explanation. "My dad flew home late last night, and they both spent the night at the hospital."

I walked slowly through the downstairs, Ryan trailing behind me.

Jan's house reminded me of a person I used to know. Rooms painted a new color, but the same creak in the floor at the kitchen entrance, which I had forgotten. Something comforting and familiar. Even if it was just a loose piece of wood. I used to share Emma's room when I slept over, a sleeping bag on the plush carpeting upstairs, but I doubted that was the plan this time around.

"You can leave her stuff in the den," Emma said.

The den had an old pull-out couch across from an ancient television. You had to step down from the kitchen, and there was a sliding door with vertical blinds leading to the backyard. I stared at that door now, at the windows. The only line of protection.

Ryan dropped my bag onto the couch, and I felt him standing behind me, his hands dropping onto my shoulders.

"Sure you can't stay with me?" he whispered.

"Ha."

He pushed the blinds aside so they cascaded against one another in their own makeshift alarm.

"How is Cole?" I called to Emma, but nobody was there.

We heard footsteps overhead, the floorboards creaking, an engine turning over down the street. There was safety in a crowd, in houses all clumped together, with eyewitnesses who could track you down.

Except. Except my mother was taken from a house like this, once upon a time. She was taken, and nobody saw. Before that, there had been years of abuse, and nobody came.

Ryan stood in the middle of the room, looking at the pictures on the shelves. "So you and Cole . . . ," he said.

"Me and Cole what?" Me and Cole hadn't spoken in three years until he'd showed up at the hospital. But I remembered, as Ryan must have, the way I pressed my body close to his, whispered in his ear, trying to stop the blood.

"Were you and Cole ever . . . ?"

"Three years ago. For a nanosecond. Before his mother told him to cut it out." He had shrugged then, and I shrugged now. "Didn't mean anything. I was just . . . there."

I looked through the slats of the blinds. There was a brown split-wood fence encircling the yard, and a tire swing dangling from a tree. And on that tire swing was the place Cole first kissed me. And in this room was where I stood, hiding behind the wall, while Jan yelled at Cole in the kitchen, and where I waited for her to drive me home after. She never said anything to me about it—apparently, I was not capable of making decisions. I just went along with things. And the situation had been handled.

"You're never just *there*," Ryan said.

"I was a girl in his house all the time. That's all."

"He still cares."

"He doesn't. He's pissed I disrupt his life. He wanted to *hand me over*."

"He wouldn't have showed up in the first place if he didn't care. He was scared. He was bleeding, and he was scared."

We were all scared. And the fear revealed things. About all of us—including me. Something I didn't really want to know. I felt it down to my bones, clawing its way to the surface.

Ryan scrunched up his nose, and he looked younger, more vulnerable. "I don't like the way he treats girls, and I really don't like that he ever kissed you."

I put a hand on my hip. "Are you going to give me a list of all the girls you've kissed?"

He grinned. Shook his head.

"That's what I thought," I said.

"Doesn't change the fact that I hate that you're staying with him," he said.

"I'm staying with Jan, who has power of attorney over me and my mother. He just lives here. We have nothing to do with each other."

He came closer, put his hands on top of his head, like he'd just run a race. "Okay, what I'm trying to say, and what I'm not doing a very good job of saying apparently, is that I want you to be mine."

My eyes must've widened, or my face must've turned as red as it felt, because he grimaced, then tipped his head back. "Okay, wait, that sounded creepy. God, why is this so hard? What I mean is, I don't want this to be a temporary thing. A thing that you're doing because I was just *there*."

I smiled, stepped closer. "You're never just there," I said, and he pulled me closer, erasing every memory I'd ever had in this house—

There was a squeak in the kitchen, and Emma stood there, mouth agape. "God, Kelsey, really? Do you have to take *everything*?"

"What?"

"Hey, hold on—" Ryan said.

But Emma was too riled up. There would be no holding on. I knew this version of her, whose emotions were too close to the surface, ready to tip over . . . "First my mother," she said, "then my brother . . . and you just keep *taking*."

"What are you talking about?" Ryan asked.

She pointed at me, her jaw set. "Our lives revolve around her and her mother. *Sorry, Emma, we can't go skiing, Mandy's had a setback. Sorry, Emma, the job at the Lodge is for Kelsey, she needs it, for legal reasons. Sorry, Emma, drop everything and get to the hospital with*

Kelsey's paperwork." She finished with a hard *k*, and I backed up—never realizing the depth of her anger. "I thought it would end when I told Mom about you and Cole, but *no*. It only made it *worse.*"

"You did *what?*" I thought Emma and I had drifted apart because of Cole, but it was the other way around. She had been the instigator. She was the reason I had been banished back to my own house. And maybe she had good reason. I was currently standing in her house with a bag of clothes, and her brother was upstairs, injured because of me.

She put her hands on her hips. "And Ryan, I thought you liked *Holly.*"

He shook his head. "I never said that. I don't even know Holly."

"You know her *fine.* So, you were just stringing her along? Like some asshole?"

He took a step back, hands held up in proclaimed innocence. "I didn't . . . I didn't do anything to make her think that I liked her."

"Well, you didn't do anything to make her think that you *didn't* like her, either."

Her words cut, and I pictured Holly in Ryan's room, in Ryan's clothes, in Ryan's bed.

Emma held up her hands, a mirror image of Ryan. "Never mind. Just. Never mind. Do whatever the hell you want, Kelsey. You always do."

She backed out of the room.

"It's not like that, Kelsey," Ryan said, turning to face

me. "I didn't . . . we never . . . If I led her on, I didn't mean to."

I stared at him, trying to see him through a different filter. Through Emma. Through Holly. Through my mother.

"I think I should go," Ryan said. "But Kelsey? Call me, okay?"

I watched him go, my arms faintly trembling, everything twisted in my heart. Everything.

I pulled open the bag, about to unpack into the drawers of the television stand. But everything smelled faintly of smoke.

I tried calling Annika again. I sent her an email. I left her a voice mail. "I just want to know that you're okay," I said for the tenth time. "I am so sorry. I am so, so sorry." I thought of what I had done to Emma and Cole just by existing, and now I wondered if I had done the same to Annika. Annika, who was fearless when it came to talking to boys, and being who she wanted—but who had been scared to go back home.

I was lying on the couch, eyes wide open, listening to the clock on the mantel, unsure what to do because of all the movement happening overhead. My mother was gone, and it didn't seem to be anyone's priority. And now the police believed my mother did not get the money where I thought she had. Had she lied about where she got the money? Or had I made it up myself, filling in the story gaps with things that made sense? Much as they were doing right now?

I had to ask Jan. Cole said that Jan knew my mother was lying, that she knew more than she let on. Jan would have the answers.

"I'm fine," I heard Cole saying. "Seriously, you guys can let go now." He was coming down the steps, surrounded by both parents.

Jan froze at the entrance of the den. "Hi, Kelsey. When did you get here?"

"Emma let me in," I said. I looked Cole over. He was in sweats, and he leaned slightly to one side, but he was on his feet and he was here and talking and *okay*.

"Hey," I said. "Are you okay?"

He gestured to his side. "Stitches." Then turned his arm over for me to see. "And an IV. Got someone else's blood running through my veins at the moment."

"We're glad you're both okay, Kelsey," Cole's dad said, then he gave Jan a look. He went into the kitchen to start cooking, while Cole eased himself onto the sofa behind me.

Jan stood before me in the den. She looked like crap. Like she hadn't slept, or showered. No, like her kid had been shot, and she didn't know what to do.

"The police think she ran," I said. "You have to tell them the truth. She couldn't, Jan. She's *hurt*."

She hesitated. Looked at Cole sitting behind me. "Come on," she said, gesturing toward her office on the other side of the den.

She had a wooden desk that backed onto a large window, and walls covered in bookshelves, a few document boxes on the floor. Behind her were the double doors of the closet of files, with the metal lock between them. She shut the office door behind us—though I'm sure Cole could hear us just fine regardless.

"The police were asking me questions. . . ."

She pinched the bridge of her nose. "I know, Kelsey. I know."

"What aren't you telling me? What happened to my mother?"

"Kelsey, I can't talk about this. It's privileged."

"She's missing and the police think she ran. . . . You don't believe that, do you?"

She looked around at the empty walls, as if searching for an answer. Finally, she said, "I think she might have."

I flinched. "You think she could've *left?*"

She reached for me, but I backed away. "I think your mother is very strong. I think she could do more than she let on. It's the only reason you were allowed to stay there in the first place. Because I believed that she was capable of more. That she was capable of caring for you."

"You're wrong." I had lived with her. She was contained by walls and limitations, nightmares and memories she could never reach.

She held up her hands. "Okay, Kelsey. Okay. The police are looking for her. They're talking to the cops in Atlanta. They're digging through her history right now."

"You think she remembers," I said.

She paused. "I think there's more to the story than what was reported in the papers. I think she doesn't want to remember."

"But she's gone, Jan. People came and she's gone. You have to tell the police."

"You know what the police think is more likely? That your mother took something that didn't belong to her. That whoever she took it from came back for it. You're safe here now. We'll talk this weekend, okay? We'll figure out what to do."

She brushed by me, but I couldn't move.

"You really think she left me?"

She stood in the entrance, the door open. "I think I made a really big mistake, Kelsey. I think I did something terrible, that almost got you . . . and Cole . . . killed. And I will never forgive myself for it."

Cole was sitting just outside the doors, on the couch I'd be sleeping on, a glass of water in his hands. Jan went to the kitchen, and he tapped the seat beside him.

"You look about how I feel," he said.

I cut my eyes to him. He was pale, and there was a tremor running through his arm, and he pressed it to his side, to hide it.

"Are you really okay?" I asked.

He shrugged, changed the topic. "So, you and Baker, huh?"

"Yeah, me and Baker."

He was staring at the blank television, at our distorted reflections, sitting on opposite ends of the couch. "I was scared, Kelsey," he said. And I thought that was an apology.

"Well, I did get you shot," I said, which I guess was mine, too.

He nodded, motioned for me to lean closer, so close I could smell the hospital soap, the astringent on his skin. His mouth was next to my ear. "She keeps the key to her files in her purse."

That night, I waited for everyone to go to sleep, rifled through Jan's purse, and took the key that was hidden within the secondary pocket inside.

Maybe I was mistaken and nobody was out there. Maybe Jan was right. That they had gotten what they came for, and left. But just in case, I checked my phone every few minutes, just to make sure I had a signal. And I picked up the home line, listening to the dial tone. A hum in my ear that promised, *You are safe.*

I used Jan's key, unlocked the double closet doors, and stared at the stacks of shelves. They were organized alphabetically by last name, but we had an entire box to ourselves. Eight years' worth of research into my mother's life. Eight years of truth, boxed up right here.

Jan had her sessions documented in shorthand inside several journals, everything written out in lists or indecipherable scrawl. Her journals also had time-stamps alongside several of the entries, but they didn't seem to correlate to time of day.

It wasn't until I reached the bottom of the box and found the digital recorder that I realized the time-stamps referred to *that*.

From what I could understand from Jan's notes, Cole was right—Jan had suspected, long, long ago, that my mother remembered everything. What he didn't tell me, what I had to find out for myself, was that Jan suspected my mother's fear went deeper than the men who had taken her. The fear was real, but misdirected.

I lay on the hardwood floor, headphones over my ears, my mother's voice filling my head. And I listened for hours to her lies. I could pick them out, just as surely as Jan could. Her voice, like warm blankets tucked up to my chin. The lies, like a burst of cold air that turned my stomach to ice.

This was the thing I kept rewinding, and replaying, that Jan had time-marked in her notes:

Jan's voice. "Let's go back to the day you were taken. Start over again."

And my mother's broken voice. "The house was dark. I was asleep. I heard glass breaking, and I screamed."

"And what did you see next?"

"I saw a shadow."

"What did you do? Did you try to run?"

"Yes, I tried to run. We fought. Things broke."

"But nobody came."

"Nobody came."

"Then what?"

"Then he hit me harder, and I fell, and then I don't remember."

"Okay, Mandy, okay. You're okay. Take a deep breath." A pause. "Ready?"

"Sorry. Ready."

"Let's start again. What woke you up?"

"The sound of glass breaking."

"And then you screamed?"

"Yes, when I saw the shadow."

I rewound it three times, heard the discrepancy. The first thing Jan must've noticed. The first time, she screamed at the sound of glass breaking. The second time, not until she saw the shadow.

Another note in the journal, three question marks, another timestamp.

I found the corresponding section of the recording. Jan's voice: "Let's talk about your home life before you were taken."

"No. I'm not talking about that."

"The newspaper reports about your father, the abuse. The medical report from when you escaped showed old rib fractures, long since healed."

"I said I'm not talking about that."

"Were you scared before you were taken? Of your father?"

"Was I scared? No. Scared isn't the right word. It's the only thing I'd ever known. But it has nothing to do with anything, and he's dead, so we're not going to talk about it."

"Well, we're going to have to. You understand why, don't you? We need to be sure of your daughter's safety."

"She's perfectly safe. It's the only thing I can do. Everything I've done is for her."

I rewound it, over and over, hearing the slip. *Everything I've done. Everything I've done. Everything I've done.*

If she could lie then, so readily, for so long—then surely she could lie now.

They came back for something, Jan had said.

But this was what I was starting to think: what if the thing they came back for was *us*?

I found her that night, in the files. The thing she was most scared of, more than anything, was not of being taken, but of being found.

CHAPTER 26

Jan asked me to drive Cole and Emma to school. This appeared to be the last straw for Emma, who grimaced and waited for Cole to put up a fight, but Cole just said, "Sure."

My head shot from Cole to Jan.

"I can't go to school," I said.

"Kelsey, you have to get back to normal. We have to try. You sitting around here won't do you any good. We're both going to work. You'd be here all alone, and for what?"

And that, right there, was enough to get me out of there.

I parked in my normal spot in the lot, tried to help Cole into school, but Emma said, "I got it," and hitched his bag onto her other shoulder.

Cole could walk fine, but he wasn't supposed to put any added weight on his side.

I was aware of the silence that followed in my wake, the way people stopped and watched. I started to feel sick.

Math class, I had to get to math. This was my routine.

I could see the empty classroom, the door open, and I started moving faster. I rounded the corner, a hand to my neck, trying to stop the inevitable. Ryan was in his seat already, his gaze drifting to the door as I walked in.

"Hi," he said, and then his face shifted. "Oh."

You are safe inside the classroom, and Ryan Baker is here, and you're fine. You're fine. I dropped my bag beside the desk, slid into my seat beside his.

"Are we okay?" he asked.

I nodded, unable to speak.

"Okay," he said. His voice sounded far, far away, even as he leaned closer, so close his lips brushed my cheek as he spoke in words I didn't process. He placed his fingers gently under my chin. "Hey, come back," he said.

"Sorry, I'm here." I gave him a smile, but he tipped his head to the side, like he knew.

I felt safer with the door closed, with the people pressing closer, with the witnesses surrounding me. With the people looking and talking and making up stories. I couldn't disappear—not with them all watching. I couldn't slip through any cracks without them catching on. I felt, for the first time, completely grounded outside our gates.

And I was sick that I only felt that way after my mother was gone.

By lunchtime, the story had grown, and the rumors were swirling. Cole had allegedly taken a bullet for me. But what were they both doing at my house? Was I playing them both? Had they fought over me, gotten caught up in a home invasion? The story had taken on a life of its own.

The whispers followed from class to class, a lie that I almost wanted to believe. It was a simpler story. It was a story that did not change the fabric of my entire existence.

I sat with Ryan at lunch, which turned out to be momentarily terrifying. Leo, AJ, Mark, and Mark's girlfriend Clara all paused to look when I dropped my tray at their table.

"About time," Leo said, and then he went back to his conversation.

Ryan grabbed a leg of my chair and pulled it toward him, until we were almost touching. Then he ran his hand down my arm, laced his fingers together with mine, and leaned back in his seat, laughing at something Leo was saying.

I closed my eyes, counted the exits: the double doors behind me, the emergency exit side doors, the windows up high, and I figured there also must've been something behind the food preparation area. I felt Ryan squeeze my hand, opened my eyes to find him looking at me.

He leaned in close. "What are you thinking about, Kelsey Thomas?"

"Exit strategies," I said, which made him laugh.

He tipped his head toward the wall, and his hair fell across his forehead. "My car is right out those doors, if you want to take me up on it."

My face broke into a smile, and I tried to view the room from his perspective: friends, people he knew, a safe routine. My eyes locked for a second with a guy sitting at the corner table, not eating. He had a phone—no, a *camera*—pointed in this direction. As soon as our eyes met, he looked down, stood quickly, made his way for the exit. My entire body went on high alert as all the voices faded away.

In his profile, I saw a hooked nose, deep-set eyes, a bunch of mismatched parts that somehow worked. . . . I had seen him before. Seen his picture, at least. On Annika's phone.

That was Eli.

Ryan looked up at me as I pushed back my chair, standing. "I'm . . ."

I let the thought trail, and I slipped away from Ryan, pushing my way between cafeteria chairs as I made my way to the exit.

"Hey," I called, but Eli didn't stop. He was lost to the crowd, weaving through the halls. I was moving fast, but he was moving faster—as if he didn't want me to catch up.

I didn't realize Ryan had followed until he was beside me in the empty hall. "What is it?" he asked, looking both ways down the corridor.

"I saw someone," I said, my breath coming in quick bursts. "I saw someone from that night."

His forehead creased, and he grabbed my arm. "Who? Where?"

"His name is Eli. A boy I've never seen here before. He was out on a date with Annika that night."

"Does he go here?"

"No, he doesn't go here. I don't think." Did he? What did Annika say? She met him . . . he worked doing landscaping . . . right? Or maybe he worked while attending school, like Ryan did. Was I panicking over nothing?

"Okay, it's just some kid," Ryan said. "He probably goes here. Call Annika to check. Okay?"

I shook my head. Not okay. "Annika hasn't answered her phone since that night." Not my calls, not my texts, not my emails.

Ryan frowned. "Let's go, then," he said.

"Go where?"

"To Annika's."

"Okay. Yes, let's go." I needed to see her anyway.

I needed to be sure she was okay. This was probably nothing. But he had moved so fast, avoiding me . . . and I needed to be sure. Because otherwise, the fears started circling, and I wouldn't be able to let go of the thought.

This was the thought: Someone was watching. Someone was still *here*.

Something was coming for me. I felt it, gathering force and taking shape.

But the thing coming for me was also coming from within. An ache in my bones, the marrow simmering. Something slowly fighting its way to the surface.

I worried as we stood in the parking lot before third period that someone would notice. That the GPS on my phone would show I was not where I was supposed to be, and someone would stop me. Before remembering that nobody was there to keep tabs on me anymore. That I had finally gotten what I wanted—freedom— and it had come at the steepest price.

Once inside Sterling Cross, we drove past my place, where there was still a cop car blocking off the driveway entrance. The news vans, at least, were no longer lingering along the roadside. The disaster had moved on. *They* had moved on. But not us.

I directed Ryan down the next driveway. Annika's car was there, and so was her mother's. I tried calling her again, but she still didn't pick up.

After my car accident, when Annika couldn't get ahold of me, she had come to the wall—waiting for me. Why hadn't I done the same yet?

Annika's house was twice the size of my own, even though only three people lived there. The front yard was landscaped to perfection, a bright patch of wildflowers beside the white porch. I rang the bell and heard footsteps approaching. Whoever was behind the door paused at the entrance. A shadow peered through the sheer curtains at the side window before opening the front door.

Annika's mom always acted business-friendly toward me—and the house reflected her demeanor. Everything inviting, but formal and orderly. When I first used to come over, I was never sure which furniture was okay to actually use and which was purely for decoration. And her mom looked like she could blend right in.

But now Annika's mom looked exhausted, like Jan had looked, and she had a phone resting on her shoulder. "Hi, Kelsey," she whispered, dark circles under her eyes, hair like Annika's thrown back in a low ponytail. "Sorry about that, the press keep showing up."

I shifted foot to foot. "This is Ryan," I said. "We came to see if Annika's okay?"

She nodded, smiled tightly. "She will be. She's resilient. Are *you* okay? Has there been any word about your mother?" She lowered her voice at the last question, as if Ryan wouldn't be able to hear us then.

"No news," I said, the words scratching my throat. "But I'm okay. Can I see her?"

She swung the door open wider. "She's in the back TV room. I'm glad you came."

Annika's house was open and airy. The common areas had big floor-to-ceiling windows, with no curtains because the only thing out there was mountains and wildlife. When I'd come over, I used to stare at them in wonder. Now Annika was in the one room with no windows. The perfect dark for movie nights, no glare on the screen. But she was sitting cross-legged on the couch, a bottle of green nail polish balanced on the armrest beside her, television off.

"Hi," she said as I rounded the corner. She held the brush over her thumb, like nothing had changed. Then she noticed Ryan behind me, and nodded once.

I could see, right away, that everything had changed. From the way she greeted me and Ryan together, to her location in the most sheltered room in the house, to her appearance. Her hair was braided down her back, small curls escaping around her makeup-free face. She was in black yoga pants, and her eyes were red, and she said nothing else.

I had done something to her, taken some of her Annika-ness. Welcomed her into my life.

"Hey," I said, sitting beside her. "I've been calling. And writing."

She nodded, concentrating on her next finger. "I

know, I know, I'm sorry. It's just—" She paused again, cut her eyes to me. "I don't know what to say."

"I'm sorry," I said, my throat tightening.

She shook her head. "I don't . . . I don't even really remember, it all went so fast. The police keep asking, and the more they ask, the less I'm sure of." She blinked slowly at me. "Is that happening for you, too?"

I thought of my mother's voice on the recordings. The police and Jan, filling the gaps with new stories, new ideas. The story taking on a life of its own. "Yeah," I said. "It is."

She looked at Ryan, who was leaning against the wall behind us. I wanted her to say something stereotypically Annika, something about me and him, teasing but affectionate, but she continued as if he wasn't even there.

"Cole's okay, right? In the paper, it said he's okay, but . . . he was so *pale*." She lowered her voice. "At least, I think he was. I can't really remember anymore. Maybe that's just the way he looks in my nightmares."

I shuddered. "He's okay. Went to school today, even."

"Good," she said. She blew on her nails, and her fingers trembled faintly.

"Annika, I have to ask you something."

But I could see her pulling back already, concentrating on the next hand, her eyes going slightly unfocused.

"Eli, have you heard from him?" I asked.

"What?" She started on her second hand without pausing. "Oh, no, the date was weird. Scratch that: *he* was weird. After you called, he insisted he bring me home. I think he just wanted an excuse to end it early. He was so obviously not into me. And the feeling was mutual."

"Can I see his picture again?"

She gestured toward the table. "My phone's over there. What's this about?"

"I thought I saw him at school today."

She shook her head, a curl escaping, and she blew it out of her face. "No, he doesn't go to your school. Dropped out, he said. I told you, he works doing landscaping." She looked out the window. "Another reason I think I'll stay inside, thanks." As if this was an argument she'd already had with her mother.

I pulled up his picture, zoomed in—it was definitely him. I handed it to Ryan so he could see.

"I'm going to send this to myself," he said.

Annika looked alert for the first time, back rigid, shoulders straight, eyes moving between me and Ryan and her phone. "What's going on?" she asked.

"Annika," I began, "can you call him?"

"Why?"

I swallowed. Looked at Ryan, who was better at keeping people calm.

Ryan came closer, lowered his voice. "We think he may not be who he says he is."

She shook her head. Shook it again. "You're scaring me. Do you think . . ." She raised a hand to her mouth. "Oh God, are you saying I was sitting in a *car* with one of them?"

"I don't know. I want to call and talk to him," I said.

She shook her head. "No. Please. Leave me out of it. I just want to forget it."

"I'll do it," Ryan said, entering the info into his phone instead.

She turned to face me. "I've known you longer than anyone, you know that?"

Annika had moved here three years earlier, but we only saw each other summers and breaks. Still, she was the person I knew best, other than my mother and Jan. I thought our friendship mostly worked one way, but it seemed it was the same for her.

"I'm always the new kid. Do you know what that's like?" she asked.

"Yes," I said. I knew the feeling exactly, of walking into a place for the first time, of feeling the vastness, the terror, the loneliness in the crowd.

"We moved around so much when I was younger. Everywhere I go, I'm scared nobody will notice."

"How could anyone not notice you?" I asked.

She grinned. "I got asked to leave my last two boarding schools, did you know that?"

"No," I said. And then I wondered why we never did this before. I thought how much easier it would've been for the both of us with somebody else who understood. I thought how alike we were, the secrets we kept.

"Oh, I got noticed all right," she said. "The first time, breaking curfew. By a few days." She grimaced. "I only went to see my brother. It's not like I *know* anyone else. This last one, though, was just a strong suggestion—end of last year they told my mother I didn't seem to mesh well with *the school mission.*" At this, she laughed. "I think the school mission was to bore everyone to death, so I can't exactly argue."

She leaned closer, her eyes watery, as if she had a bigger secret. "But now . . . now I want to disappear. I just want to go back to school. I can't sleep. Every noise makes me jump." She placed her hand on my arm, her cold fingers circling my wrist. "I'm sorry, Kelsey. I am. I know it's worse for you, and I feel awful, but I just want to leave this all behind, forget it ever happened. I need to for a bit, yeah?"

"Yeah," I said. "I wish I could, too."

She sighed. "I'd hug you, but." She held up her hands. "You'll let me know, right? When they find your mother?" She tipped her head against my shoulder. "I'll be back, I promise."

Ryan lowered the phone.

"What?" I asked.

"The number is disconnected," he said.

Annika's eyes grew wider. "Oh God," she said, and her arms began to shake.

Ryan held up the phone again, Eli's image on the screen. "I'm going to bring this to the police. Just . . . if you see him, call, okay?"

Annika wrapped her arms around her knees, streaking one of her nails. "I just want to go," she said. "I need to go."

She buried her face in her knees, and I wrapped my arms around her from the side, and I said, "It's over, Annika. It's over."

Little lies. The safest lies.

"I need to get back to school," I told Ryan as he sat frozen in the driver's seat. "I have to drive Cole and Emma home."

But Ryan looked at me like I didn't understand. Except I did. Someone was out there, and I wasn't safe. This wasn't over.

"I'm following you back to Jan's, and then we're going to the police together."

As Ryan drove to school, I saw him checking the rearview mirrors every few minutes. A fear he couldn't see and couldn't shake.

"I want you with me," he said.

"What?"

"Now. Always. I want you *with me*." But what could he do? If walls and bars and locks couldn't keep me safe, how could he?

The danger is everywhere.

It's everyone.

It's the parts we keep hidden, and the darkness inside, fighting to get out.

The only thing I did was take people down with me. They tied themselves to my anchor, and we fell.

CHAPTER 27

Detective Mahoney stared at the photo on Ryan's phone. "Who is this again?"

"We don't know," Ryan said. "He was there the night her mother disappeared. He was taking Annika out on a date, and he brought her home after Kelsey called her. He said his name was Eli."

The detective paused, seemed to think it through. "So this would be before the cell phones were blocked?"

"Right. We didn't think it was related until Kelsey saw him at school. He's not a student there."

"There are twenty-five hundred kids at the high school. How can you be sure?" Detective Mahoney asked.

"We called the number, but it's disconnected. We think Kelsey calling Annika tipped them off that Kelsey was back at the house, and that's what triggered everything."

"Hold on, so you think they came *because* she was

home, not accidentally?" The detective looked at me as he asked this.

"Why else would the cell phones be blocked?" I said.

"I don't know. It's not so hard to get a cell jammer. Maybe they didn't want any witnesses to make a call during the burglary. I will definitely look into it, but what I'm thinking is that it would be very bold for anyone to come after you now. Not with so many witnesses."

"There were witnesses before," I said.

He sighed, ran a hand through his hair, making him seem younger than he actually was—which appeared to be closer to my mother's age. "They're after the money," he said.

He opened a file on his desk. Pulled out a photo. "We traced the money in your house to part of an unsolved crime spree. A good chunk of the money your mother had in your basement was in sequential order, which raised some flags—it's surprising to see outside of a bank. It can indicate a shipment of new money, in which case it can be traced back, if it was logged. If it was stolen . . . So I made a few calls to some colleagues in Treasury, and turns out this specific batch was linked to a violent bank robbery more than seventeen years ago." The photo was a pixelated shot of two men in masks with guns. "But there was more money. A lot more."

I leaned closer to the photo, tried to read something in the image. "That's not my mother."

"We know that. But then how did she come into possession of the stolen money?"

I didn't know, but I saw their story forming. "You think she was with them?"

"We think she must've been."

I sat up straight, my hand flat on the image. We had them. We *had* them. "So this is them, then. These are the people who took her."

He tapped his pen on the desk. "It's possible she went willingly now." He paused, tapped his pen some more. "And so we have to operate under the possibility that she could've gone willingly *then*."

No, no, no. They didn't understand. My mother was not capable of that. My mother was *not*. "She had chemical burns on her back. She was found running, smelling like gasoline. She was panicked and delusional and she has *nightmares*," I said. "Something terrible happened. And they came for her. And now they're coming for me." Couldn't they feel it? This wasn't even close to over. Couldn't they see the danger everywhere?

"This money was with you in the safe room," he said. "It's possible they expected more. It's possible they asked for you by name because they thought you might know how to get it."

Ryan sucked in a breath. "So it's possible they think she still might know, right?"

The detective looked pointedly at Ryan. "I think that's a stretch."

I was going to be sick. *Violent robbery. Crime spree. Willingly.* Everything I thought I knew about her: a lie. Everything I thought I knew of myself—that only half of me came from terror. But that wasn't true.

I was made of terror and lies.

I was shaking in my chair, and I thought Ryan was saying something, but his words weren't coming through, not with the buzzing in my head. "Do they know who that is?" I asked.

"No," he said. "This happened in Virginia. And it's a cold case," he said.

"Doesn't this change things, though?"

He tilted his head slightly. "How would this change things? We still don't know anything about their identity."

"Because." He was going to make me say it. Or maybe he didn't know. "Did you talk to the police in Atlanta about my mother?"

"Briefly. Your mother went off the grid pretty soon after reappearing. They didn't have much to go on. No statement at all, really. She said she didn't remember anything, and she didn't want to talk."

Were her medical records sealed? Maybe. Maybe he really didn't know, because he was missing something major. Me. He was missing me.

"You want a lead? Here it is." I held my arm on the table, pushed my sleeve up. Ryan looked away, eyes closed. The detective narrowed his eyes.

"My blood," I said. *It's not my fault. It's who I am.*

"His DNA is in here. Subtract my mother's. It's all that's left."

Ryan finally agreed to leave me at Jan's front door, but only after making sure Jan was home and wouldn't be leaving, and that Cole and Emma were home. He didn't say anything at all about what the police said—because what could he possibly say? *Kelsey, sorry your mom was lying her entire life. Sorry she abandoned you. Sorry she was not who she said.*

"I'll be here tomorrow morning," he said.

"I'm driving this week. I don't need a chaperone."

"I know you don't, but it will make me feel better."

I gave him a look.

"Okay, don't look at me like that. It's not my fault. It's in my blood. This is what we do for . . ."

"For people in danger?"

We heard voices behind the door. "I wasn't going to say that," he said.

Jan opened the door, looked between the two of us. "I thought I heard you," she said. "Ryan, right? We're ordering dinner. Would you like to join us?"

He nodded. "I would," he said.

"Oh, come on," I said, dragging him behind me.

That night, I couldn't sleep, like always. Imagining Eli out there somewhere. Watching. Reporting back. And for what? For *what*? I felt I was missing a major piece of the puzzle. Either my mother had left, or they had her. What could they possible want with me? They didn't want me to leave that house. They asked for me by name. My mother was gone, and they were after me.

My mother was gone and they were after me.

I was collateral.

Eli taking my pictures, following me. A warning: *We know who she is. We are watching her.* A threat.

And my mother, where was she in all of this? If they were taking pictures of me, they knew where to reach her.

Because they had her. "Mom," I whispered.

I went back to Jan's office. Tore through that box again. Sat between a heap of papers and reports, trying to find her. Digging deeper, growing more frustrated, my breath coming in short pulls. It took a moment to realize I'd been crying.

"You're going to wake everyone up." Cole stood in the doorway, eyes roaming over the mess I'd made.

"Oh." I looked around the room. Wiped my eyes with the back of my arm. "Shit," I said.

He laughed. "Looking for something in particular?" he asked.

"They think she was never kidnapped," I said, begging him to argue.

But he didn't. "Is that what you think?"

What did I really know? The police painted one picture; my mother, another. "She was seventeen, and she had a terrible home life, and she wanted to escape, it's true. But she also taught me how to escape being captured. She was obsessed. She . . ." I looked up at Cole. "She had to have been held. She was held against her will, with spiders she could not escape."

He shrugged, and it almost made me smile. "Okay, so it doesn't matter then, the stories they tell. *You* know." As if it really was that simple. And maybe it was. "You want some company down here?"

"No thanks," I said, actually smiling now. "Hey, Cole?"

He turned at the doorway.

"I was wrong about you," I said.

He smiled, and it was sad. "Yeah, well, I was wrong about you, too."

He left me with the heap of papers, and I started cleaning up after myself when I found it—that study on fear.

I read through it once more, wondering: What was truly buried inside of me? A fear so deep, it was the iron gates, and I was the ivy that grew around it. I did not exist without its foundation. It was the place from which I grew.

The scent of harsh chemicals as she lay tied up in a basement, with spiders crawling over her skin. A scream that nobody could hear. A life that, a year later, and before she escaped on her own, was reduced to nothing more than an article buried at the back of a newspaper.

The fear: that we could disappear, and nobody would find us.

And wasn't that what I was afraid of, too? That nobody knew I lived behind the bars. Nobody saw me. I faded to nothing in the halls. I could be taken, and who would've missed me? Who would've noticed? I'd have to fight my way back, because nobody else would do it for me.

Nobody else would do this for my mother, either.

I lay on the couch, the springs of the thin mattress digging into my back, imagining all the places she could be. Hidden, taken, hurt, buried. Too many possibilities, out in the vastness.

I sent Ryan a text instead of calling, because it was the middle of the night and I didn't want to wake him: How many missing people are never found?

My phone rang immediately, and I answered it before anyone else could hear, pulled the sheets up over my head, carving out a piece of the world with just the two of us.

"Want me to come over?" he asked.

"I can't sneak you in. There's not even a door to my room."

"That wasn't a no, I'm realizing."

I smiled in the darkness. "Good night, Ryan. Sorry I woke you."

"Swear to God, I can be there in five minutes flat. Just say the word."

I laughed under the sheets, the words spilling out. "Oh God, I love you." And then I choked on my tongue. Figuratively. Metaphorically. Died, either way.

I pushed myself to sitting. "Oh God oh God oh God. I didn't mean to say that."

"Oh. Okay, I guess you can take it back, but that would hurt."

"I mean, I didn't mean to say it on the phone. Just blurt it out like that." *Seriously, Kelsey? Seriously?* "This is one of those things, isn't it? That scares people off? That makes people hang up the phone and pretend it was a bad connection. Oh God, did you already hang up?"

"Kelsey, it's okay. I hung upside down in your car. I was trapped in your basement. Words aren't going to scare me off."

I paused, tried not to die of embarrassment. "Okay."

"It's three a.m., these things happen."

"Misguided declarations of love?"

"Honesty. And honestly, I'd tell you the same, but I'd prefer to do it when you're not having one of the worst days of your life, and I want to say it to your face, with you standing in my room. Wouldn't hurt if you were in my clothes again. I'm saving myself."

The silence stretched between us, filling itself with promises.

"I mean it, then," I said. "I don't take it back."

"I mean it, too."

"But you didn't say it."

"But I will."

"Is that Ryan Baker's car?" Emma asked as Cole handed me his keys.

I waved from the driveway. Ryan's arm was hanging out the window, and he waved back. "Morning, Kelsey. Emma." After a pause, "Cole."

"Seriously?" Cole asked. "He's going to escort you to school? This is ridiculous."

Emma tossed her bag into the backseat. "I'd think it was romantic if he hadn't ditched my friend for her."

But it wasn't romantic. It was terrifying. Because Ryan thought something could possibly happen between here and school. Because he didn't trust that Eli wasn't still out there, watching. He didn't believe the police line, either. He felt the danger everywhere.

We were, all of us, trapped in my mother's world.

Cole turned to face me. "You're going to tell me why he's doing this, right?"

I pulled out my phone, showed him a picture of Eli. "Ever seen him before?"

"No, I don't think so."

"If you do, you should call the police, okay?"

Cole's jaw was set, and Emma was watching us closely from the other side of the car, just out of earshot.

"Please, Cole. Just promise me you'll call."

"Should we be worried?" he asked.

"I don't know."

Emma groaned from the other side of the car. "How long will you be staying with us again?"

I didn't know. We were supposed to talk this weekend. What happened to seventeen-year-olds with missing parents? Who had no other living family? Where the people who housed her did not want her to stay?

Were they the ones ultimately taken, or hidden, or kidnapped? Were they the ones lured away, because there was nothing worth staying for? I shivered in the breeze.

Cole peered over his shoulder. "Your boyfriend doesn't like me," he said.

I shrugged.

He got in the car.

It was becoming a new sort of typical day, a routine, a cycle that I worried we would never break.

Another day to and from school with Emma and Cole, Ryan following behind.

Another day with no other news of my mother.

Another day of me looking over my shoulder, scared to walk to the bathroom alone, terrified of what lay outside the walls that held me.

I was becoming like her. Like my mother. Step by step, little by little, the fear was chipping away. And I couldn't break free. None of us could.

This was never going to stop. Did I have to depend on Ryan escorting me to and from school? And keep Jan and Cole and Emma in constant danger?

It was the same thing I felt hanging from the car, and being trapped in my basement. I felt it starting up then, and it had never stopped. I had only been prolonging the inevitable.

I had to be ready. Something was still coming. We were in the middle of it, still. Hanging, slipping, falling in slow motion.

CHAPTER 28

Friday. **Another day,** same routine.

"Oh look, it's your shadow," Emma said, tossing her bag into the backseat again.

Ryan waiting for me as I drove Cole and Emma to school. The four of us like a battle shield—a protection in numbers, for each of us. Witnesses at school, and safety in the exposure.

"Wait, he fell a car behind," she said, craning her neck. "The universe is going to collapse."

I was trying to cut Emma some slack, because I had, effectively, replaced her in the car hierarchy. That used to be me back there, with her up front beside Cole. Now I had usurped Cole, and he was riding shotgun, and she was relegated to the back, out of the loop.

I thought of Emma, and people like Emma, completely unaware of all the dangers surrounding them. I was sucking her in, and she didn't even realize it. She was in danger just by sitting in this car, with me.

Ryan met us beside the car in the school parking lot, leaning down to brush his lips against mine as Emma mock-gagged behind us. He slid an arm behind my waist, and I decided I loved the new routines we were forming. Or better yet: the surprises. They felt fresh and right and mine, and I wanted them, the things I wasn't expecting.

Another day when I tried to lose myself in moments like this, before reality came slamming back.

Another day when I looked over my shoulder as we walked inside together, wondering—but seeing nothing.

Another day when I started to fear not the shadows, but their absence instead.

Ryan and I walked to math class together, his arm around my waist, and I wanted this, I wanted this to be my new normal.

But the dangerous truth was that I also did not want the shadows to leave. If they disappeared, she would go with them. When I was safe, she'd be gone for good.

The fears were a familiar comfort. They were a reminder of who we were, and who we had been, and that we existed—and continued to exist. Who was I without them?

"So, I was thinking," Ryan said.

"What were you thinking?"

"I was thinking about this weekend, and whether I could take you out, except by *take you out* I mean *have you over*, just so we're clear."

Because taking me out might not be safe. Because he needed to keep me hidden away, too.

"Don't you have work?" I responded, feeling like I was watching the conversation play out in front of me, my mind somewhere else.

"They want me to take some time off, after everything. Normally I'd complain, but I'm choosing to see the positive here."

I nodded, and he smiled, leaning closer. "Yeah?" he said.

Then Mr. Graham poked his head out of the room and said, "Care to join us?" and we followed him in.

I got the message in the middle of class, feeling my phone vibrate in my bag. I asked to use the bathroom, and took my bag with me when I left. The message was from Jan. The police had called and had finished their processing at my house.

The house was mine again.

She said she'd come home early and meet us at her place, and then she'd take me over, for anything I still needed.

But I thought of what the police had said: that there was something more that my mother had taken. Where else would she go? The house was her entire world. The house would have all the answers.

And if someone was out there, watching and

waiting, it was possible—no, more than possible—
that I wouldn't be the only one looking for it.

I could not be collateral anymore. I would not be
used against my mother. There was something in
that house that they would eventually be back for,
and I had to get it first—before they found it and disappeared for good. I could bring it to the police, as
proof. I could convince them my mother had been
taken. They could use whatever it was to lure them
back. They could find her.

I left Ryan after math, kissing him in the hall, even
though people were passing and everyone saw. Even
though Mr. Graham cleared his throat and told us to
move along. "See you at lunch," Ryan said.

"See you," I said, and I turned around, biting my
cheek so he wouldn't see the lie.

I hoped he would forgive me for it.

I hoped this was the right choice. That keeping
this to myself was the best way. That some secrets
were meant to be kept, and some lies were the safest options. Because the more I stripped away from
my mother's lies, the more truly dangerous the world
became.

I had never been alone in Cole's car, and it felt too big,
too wide, too silent and empty and cold. The day was

gray, the sky overcast and the clouds descending, the woods covered in a light fog that turned everything muted and dull. The cool air sharpened my senses.

There were too many cars in the lot, too many possible eyes. I started to drive, and the fears set in. Would someone try to run me off the road? Were they following, right this second? There were too many unknowns, too many possibilities, and I kept my phone in the cup holder, as a comfort.

I caught glimpses of sky and trees in the rearview mirror, the shadow of something following—but when I looked closely, there was nothing there. Just wisps of fog and shadowed curves. I had to believe that the unexpected would work in my favor. That Eli was not watching while I was supposedly in class. That he'd gotten what he needed in the form of a photo, two days before.

I was supposed to be accounted for until three p.m., and this wasn't even my car. Still, I couldn't shake the fear that there were eyes following, eyes everywhere.

There was no familiar comfort in pulling into my neighborhood. Nothing that promised *home* and *safe*. Instead, there was only the unknown, a shiver working its way to the surface. I paused at the entrance to our driveway, heard my own heartbeat echoing inside my head. There were no cars—nothing I could see down the road, or in the rearview mirror. But the police were gone. And now it was just me and the house, everything that had happened, and everything that might.

I drove past the entrance, instead parking at the start of Annika's driveway. Out of sight of both her house and the road. Outside, the breeze was turning stronger, the leaves rustling up above, a few falling to the earth around my feet. I stood outside the car and listened. Nothing but the wind and the leaves echoed back.

Just like that night when I heard Ryan's Jeep idling in my driveway, I inched down the side of my road, preventing the noise of my feet kicking up gravel. I felt, for once, like the eyes in the woods instead, hidden inside the fog. The things my mother would look for from behind the safety of the tinted windows.

I slipped into the trees, just in sight of the front door, and watched. I listened, but heard nothing. No cars, no voices, no presence. It was just me and the trees, and the emptiness.

To be sure, I circled the house on foot, tracing a path between the stone wall and black iron gates.

I wrapped my hands around the bars of the gate around back, but heard a noise in the woods—a snapping of a branch, like a footstep—and I froze. I stared into the woods until a small animal darted out of sight. The hinges cried in the breeze, unlocked and unlatched, as I pushed them open.

The house beyond was dark, but the web of cracks where the bullet had lodged stood out in the otherwise smooth surface. I cupped my hands over my eyes and leaned in close, but the curtains were pulled shut. I held my ear to the glass instead, listening for movement. I didn't let myself in through the back door until I was convinced I was alone.

The scent overwhelmed me as soon as I stepped inside the kitchen. The hazy smoke was gone—the house had been cleaned. Instead, the scent of industrial cleanser filled the room, and my stomach rolled with nausea. An instinct. Nothing more. Or maybe it was something else: that I was standing in the kitchen of what had been my house just a few days earlier, and now we had been stripped from its surface.

All I felt was the emptiness.

I understood that this was what we both feared. Not the scent of the chemicals, a burn that would scar but eventually heal. We feared the thing that could erase all evidence that we had ever existed. We feared that the people we were had never been real. That we would be reduced to nothing more than a story.

Nothing inside was quite as I'd left it. The police must've been through all of our things, searching for evidence that my mother was not who she claimed to be, that she was someone other than the person I'd known my entire life. I heard Detective Conrad's voice in my ear, saw the house as he might instead: cameras to see if the police were coming; a go-bag with stolen money and forged passports to take as we ran; an alarm system that told us someone was near, but did not call for help; walls and gates, marble and steel—all to hide behind.

I had been taught the protocol. *If the alarm sounds, get into the safe room.* But now I wondered whether it was supposed to keep me safe, or whether it was supposed to be the start of an escape. And I wanted to know exactly what we were trying to get away from.

And yet, when it came down to it, my mother had not followed protocol at all. I imagined what must've happened that night: *It's nighttime, and the gates are locked. The lights are on, the alarm is armed. There's a noise at the back gate, men in hoods trying to force entry. She picks up the phone, but the line is dead. She runs to my room, but it's empty. She notices the open window, pushes at the grate. She sees my phone, but I am gone. Maybe she tries to make a call with it, but it won't go through.*

She was supposed to get to the safe room, but she hadn't. Instead, she disarmed the alarm and pressed the button opening the gate. . . .

And suddenly, I got a glimpse of someone new. Her, but not her. *Your mother is very strong. She's capable of more,* Jan had said. I had seen glimpses of this person before: the little lies she told for our protection, the moment when social services came to take me away and she froze, wavering. I saw the moment in a new light: the decision to run or stay. Escape, or take the risk.

She let them take me not because she saw no other

choice, but because this *was* the choice. The long game. The risk that she would get me back.

Or this: That I would make my way back to her.

And I did. Over and over, I did.

The stories I told to, and kept from, Jan. Hanging from the car, with nothing but the strength in my fingers and some hope.

My mother knew. She knew I'd find my way back to her. I always did.

I started rummaging through drawers, tearing through her things. She had to have left me something here. She had to have left me a way.

I checked her bedroom, the bathroom, the bedside table. I ran my fingers between the mattress and box spring. But there was no place to hide.

I went to her office, where she spent most of her time—but her computer was missing. My heart sank as I imagined the police digging through her history instead, looking for the wrong thing. Her emails, her searches, the things she feared . . . All those times she'd read up on stories of missing children, acts of violence—I wondered if all along, she'd been looking for *them*.

I opened her filing cabinet, thumbed through her labeled folders, each of her clients in alphabetical order. From the haphazard way they were lined up, I knew the police had been through here, too.

Where, Mom? Hidden. It would have to be hidden.

There was no rug to peel back, or ceiling tiles to remove. I ran my fingers over her desk, looking for hidden compartments—but nothing. Only the walls remained. I took our pictures off the hooks, but the wall was smooth behind them. Even the finger-painting artwork, which had been here forever, for reasons I could never understand, in a frame too big for its paper.

My fingers tingled as I held the shadow box in my hand. I shook it gently, heard a faint rattling inside. I dropped to my knees, pried open the back, and saw a small piece of paper, folded over and yellowing at the edges.

I flattened it against the floor. It was a car registration. For the state of Georgia, issued eighteen years earlier, and held in the name of a man I'd never heard of before: Samuel Lyter.

And there was an address.

I stood, tucking the paper into my back pocket, my hands shaking, my entire body on edge. The name, and all it might represent. The man she had escaped. A name to the nightmare. But a name my mother *had always known*.

Why had she kept this, if not for me? Trace back my blood, trace it to him. Trace it to her, *right now*. In case of emergency, I could find her.

I'd take this to the police, and we'd have a lead. I could give them a name and the car registration, see the face pulled up with the driver's license, tell them if it was a match to the man I'd seen in my house.

I could bring the shadows to life.

I stood too fast, my mind spinning—and I heard it. A muffled voice, a shuffling of steps, a pause. I pulled my phone out, held it in my shaking hand, quickly dialed 911 and waited for it to connect.

No service.

My stomach dropped. Everything within me went on high alert. Goose bumps rising to the surface of my skin, a slow sickness making its way through my stomach, my vision narrowing to a point.

Fight or flight, Kelsey.

The sound was coming from the front, but the back door was within range. I could make it. Maybe run straight for the wall, maybe make it over before anyone saw. Maybe make it back to Cole's car and out of the development, to where I had a signal. And maybe then the police would get here in time.

But then I heard something higher, more familiar. Not words, not anything so clear. But a voice that I knew. My mother. My mother was on the other side of that door, and I had found her.

I crept behind the open office door, trying to make myself small. Heard the front door creak open, the footsteps in the foyer, a grunt. My shoulders tensed as I imagined all the possible things that could be happening on the other side of the wall: my mother, forced inside the house, being hurt, being terrified.

Careful.

I held my breath, held my body perfectly still.

"Show us, Amanda." It was the voice from the walkie-talkie, now too personal, too close. I pictured the down-turned mouth that had begun to say my name. And the name on the car registration in my back pocket. *Samuel.*

But then, a second voice. "Make it quick." Not the voice of someone my age, not Eli—someone older.

"Relax, Martin. The kid's keeping watch."

So, there were three. Martin. Samuel. Eli outside somewhere, watching.

"The basement," my mother said. The breath rushed from me at the sound of her voice. Just a few steps away. So close I could reach through the wall and touch her.

I heard them moving down the hall, the familiar sound of the basement door opening, my mother's voice pleading "Don't"—and then a door swinging closed.

The person I knew was real—the one who could not manage the thought of being trapped inside a basement with these men. No matter what the police said, she was real.

I eased out from my hiding spot behind the door and tiptoed toward the top of the stairs, just to listen. I pressed my ear to the closed wooden door.

Voices came through in snippets—"No," "Here," "I didn't"—half of it lost to the dark. But then I got some clarity. They must've been standing right at the base of the steps now.

"She told us she buried it. What the hell are we even listening to her for?" That was the more unfamiliar voice. Martin, I assumed.

"I *did*," my mom said. "But then I went back for it."

"You're getting sloppy with your lies, Amanda," Samuel said.

"Listen, Samuel, please. She doesn't know. Call off the kid."

The hairs raised on the back of my neck. Me. They were talking about me.

"She doesn't know *what?*" Samuel asked.

"Anything. She can't hurt you. She doesn't even know who you are. I'll give you anything. Anything you want. Just. Don't do this."

His voice rose. "How could you *possibly* give me what I want now?"

"I'll get you the money—"

"Money! That might work for my brother, for the kid, but me and you have a little more history to work through, sweetheart."

His brother. Martin was his brother. The same blood running through them, and me. As if the thing that turned them dark was not a quirk of fate, but something deeper, something I could feel simmering within my bones, too. . . .

I had to get out. I had to get *help*. They weren't just here for money. Samuel wanted something more, and he was still using me to get it. I had to run. I had to *try*. Had to get to the road and make a call, and then come back for her.

Front door, back door. I checked out the window of the dining room, looking for Eli's shadow, out in the trees. Saw no sign of him at the gates. The fog might be hiding him deeper in the trees, but it could hide me, too, if I made it that far. *Front or back, Kelsey.* A fifty-fifty shot, but I had to *try*. . . .

I turned the front door knob slowly, slowly, trying not to make a sound. Pulled the door inward, and gasped. There, standing in the open doorway, facing me, was a boy about my age.

"Hello," he said. Eli, with his deep-set eyes, mismatched parts, and now a crooked smile, blocking the front door.

I backpedaled until I was in the middle of the living room. Eli closed the door behind him, stepped closer, walking toward me like I was an animal he didn't want to spook.

The entire room hummed. I stood frozen in the middle of the living room, moved my arm slowly to my back pocket for my cell, but Eli shook his head.

"Won't work," he said. "It's useless."

All the hairs rose on my arms, the back of my neck, and the room narrowed into focus.

Everything I thought I wanted—answers, my mother—was replaced instead with the simple basic instinct: *Run*.

The back door. The bedroom windows. The hole in the safe room floor.

The back door was closest. I still had the phone in my hand—*useless*, he'd said. But it wasn't. I hurled it at his head, and as he ducked, I spun around, sprinting for the back door. Three strides, four, my hand on the knob, pulling it back—and then a hand was flat on the door beside me, slamming it shut. Slamming my body against it at the same time. My front was pressed up against the wood, and Eli was pressed up against my back.

I felt him breathing against the side of my face. "Not this time," he whispered. He smelled of sweat and stale cigarettes, and I fought back a gag.

He wrenched one of my arms behind my back, still using his weight to pin me to the door. I stomped on his instep in a move that was second nature, and he released his grip enough for me to spin around and grab the handle again. But I couldn't get it open in time. He backed me against the door again, jamming his forearm into my neck. I couldn't breathe. I started clawing at the skin of his forearm, drawing blood, the world turning hazy, and then he suddenly released me, breathing heavily.

I slumped to the floor, preparing to kick him in the knee as he came closer.

But then I heard her again.

The high-pitched voice. The word *no*. All the tension, transferring from her to me. I twisted my head toward the hall, toward the basement, and in that moment of distraction, I didn't notice the fist coming for the side of my face until it was too late.

A sharp sting, my head ricocheting off hardwood, and the world gone black.

It must've only lasted a moment or two, because I opened my eyes to see Eli crouching in front of me, his face contorted into panic. I was slouched against the back wall, but this time he was holding me up.

"Come on," he mumbled. Then he glanced over his shoulder, and I fought for clarity.

He must've felt the tension come back to my body, because he hauled me up to my feet.

"Who are . . . where are . . ."

But I didn't fight him as he walked us toward the basement, floating on my feet. I didn't fight him, because I knew where we were going. I was still falling— only now I was doing it willingly. I was doing it to find the person at the bottom.

CHAPTER 29

The voices stopped as we stumbled down the steps. From this angle, I only saw shadows elongated across the basement floor from the spotlights set up in the corners. Like ghosts stretching across the distance.

"Look who I found," Eli said, pride in his voice.

I couldn't see the people yet, but someone saw *me*. "No." My mother's voice, echoing across the concrete, off the cinder blocks, cutting straight through the chill.

"Mom?" I shook out of Eli's grasp at the bottom of the stairs, barely registering the two other shadows, unable to see her clearly through the tears as I raced across the room to where she stood. I fell into her arms, felt her inhale suddenly as her arms came around me, one hand over my hair, a face buried close to my ear.

She was so slight, and cold, but she was standing and here and *alive*.

"I'm sorry," she whispered. "I'm so, so sorry." Her whole body was trembling, and I fought to hold her still.

It was only when I pulled back slightly that I noticed the bruises on her face, the cuts on her hands, the dried blood caked under her nails as she reached for my cheek, her fingers resting on the spot Eli had hit me.

Eli had me by the back of my shirt again, tugging me out of her grip.

"What did you do to her?" a low, calm voice asked from the corner. He stepped forward, into the light, and I recognized him from that night. Large frame, down-turned mouth, eyes that were the same as mine, like looking in the mirror. Samuel. Samuel Lyter, his name humming through my blood. Was it possible to want to come face to face with someone while also wanting to wipe him from existence? To bury him in a dark room of my mother's mind, and let him stay there?

His eyes darted from Eli to me and back again, and he stepped closer. "I said, what did you do?" His voice, I now noticed, had the faintest hypnotic drawl to it. Something that pulled you in, made you want to lean a little closer, hear a little better.

"Nothing," Eli said. His hands were held up as if he were surrendering. "I caught her. She was inside the house, and she tried to run, and I caught her this time."

Samuel grabbed my chin in his hand, turning my face from side to side. His hands were rough and callused, and I wanted to move back, wanted to smack his hand away, but I held my breath, held myself perfectly still. He smelled of leather and something sharper, a faint whiff of gasoline, and my instinct was to jerk back. *Careful,* I thought.

"You did more than *catch her,*" he said. I felt the burn on the side of my cheek, the constant throbbing, the ache in my head.

He pressed his lips together, gave Eli a look that made even me wither, but then he refocused on me and smiled. "Kelsey, then. So nice to finally meet you." He spoke through his teeth, the smile firmly planted, a cat with a bird caught between his teeth.

Whatever I'd been fighting against, the hum in my blood, it was here now. The truth. The mirror. A tangle of lies, my entire existence, the dark basement from which I grew. The lies that were woven into my bedtime stories, the fears that were planted to keep me safe, the truth staring me back in the face. And now rage, clawing its way to the surface, balling my hands into fists.

"Let go of her, Samuel," my mother said, and I noticed her fists were clenched as well. Sometime during the conversation, Martin had grabbed my mother around the shoulders, restraining any further movement. He was a little shorter than Samuel, and he had a scar over his lip. But the similarities were otherwise too strong to deny. This was his brother, and this was my origin. An entire family of bad blood, currently coursing through me. If fear could be inherited, couldn't this, too? It was not a random turn of events, but a thread running deep inside the both of them, and so it could in me as well. I felt sick, and it wasn't the fear. Not this time.

Samuel listened to my mother, dropping his hand from my face. But he didn't move. "Tell me, Kelsey. Do you know who I am?"

"Yes," I said, feeling the taste of acid rising in the back of my throat. *The other half of me.* "You're the man who held my mother."

He looked over his shoulder. "Amanda, is that what you told her?"

He turned back, his gaze lingering on my chin, my nose, my hair. He faced my mother again, gave her half a smile. "She looks more like me."

My mother frowned. Of course she knew that. She saw it in me always. What else did she see, that she felt the need to hide? Did I act more like him, talk more like him? Did she teach me to be more like her, because she saw what else I might become?

My eyes burned. Everything burned. I wanted to step outside my skin, become anyone other than who I was.

He took a step closer, the light behind him, as if he were the moon eclipsing the sun—and all that remained was darkness. "Your mother is a thief and a liar," he said, his voice like music, though it dripped with acid. "Don't listen to what the papers said. She came with us because she wanted to."

"Because I didn't *know*!" she yelled from behind him. "I didn't know who you really were!"

He shook his head. "You knew exactly who I was," he said. "We were together for months before I offered to bring you with us. *Months.* We are the same, you and I. I was the only one who understood you. I *saved* you from your life of misery. And this is how you repaid me? By leaving and taking our money? I loved you, Amanda. I really did."

"You did not. *You did not.* I was young and naïve and you preyed on me." She pointed to Eli. "Same as you're doing to him." She shook her head, pleaded with Eli. "Don't listen to him. Don't. You can go back home. Your home is better than this, I *promise.* It's not too late—"

Eli jerked back. "You know nothing about me."

"I know *everything* about you. You're a kid who was looking for a way out of a bad situation, and they took you in, am I right? And the way they live, the things they do, the things they ask *you* to do, they just seem like little things at first. *Just watch the doors,* I bet they told you. *Just keep the car running.* Let me tell you, kid. It's going to change."

Eli shook his head, but he didn't disagree.

"It already has, right?" she asked.

Eli slid his battered fist behind his back. Set his feet,

and his jaw. "I know all about *you*, Amanda Silviano. You took their money, and Sam's *kid*, and let the world think you were their victim." His spine straightened, and his voice grew more assured now. "They took me in. I ran away and they took me in when nobody else would, and I wouldn't trade it for anything."

Samuel smiled. "See? Eli is nothing like you. He is not so weak. He would not betray us."

"Want to know what they'll do to you if you change your mind, kid? When you find out what they're really doing, and want to leave?" She pulled her shirt over her shoulder, exposing her scars. Leaned toward Samuel, and yelled, "You burned my back when I tried to leave! Poured it on me one drop at a time! You kept me locked up in a basement after! For months. With nothing but the cold and the containers of cleaning fluid you stored in the corners. And the spiders. The goddamn spiders were everywhere." Her face broke at the memory.

"It was your own fault," Samuel said, and he was losing his composure now, his features hardening, the lines around his eyes deepening. "You don't get to change your mind whenever the hell you feel like it."

My mother was shaking her head. "We just needed a little money to get by, you said. Just one thing, to get us started. It was all a lie. You had no intention of stopping. I hadn't realized you'd been *hurting* people. I didn't know that I . . ." She raised her hand to her mouth, her eyes watering over, the words stuck inside.

"That you were just as guilty?" He smiled. Crouched so he was at her level. "I don't know what you think would've happened if you had left back then. What, would you have gone home, said you left on your own and had been involved in a little crime spree, no big deal? You would've given us up, because it was the only thing you could've done. I couldn't do that to my own brother. You left me with no choice."

Martin jerked to attention.

"You took something from us, Amanda," Samuel said. "And you will give it back now."

"I didn't know," she said, shaking her head. "I didn't mean to."

"And yet, here we are," he said.

He turned to me. "She took our car," he said. "She took everything inside of it, all that money. And you know what she first said she did with the money? That she buried it. Can you believe that, Kelsey? She is *such* a talented liar, your mother. But then, you must know that already. Now, of course, she sings a different story."

His words, circling into my mind. They were weaving a spell, digging in and refusing to let go. "The police have it," I whispered, and Martin let out a string of curses. I pointed to the safe room. "It was in there, and the police took it."

"How much?" Martin asked, his voice growing louder. "How *much*?"

"Twenty thousand," I said.

"Where's the rest, Amanda? What have you done?" Samuel asked.

"I did bury it," she said. She looked at me, lowered her voice, like it was just me and her and this was a bedtime story. "I escaped on a Friday—they came back drunk and celebrating, and didn't check on me. Didn't know I'd finally gotten free of the restraints, had used a mattress rail to pry the bolts from the door hinges. The key was on the kitchen table, and they were in the next room, and I took it." Martin jerked her head back, his fist tightening in her hair, but her mouth stretched into a smile instead, at the memory. "I drove that car as far as I could, until I'd nearly run out of gas. I popped the trunk, because they used to bring gasoline with them"—she started shaking, and I realized what they must've used that gasoline for—"and I saw the money. There was stolen money and the car had my prints, and I didn't know what to do. I was near the woods, so I ditched the car, and I buried the money. And that's where I was found, running down the side of the road. . . . I was so scared, being alone for the first time. And then, all of a sudden, I wasn't."

Then she turned back to Samuel. "After Kelsey was born, when I was sure nobody was watching, I went back for it, just to check. And it was still *there*. I told you: I buried it, and then I took it back. That's not a lie." She looked to me, pleading. "What choice did I have?"

But what she didn't say, what only I knew, was she had also taken his registration, as proof. A trail leading to his car, wherever it was abandoned. A trail leading to everything she had done, and everything that had happened to her. A way out, if ever she needed it. There was always a way out.

She started to laugh then. Raised her arms. "You want that money? I told you I'd bring you to it. Here it is. You're looking at it."

The walls of concrete, the gates of iron, the bullet-proof windows . . . all of it could be traced back to them. This house was never ours. This house had always been the lie. We had been living in this place built on blood money.

Martin jerked her head back by the hair again, but Samuel held out his hand. "Martin," he said in warning.

"No," Martin said. "She's always been a weakness for you. You said they'd have the money. You *said*."

But Samuel looked unaffected. The others may have been here for the money, but I had a feeling Samuel was here for something more. I'd heard him from my hiding spot upstairs: that there was no way my mother could get him what he truly wanted. He was here for something more. For us.

"You are so small," Samuel said to my mother. "I always underestimate you."

He slid a knife from his back pocket as he walked

toward her. I saw a gun tucked into the waistband of Martin's pants. And Eli . . . what did Eli have? The scent of cigarettes . . .

I didn't have to overpower them. I didn't need muscles and doors. There's a way out of everything. She had taken it, once. It wasn't perfect, maybe wasn't even *right*, but she saw the chance, and she took it.

She built our life out of blood money, and I existed because of it. Everything that sustained me, from the walls that surrounded me to the blood running through me, came from darkness and lies.

But this is what nobody else understood except me.

She had built herself a cage, with bars and concrete and locks. She had been serving time for it. Seventeen years' worth. A life sentence.

For me.

Stories take on a life of their own, but this one was mine.

I lunged for Eli, my hands going around his waist, dragging down his body, trying to force us both to the ground. There was yelling—someone calling for Eli to stop, someone calling for *me* to stop, but I didn't. He stumbled, braced himself against a wall, and he fought me off easily. But he didn't hit me, wasn't too rough, and I thought it was because Samuel was watching.

From the ground, I saw Samuel and Martin exchange a look. A frown. The room filled with tension, but I stayed curled up on the ground, trying to catch my breath. I kept my hand tucked against my stomach.

I needed one thing. Just one. And now I had it.

"What are you doing?" Samuel asked as I pushed myself to standing. His face twisted in confusion.

I let out a noise that sounded almost like laughter.

I felt the dust and grime from the basement floor like a chill on my skin. Felt the bruises like a challenge, the fear like something whispering my name, urging me on.

"Find something to bind her arms," Martin barked at Eli.

"Wait," I said, and everyone froze. I felt their eyes shift from my face to my hand—at what I was holding out in front of me, over an open box. My hand was trembling, but I didn't know if it was from the fear or something else. Something stronger, simmering in my blood.

"Do you know," I said, "what you're standing in the middle of?"

Samuel turned the knife in his hand, the blade catching the light in the corner.

"My entire basement is combustible."

I thought of Ryan, slowly backing away. The fire extinguishers throughout the house. As if all of it was waiting for a spark.

There were the stairs behind me, and the hole in the floor in the room to my right—and then there was this.

I held Eli's metal Zippo lighter in my hand, flicked it once, watched as the flame danced over the metal. "Nobody moves," I said.

Martin had his gun aimed at me, but Samuel raised his hand. "You want to play, kid? Let's play."

He took the gun from Martin's hand and pointed it at my mother.

"What will you do, I wonder," Samuel said. His head was faintly cocked to the side, as if he really was that curious. Curious to see what I was made of. And I was scared to find out. Fear reveals things, but so does what we do with it. So does this.

What was I afraid of?

That I would not be forgiven.

That I might make the wrong choice.

That I had taken too great a risk.

That nobody would truly love me, once they knew me.

That I might be made of too much darkness.

"Kelsey," my mother gasped in warning. But wasn't this what she had prepared me for? Not just to run, but to stand my ground? She taught me, above all, to survive. She taught me to weigh risks, and dangers—to see them everywhere. To act.

And I was doing it.

Eli's head twisted toward the stairs first. Then Martin's. And then I heard it, too. Sirens, faintly calling. Getting closer. But I didn't feel any relief. Instead, the tension grew, the room practically tingling with a new blind rush of terror.

They had no reason to hand us over. They were violent, the police had said. It was the reason my mother left them in the first place—because they had blood on their hands, and now so did she.

This was about to become a hostage situation. And they had no remorse, nothing worth bargaining for. They had a gun, a knife, two hostages, and walls closing in on them.

All I had was the lighter and some hope.

"How did you get out of here the last time?" Samuel asked. He seemed too calm, like the fear could not touch him—and that made *me* suddenly more afraid. As if he was missing some basic human emotion, and its lack had turned him cold and remorseless.

"Drop the gun and I'll show you," I said.

He smiled. "You know I'm not going to do that."

I looked from him to my mother to the stairs. I could not go with him. I could not. If we went with him, we were dead, or we were taken. Either way, we were gone. This I was sure of.

Everything my mother had taught me, all the things she'd fought to keep hidden, all of it was leading to this. Right now.

"Mom," I said in warning.

Martin still had ahold of her.

My mother closed her eyes.

I had become the thing we always feared. The danger in the world. The unknown, existing out in the vastness. An unforeseen turn of events.

A shadow in the corner of your eye—blink and you might miss me.

The flame still flickered in my hand. And then I dropped it.

CHAPTER 30

In the event of a fire. Stay low to the ground. Know the exits. Crawl toward safety. Know the way by heart, by feel.

But nobody prepared me for the thickness of smoke, how it suffocates even as you escape.

Nobody prepared me for the heat.

Nobody prepared me for the sound. A crackling. A whoosh. The screaming.

Nobody prepared me for the thousand doubts that piled one on top of the other in the moment that followed, insisting I had made the wrong choice. The fear that threatened to paralyze me once more.

There was a series of explosions as one box ignited, and then another, and another—chemicals bursting as the fire spread throughout the room.

I heard footsteps on the stairs, and I called for my mother. Her name scratching against my throat. The smoke choking me as I sucked in air to call for her again.

I sank lower, my face pressed to the concrete, and I wondered what I had traded my shot at safety for. What we all had traded.

Somewhere, a fire alarm blared. Somewhere, sirens approached. Footsteps fled. The heat radiated all around me.

Move, Kelsey.

I started crawling in the opposite direction from the footsteps—to the closest exit. I felt for the sides of the open safe room along the floor, the metal hot to the touch, and scrambled for the compartment in the floor. *Shut the door against the fire. Shut the door against the smoke. It's the safest choice.*

I couldn't do it. "Mom!" I called again, but the fire was too loud—I was shrinking into myself, my world growing smaller—

I couldn't see anything, just felt for the compartment—my hands connecting with warm flesh, jerking back.

"Kelsey?" A low voice, a cough.

"Mom?"

The safe room door slammed shut, the noise trapped behind it, though the smoke and heat lingered. I couldn't see her in the dark, with the smoke billowing all around us.

Her hands brushed mine on the floor, and she said, "You found it." She coughed again in the thick smoke, even though the door was closed.

"Kelsey, listen," she said. But then there was yet

another explosion from just outside the door. The entire foundation shook, rattling my bones.

"We have to move," I said.

I made my mother go first, because I remembered the feeling I had, sitting on the ledge. Debating whether to go. I didn't want to give her the choice. I didn't want to know which one she'd pick.

I slid down after her, breathing in the smoke-free air. Her hand connected with the side of my face first, then gripped my shoulder. "There's a tunnel," she whispered, leading me in the darkness.

"I know."

She paused, the muscles in her arm stiffening. "When Samuel asked how you got out, was he talking about this?"

My eyes watered, tears rolling down my cheeks— from the smoke, or something more. "They got in," I said, and the words pushed their way out with a sob. I hiccupped, trying to force it back, but even my breath rattled. "Ryan, Cole, Annika, and I were trapped in the safe room, and they were right outside the door."

"But you found it," she said, sounding breathless. "You got out."

I pulled away from her, started crawling through the tunnel, hearing the crackle of foundation somewhere above. "Cole was *shot*. And you were *gone*," I said. "You just *left* me there, and I didn't know what to do." My hand over my mouth, my head shaking back and forth. I was glad for the darkness, for the noises above. I sat back on my heels, feeling her somewhere nearby.

"No," she said. Her hand was around my elbow, and she was holding on tighter. "*No. I ran, Kelsey. Because it was the only thing I could think to do. It was my biggest fear, Samuel coming back. Samuel coming back for *you*. I ran to draw them away from the house. So they wouldn't find you as you tried to come back inside."

I didn't move. Didn't know what to believe after all the lies, all the stories. The version from the police, from Jan, and now the one from her.

"Kelsey, we're running out of time."

I pressed my face closer, made my voice lower. "They're going to arrest you, Mom. The money . . . they know."

"It's okay, Kelsey."

"No, it's definitely not okay!" If I had no father, and no mother, and nowhere else to go—how was that possibly okay?

She nudged me on the shoulder, a little rougher than I expected. "*Move*, Kelsey." Her words rang in my ear, as they had earlier. Instinct. Muscle memory. We had no light, and the tunnel was endless. I started moving faster, more frantically, thinking the tunnel was longer than I remembered—wondering if there was a fork I didn't know about, if I was heading in the wrong direction.

And I was overwhelmed by the feeling we were not alone in this tunnel. It was the noise that echoed, the *feel*—like the opposite of when I arrived home to my empty house.

Maybe it was just the fear. My imagination, running away with me. But I kept feeling something more. A shadow in the darkness, that you could feel but never see. A breath at the back of your neck—look over your shoulder, but nothing's there.

But then I heard a shuffling in the tunnel somewhere *ahead*, and I froze. My mother collided into my back, and she let out a grunt—and the noise stopped. I started pushing her the other way before realizing there was nowhere else to go. I groped for anything I might use. But it was just me. Me and her.

I slowed my breath, and I waited.

A bright beam of light shone from the corner ahead, and I tried to make myself smaller. Make myself *ready*. My mother started moving backward. We were trapped. The fire behind, the light ahead . . .

I heard the crackle of a radio. "Baker," it said, and his name echoed off the walls of the pipe, straight to my gut. "Come in. Where the *hell* are you?"

"Ryan?" I called.

"Kelsey?" His voice echoed around the corner, and then the light hit me full on, so my eyes squeezed close on impulse. But then his hands were on my shoulders, and I moved by feel, by instinct. My arms circling around his shoulders as his arms pulled me closer. He took in a shuddering breath. "Holy shit. I've got you," he said.

And then he shined the light past me, at my mother. He fumbled for his radio. "I've got them," he said.

And then, to me, "I told them," he said. "I told them there was another way in."

We stood huddled beside Ryan's Jeep, waiting for the team to meet us there. He'd left his car just off the road, across the street from the sewer, in a small clearing surrounded by trees and fog. My mother had her eyes closed—as she had since we emerged from the tunnel—and I could see her mouth moving, as if she was listing off the things that might still keep us safe. She slumped to the ground with her back to Ryan's car, her head between her knees—and I went with her. The ground was cold and damp, and I held her hand as Ryan paced in front of the open sewer grate we'd emerged from, still holding his flashlight.

Ryan was speaking into his radio, directing them, repeating what he'd said before. He had us both. *Both*, and we were safe.

I could see the smoke now over the trees.

But there were still secrets to learn, and to keep.

When they arrived, my mother would be gone. Even now, even free, there were so many ways I could lose her.

I pressed my shoulder up against hers. "Mom? I

need to know what to say. What to tell them." I knew we would need to be *careful*. And I would do it still, for her.

She raised her face to mine. "No more," she said. As if she knew that this was the end. That something was shifting, for her, and for me. The vastness, and all its possibility, stretching before the both of us.

"You never told me," I said. "You knew, and you didn't tell me." The truth was, I was angry. But under that, I was hurt. It stung to realize the secrets that had been kept, the lies that had been told.

"I was going to tell you," she said. "At fifteen, I decided. Then sixteen. And then at seventeen. But I didn't know what it would do to you. I didn't know what good it would do, as long as I was there to protect you. I thought it was the safest thing, to keep it from you."

My throat tightened. "Then tell me *now* where you've been. The police think you went with them on purpose. Tell me the truth. All of it."

She looked at me like surely I must know this. "He rang the doorbell. Just rang it, and waited. I saw his face on the video screen, and I couldn't find you. I tried to call you, but the line had been cut. And you'd left your phone. I knew it was too late for anything else. All I could do was run. So I ran, and I kept running."

She left on her own, like they told me. Even though I thought she wasn't capable. These men had been her nightmare. The scars on her back, a year of horror and guilt and fear—but she still took the risk and drew them away from me.

"They caught me, deep in the woods behind the house. Got that kid Eli to take me back to wherever they were staying, tied up underground. They kept showing me *pictures* of you to get me to behave. To talk."

"They hurt you?" I asked, remembering the bruises, the blood under her nails. Her history repeating itself.

She shook her head, like I didn't understand. "My worst fear was coming true," she said, and my heart dropped.

"That they would find you again?" I asked.

"No. *No.* That they would find *you.* I didn't know what else to do. It was the *only* thing I could do. So I did it."

Everything I've done, she'd said on Jan's tape.

"But when that didn't work, when they threatened to hurt you even after they had me, I told them the money was still at the house. If I was at the house, I thought I could figure something out. I thought I'd have a chance. . . ." She lowered her voice. "Don't you understand? I took you from him." She shook her head, her eyes filling with tears. "You can't take something from a man like Samuel and get away with it. So I made a choice, and I hoped it would save you."

"It did," I said. It gave us time to make a plan, to fight, to defend ourselves.

"No," she said. "You did that all on your own."

Ryan paused in the middle of the road—calm, finally—listening to my mother's secrets, too. "What happened back there, Kelsey? They got two people in custody as they were trying to escape the fire. But they couldn't find you." I noticed the slightest tremor in his hand, the way he still gripped the flashlight, and the way it trembled as he looked down the gray shadowed road, waiting for help to arrive.

I slowly pushed myself to standing. *Two people in custody.* "There were three," I said.

Ryan paused, lowered his voice. "The fire's pretty big, Kelsey." Implying something more. He took a step closer. "What happened?"

I set it. I destroyed my home, the only place my mother felt safe. The fire that someone couldn't escape—

My mouth hung open, the breath stuck in my throat. "Get away from the sewer," I whispered.

"What?" Ryan looked over his shoulder, at the dark sewer entrance at the edge of the road behind him.

I felt my mother reach for me as I stepped away from the car. Ryan wasn't moving, and I remembered that feeling in the tunnel. The feeling that we weren't alone. The sound of the door closing in the safe room, the smoke filling up the room so neither of us could see anything.

You don't just get to take something from a man like Samuel and get away with it.

"Move," I whispered. My legs were leaden, and Ryan

wasn't moving fast enough. "Move!" I yelled. "He's in there. He has a gun. He's still *in there*."

Ryan switched on his flashlight and swung it toward the opening—bare, empty. Still, he stepped aside. "There's nobody," he said.

Residual fear. Leftover adrenaline. My mind playing tricks on me. I took the flashlight from Ryan, pointed it deep into the sewer, leaned over the edge. The tunnel kept going. Running along the edge of the road . . . I quickly checked down the road, but couldn't see past the curve in either direction. Couldn't make out the shadows of the trees in the distance, now covered in a fine haze of fog.

"Hey," Ryan said, placing a hand over mine. "Help is coming, okay?" But even he was moving us back toward his car.

My mother was crouched in front of the car, on her feet, but low to the ground—as if she was expecting Samuel to spring from the sewer at any moment.

"Let's wait in the car," Ryan whispered, as if that could offer protection.

A crunch of leaves in the woods beyond the car, and I froze, my gaze fixed in that direction, searching for movement. The outline of a shadow hidden just inside the fog. A nightmare. A name.

Samuel Lyter remained perfectly still with one foot in front of the other, and then he stepped forward, smiling. He was covered in soot and smoke, and I realized I must look the same as him.

His eyes darted quickly from me to Ryan, and I saw him taking it all in. We were two kids. Two kids with no weapons, clinging to nothing but each other and a flashlight. "Hello again," he said.

Ryan's grip tightened around my back.

"Don't come any closer," I said.

A gun hung limply at his side. He tapped it twice against the side of his leg, as if he was thinking something through. God, where were the police? The firefighters? We were not that far from home—they should be here already. Unless they thought there was no reason. Ryan said he had us, that we were fine. . . .

"You're really something," he said. "Willing to trade your own mother?" His mouth twitched, the thought bringing him pleasure.

I made myself stare straight at him, not looking where my mother remained hidden. Not giving her away. "No, I wasn't," I said.

"You set the house on fire."

I felt Ryan tense beside me. Wondered if he saw me in a different light. As something made of darkness and destruction. Willing to trade lives, when he had not.

"That's not true," I said. To him. To Ryan. To myself. Realizing as I said it what I had known all along. "She knew what to do. She knew, because she taught me the same thing. It wasn't a trade at all." It was an action. It was a move.

And I had to make another one, right now.

"I realized something earlier," Samuel said, ignoring my argument. He tapped his gun once more against his leg. "I pointed this at the wrong person."

Through the shadows of the woods, I saw the gun rise to meet me. Samuel eyed Ryan as he stepped closer. "You will back away now."

Ryan sucked in a breath, unsure, undecided. There was no good option now.

Ryan would not leave me on his own. I wished for darkness that I could hide within. Walls and gates that would keep us all safe. We were too exposed, and there was no way left to hide who we were. There was nothing but the fog surrounding us, and the light in my hand.

I stepped away from Ryan instead, closer to Samuel. "Where's your lovely mother?" he asked.

"Went for help," I said. "Should be here any minute." *Come on, come on.*

"Fitting then," he said as he came closer, his steps crushing the dead leaves underfoot, brittle and crackling. "Can you think of anything better for her to return to? Come now, Kelsey, before I shoot your boyfriend. Or is that not reason enough for you, either?"

"Okay," I said, taking small, cautious steps in his direction. Ryan's yellow flashlight remained in my clenched fist.

"Kelsey—" Ryan said from somewhere to my right.

"Ryan, everything's okay."

But everything was not okay. There was no situation

where I went willingly and we survived. Samuel would not leave Ryan alive, I knew this.

I saw a shadow moving in the corner of my eye, something turning solid through the fog—blink and you might miss it. And in that moment, I raised my voice, to mask what was happening behind him.

He was just a man. Nothing more. "Before I knew who you were, I used to be afraid of you," I said.

He paused. "You don't fear me now?"

"I've seen your face. You're just a man."

"I'm a man with a gun right now, Kelsey."

But he couldn't see everything happening all around him. He didn't know us at all.

I saw the shadow closing in before he heard it, and I flicked the flashlight on, shining the powerful beam directly in his eyes. He instinctively raised his other arm to his eyes just as the shadow launched itself at his side.

I dropped to the ground as a shot rang out.

My ears were ringing, and the pavement stung my cheek. I pushed onto my knees, trying to orient myself. I called for my mother. I called for Ryan. But I couldn't even hear my own voice over the ringing.

And then the flashing lights lit up the fog and the roadside. I saw fragments—Ryan scrambling toward me from one direction, his mouth moving; my mother and Samuel on the ground in the other direction. Her body flat and unmoving on top of his.

The EMTs sprinted toward my mother and Samuel,

gently lifting her, gesturing for others, bringing out the gurneys and strapping her down while police rolled Samuel over on the ground. They ran my mother to the nearest ambulance, the doors shutting—my mother gone once more.

Ryan had me under the arms, pulling me toward him, running his hands over every inch of me. His mouth moved, and even though I could only hear the ringing, I saw what he was saying—*You're okay.*

I moved my hands to his face, to his shoulders, his face bathed in the colors of the ambulance siren. "You're okay?" I asked.

The corner of his mouth twitched, and the ringing in my ears died down. "Yeah," he said. He pulled me to his chest, where I heard his heartbeat pounding, felt the faint tremble in his arms as he held me close.

Another EMT was heading our way, and Ryan called, "We're good," as she approached.

"My mom?" I asked as she crouched in front of us.

"She was shot in the shoulder," she said. "She's stable. You can meet her at the hospital."

"What about . . . the guy? Samuel."

"In custody," she said. "Had the wind knocked out of him pretty good when your mother landed on top of him. But otherwise, he's fine." She used a rag to wipe something off the side of my face. "Soot," she said. "Not blood. I was just checking."

"Can I take her?" Ryan asked.

The medic looked at me closely, pulled me to standing. "You're sure you're not hurt?"

"I'm sure," I said.

Ryan led us toward his car, sending a message through his walkie-talkie, letting his team know he was okay, and where he was going, and then adding, "Yeah, yeah, I know. I'll call my dad."

A car braked to a halt beside Ryan's Jeep, and Annika spilled out, leaving the door ajar, her hair untamed, her eyes wild. "She's okay?" she called. "You're okay?"

I barely had time to turn in her direction before she was falling into my arms, burying her face in my hair. "They wouldn't let me back down your street, or mine. Nobody would tell me *anything*." She lifted her head, stared at Ryan. "And *you* weren't answering your phone." She reached around me and smacked him on the upper arm, which made Ryan smile. "And then I heard sirens and followed the lights. . . ."

"I'm okay," I said. "Where were you?"

But Annika was just shaking her head, her curls tickling my cheek.

"She called," Ryan said.

"You saw the fire?" I asked.

"Before," Ryan answered again. "Apparently couldn't get any signal on her cell, which tipped her off."

"I looked over the wall to your house," she said, "but I couldn't see anything. Still. I knew. I took my car and saw the other one parked at the end of my driveway, and that's when I was *sure*. I drove until I got signal, but the police thought I was crazy. Apparently no cell signal is not exactly an emergency. And then I called Ryan—but turned out he was already on his way. . . . He said he'd call it in. Oh my God, I was so scared." She shook her head again, and I held her tight.

I turned to look at Ryan, who raised one shoulder in a shrug. "You weren't at lunch," he said. And then he frowned. "I wish you'd told me. You could've told me."

"I didn't want to drag you down into this. Not any more than I already have."

"Kelsey, you don't have to drag me anywhere."

But I thought of the way he had looked at me when he realized I had started the fire. Now he knew all of the truth, and I wondered if everything was about to change. "I set that fire, Ryan. I did it."

He pulled me from Annika. Held me close. "And I wish I had been there with you. I wish you hadn't had to do it all alone."

But I didn't. Annika and Ryan had gotten help when I could not. And I thought how lucky I was—that even when I believed I was alone in that house, I was not.

Annika followed us to the hospital, waited with Ryan out in the lobby while I was taken to see my mother. The police were already in there, and so was Jan, but I pushed through them, pushed straight to the side of her bed, my heart breaking as she smiled. She reached a hand for mine.

"You're okay?" I asked.

"The bullet went straight through," she said, gesturing toward the bandage on her upper arm. I knew it would scar, though. That there would always be a reminder. I hoped when she reached her hand for it, when she felt the rough skin that would remain over time, she would remember what she did.

"Okay," my mother said, taking a deep breath. She turned to the man standing at the foot of her bed. Detective Mahoney. "I'll tell you everything. But my daughter stays."

All the stories, all the secrets, came out in the long hours that followed, as I kept watch beside her hospital bed. Jan had called a lawyer, but my mother wasn't interested in his advice. I didn't leave her side. This was my story, as well as hers.

Samuel Lyter was his name. A ghost to me, brought to flesh. He was three years older than my mother. He was her boyfriend, and she went willingly. She did. She thought it was her only way out. She wanted to leave behind her terrible past. She wanted her father to come home and see that she had destroyed the house. She wanted him to pay. She did not mean for it to look like a kidnapping, but she couldn't go back. The story took on a life of its own, as stories tend to do.

Her testimony and my DNA should be enough to bring him to justice, easily. It had started with petty theft, she said. How they survived. *Just wait here*, they'd tell her, and she blindly listened. Samuel and his brother Martin would leave her waiting in the car, ready to drive off quickly. She did not realize at first what was happening inside.

The lawyer told her—and still she did not listen—that she would be held liable for those crimes as well, whether she knew about the violence happening inside or not. But it didn't matter: she confessed them all.

By the time she *did* realize what was happening, around the time the media had also turned on her father, she found out she was pregnant—and she tried to leave. I hoped that counted for something. I hoped that counted for a lot. And that's when they tied her up, kept her in the basement, burned her back with industrial-strength drain cleaner, doused the room in gasoline, holding up a match as a threat.

And then one day, she escaped.

Her father was dead.

She was guilty.

The media would vilify her too if they knew the truth. And she had something more, now. I was just an idea then, she said. But still, something more.

These were not simple choices. Most things weren't.

When she finished her story, the lawyer said he wanted to discuss things in private. The police left, but I remained. My mother looked me in the eye, then at Jan. The room smelled like smoke, and I realized it was me. That I was covered in soot and smoke, and there was still half a story that needed to be told—mine. And that this part I would have to do on my own.

Jan placed a hand on my shoulder. "It's time to go now," she said, but I shook her off.

"Go, Kelsey," my mother said. She brought my hand to her face, which was warm and familiar, and she whispered into it, "It's time for you to go now."

She released my hand, my fingers slipping from her grip, but I couldn't back away. "Mom," I said, but it came out sounding like a plea.

"You'll be okay," she said.

I closed my eyes. "Okay," I said.

One foot in front of the other. Out the door, through the bright hall, into the lobby where Ryan and Annika were asleep in chairs, side by side. "It's time to go home," I said, jarring them both awake.

Never mind that I didn't have one. Never mind that I didn't know where I was going, or what would happen to my mother, or me, or the three who were in police custody.

All I knew was that tonight I would be going back to Jan's, and tomorrow she'd meet with my mom's lawyer. I'd give my statement to the police, and Ryan would come see me, as he was currently promising to do. Annika would call, and we'd figure it out—that's what Jan was saying. We'd figure it out tomorrow.

Tomorrow, anything could happen.

CHAPTER 31

I **was going to see** the house today.

The house would become a rubble of debris and ash, a flat piece of land, as if it had never truly existed. It was built from blood and fear, but at the core, it was all still just wood and bolts, glass and concrete.

Whatever remained after the fire would be demolished. They said it was the safest way. I couldn't live in it, anyway—not after I knew what it had been made from, and for. Guilt. Fear. A self-imposed confinement. The money wasn't hers anyway. The house did not truly belong to us.

Samuel and his brother, Martin, were in jail awaiting trial, no bond. Eli, it turned out, was only seventeen. Had been missing from his home for nearly a year. His case would be more complicated, and I felt some sympathy for him—for a boy who saw nowhere else to go, who believed there was no choice except the one that had chosen him.

I saw their faces on the television screen at night, but they were starting to feel more and more like strangers.

To have a chance at freedom, my mother will have to testify. Even then, Jan said she may have to serve some time. The question was where. She's been serving time, in one form or another, ever since. Anything can happen, Jan said. But she said it like it was something to hang on to. Like hope. And I thought of all the things that were happening right this very moment:

Annika, safe and heading back to school—*I'll be back soon, Kelsey darling, promise*. Cole and Emma in the backyard while their father grilled burgers. Jan, down at the courthouse with my mother and the lawyer and a judge, deciding on the terms of her deal, and our fate.

I heard someone laughing down the street, from where I sat on Jan's front porch. And then the rumble of a familiar engine. I stood, already walking down the driveway before his car pulled into view. Already smiling. Already picturing the smile on Ryan's face as I slid into the seat beside him.

The house looked the same from the drive up, until you got close enough to see it, set down the slope. It had mostly burned, the walls caving, the interior charred. The only things still untouched were the black iron gates, the fence encircling the property, and the wall beyond. Ryan stood beside me as I wrapped my hands around the cool iron bars.

It was the first time either of us had been back here. "Wow," Ryan said, "it's . . ." His throat moved as he swallowed. "I can't believe you got out of there."

"I think it looks worse than it was."

He shook his head. "No, it doesn't." He sucked in a breath. "It looks exactly as bad as it was, Kelsey."

I looked over at him, his shoulders tense, his jaw set, staring down the house before us. "You're mad," I said. I had done something reckless, and now he was seeing exactly what it was. What I'd done. What I was made of.

"No," he said, turning to face me. "I was scared."

"So was I," I said.

His hand brushed my hair, and I stood a little closer. Leaned a little nearer. Felt a little deeper. And for just a moment, everything felt close, and possible, and mine.

Once upon a time, my mother was a girl who risked everything to leave, risked everything for something that was still just an idea. She took on her life alone, and I couldn't think of anything braver.

I thought I should feel more scared, because I was alone for the first time, too. But it's hard to feel that way with the footsteps overhead at night, and Jan cooking in the next room, and my mother's voice over the phone, and Emma arguing about how long was I staying exactly. And Ryan picking me up, keeping every promise he made to me. Standing beside me as I looked at this house one last time. It's hard to feel alone when, truth is, you aren't.

I didn't know what would happen next. A thought that used to fill me with the greatest fear. But, as Ryan pointed out, maybe I was wrong.

"I'm ready," I said, tapping the bars one last time. *Goodbye*, I thought.

Ryan's hand was warm in mine as we walked down the gravel driveway, away from everything my life had been. But we were something other than the sum of our parts, something bigger than a story.

"So, tomorrow," he was saying, and his words were music. "I'm thinking you, me, pizza, maybe a movie."

I stopped him in his tracks, pulled him closer, rose up on my toes to kiss him.

"Oh. I like your plan, too," he said, which made me laugh. And then he was laughing, too.

I heard the wind coming through the trees before I could feel it.

Like a whisper, getting louder. Something simmering, an idea coming to life.

Like an echo in my head: *Out here, anything can happen.*

Out here, everything can happen.

It felt, this time, like a promise.

ACKNOWLEDGMENTS

Special thanks to everyone who helped guide this book from idea to finished product:

My agent, Sarah Davies, whose thoughtful advice helps shape both ideas and careers. I am so thankful for your guidance.

My editor, Emily Easton, who always sees what an idea can become and shows me how to get it there. I've been so fortunate to work with you on five books now!

Phoebe Yeh, Samantha Gentry, and the entire team at Crown Books for Young Readers/Random House.

My critique partners, who provide invaluable feedback at every step of the process: Megan Shepherd, Elle Cosimano, Ashley Elston, Jill Hathaway, and Romily Bernard.

And, as always, my family.

WHAT IF EVERYTHING YOU THOUGHT YOU KNEW ABOUT SOMEONE WAS A LIE?

Uncover the truth in Megan Miranda's
next psychological thriller. . . .

FRAGMENTS
OF THE
LOST

Coming soon.